HENRY HANDEL RICHARDSON

The Getting
of Wisdom

With a new Introduction
BY GERMAINE GREER

Published by VIRAGO PRESS Limited 1981
41 William IV Street, London WC2N 4DB

Reprinted 1982, 1985

First published 1910 by William Heinemann

British Library Cataloguing in Publication Data

Richardson, Henry Handel
  The getting of wisdom – (Virago modern classic)
  I. Title
  823[F]   PR6035.1354

  ISBN 0-86068-179-3

  Printed and bound in Great Britain
  at Anchor Brendon Ltd, Tiptree, Essex

ETHEL FLORENCE LINDESAY RICHARDSON

was born in Melbourne, Australia in 1870. Her father was Irish, and a doctor, and her mother an Englishwoman who had emigrated to Australia in the early 1850s. Her father died in 1879 and in 1880 her mother became post-mistress in the gold-mining town of Maldon in northern Victoria. Ethel Richardson was educated at the Presbyterian Ladies' College in Melbourne, which she later described in her novel, *The Getting of Wisdom*. In 1888 the family moved to Europe so that Ethel could study music in Leipzig. She spent most of the next sixteen years in Germany absorbing the musical and intellectual life of the day and reading widely in European literature. It was there that she met her husband, J. G. Robertson, whom she married in Dublin in 1895. Unable to make a success of her music, Ethel Richardson turned to writing. Her first novel, *Maurice Guest* (1908), also published by Virago, was based largely on her experience in Leipzig and was published under the male pseudonym of Henry Handel Richardson. In 1904 her husband was made the first Professor of German Literature at the University of London and they moved to London where they lived in Regent's Park. *The Getting of Wisdom* was published in 1910 and her famous trilogy *The Fortunes of Richard Mahony* between 1917 and 1929.

After the death of her husband in 1933, Henry Handel Richardson moved to Sussex. She published *The End of a Childhood and Other Stories* in 1934 and *The Young Cosima* in 1939, and began her autobiography *Myself When Young* which remained unfinished at her death in 1946.

VIRAGO
MODERN
CLASSIC

NUMBER
48

Introduction

Henry Handel Richardson was the name in which Ethel Florence Lindesay Richardson chose to make her bid for fame as a novelist. *The Getting of Wisdom* was begun while she was finishing her first published novel, *Maurice Guest*, as a relief, she wrote in 1940, from that book's steadily deepening sense of gloom. The nom de plume was assumed, she explained, because 'there had been much talk in the press about the ease with which a woman's work could be distinguished from a man's; and I wanted to try out the truth of the assertion'. The truth of the assertion had been repeatedly tried over the century that had passed since the Brontë sisters had shyly appeared before their public as Ellis, Acton and Currer Bell, only to abandon their pseudonyms with alacrity after they had won recognition. George Eliot succeeded so well in transcending her femaleness that her first novel, *Scenes of Clerical Life*, had actually been attributed to a Mr Joseph Liggins who did not scruple to profit by the mistake and fooled many people for more than a year. Marian Evans needed her masculine disguise not simply because she wished to write with the breadth and authority considered appropriate only to men, but because she had to shield her scandalous private life, which, if it had become common knowledge, would have undermined the impression of high moral tone for which her books were universally esteemed. Why Henry Handel Richardson should have assumed her more ponderous male mask is not so readily apparent, but once it was assumed she clung to it fiercely and bitterly resented any disclosure of her actual, legal identity.

Any discussion of *The Getting of Wisdom* must begin with the book out of which it grew. *Maurice Guest* was published in 1908 and had a modest success, going to its second impression within the twelve-month. The author was then the thirty-eight-year-old wife of J. G. Robertson, the first Professor of German at the University of London. It was fifty years since George Eliot had disgusted her most devoted readers by describing to them how Stephen Guest, overcome by lust, had covered Maggie Tulliver's upraised arm with kisses, but Mrs Robertson's grand design involved her in going much further than a respectable female novelist could yet permit herself to venture. Henry Handel Richardson meant not only to write in a manner which displayed the masculine virtues of power and authority, she wished also to write the story of a degrading sexual obsession from the point of view of its masculine victim. There was to be no hypocrisy in the telling, for the object of his passion was both in love with and had been abandoned by another man. She would accept him as a substitute and lead him into a maze of depravity while Henry Handel Richardson would keep pace with him all the way, to morgues where female suicides lay destroyed by homosexual lovers, to drunken debauches and the seamy bed of a prostitute, until his suicide, when she would look through his eyes at his last glimpse of this world. To attempt all this as Mrs Robertson would be even now to court disaster in the shape of ridicule; in 1908, she would have been sure to attract limelight of the most unpleasant sort and perhaps to ruin her husband's career as well. By taking shelter beneath her uncle's name, Henry Handel Richardson felt secure enough to court prurient speculation by dedicating her book to *Louise*, in the full awareness that her sluttish anti-heroine, who spends the greater part of the book either in bed or in her dressing-gown, like the preferred subjects of Klimt, sallow, languid and rapacious, is also called Louise. The reader is not born who could resist speculating upon such a coincidence, and Henry Handel Richardson, who all her life disingenuously claimed to abhor publicity, had no intention that we should.

The Getting of Wisdom has been called an autobiographical novel, presumably because Richardson drew upon her own experiences at the Presbyterian Ladies' College in Melbourne and it is comparatively easy to identify Laura Rambotham as Ethel Richardson if only in certain fairly superficial particulars. If the autobiographical element in *The Getting of Wisdom* has been overemphasised, the simple fact that the protagonist of *Maurice Guest* is male has obscured the importance of Richardson's own experiences as a music student in Leipzig and Munich, where she spent most of sixteen years of her life, in the development of her main themes. In later life she was to recall every compliment and encouragement that she received from her teachers, but the picture drawn in *Maurice Guest* is harsher and truer. The novel is set in the 1890's, when the tide of eager and mostly misguided young people who converged on the cultural centres of Europe was at its height. Although Richardson does not question the ideal of high art for which so many insufficiently gifted students endured hunger, privation and cold, her characterisation of the teachers who made a good livelihood out of them is as damaging a comment. They convey their brutality, arrogance and vulgarity in every jolt of their Prussian voices, while their susceptibilities, to vanity, intemperance, lust, favouritism, greed, jealousy, pettiness, unfairness and boredom, are all pitilessly displayed. What Zola had accomplished in *L'Oeuvre*, which had stripped the glamour from the French Fine Art establishment, may have provided her inspiration: certainly she fills in the same broad canvas showing a cross-section of the student population of Leipzig in the 90's, with certain figures whose vicissitudes are traced in detail in the foreground. More shocking than the exploration of Guest's degradation is the implication of gross cultural fraud which parallels her merciless depiction of the worthlessness of the education afforded middle-class Australian girls.

Like Laura, Maurice Guest must get wisdom, for he comes from four years as a provincial schoolteacher to Leipzig brimfull of dreams no less fantastical than hers.

> In a vision as vivid as those which cross the brain in a sleepless night, he saw a dark compact multitude wait, with breath suspended, to catch the drops that fell like raindrops from his fingers; saw himself the all-conspicuous figure, as, with masterful gestures, he compelled the soul that lay dormant in brass and strings, to give voice to, to interpret to the many, his subtlest emotions. And he was overcome by a tremulous compassion within himself at the idea of wielding such power over an unknown multitude, at the latent nobility of mind and aim that this power implied.

What he encounters is not exaltation and inspiration but coarseness, greed and ambition, as well as a certain crude energy which sustains the tougher students, of whom he is not one. His teachers have an easy task, for they insist upon technique, wearing him out in tedious exercises for all the hours of daylight. No attempt is made to draw out any latent talent which he might have had, for there is no shortage of gifted students, most of whom seem to have come to Leipzig ready-made. Guest's function is that of all the foreign students who came to Leipzig in search of a dream. He helps to make the prodigious musical activity of the town possible, by paying for it, paying to attend concerts, paying to be snorted at by his teachers, paying to eat and sleep.

Towering over the hoi polloi of students is the resident genius, who bears some resemblance to a bitter caricature of Richard Strauss. He is a Polish violinist called Schilsky, who can play almost all instruments with great dexterity and is writing a symphonic poem called *Zarathustra*. He is a dandified cad, a deceiver, seducer and exploiter of women, always hard up and unable to refuse money from any source, loose-mouthed and coarse-grained. His muse is the languid Australian *belle-laide*, Louise Dufrayer, whose exotic appeal captivates the naive and priggish Maurice Guest, who in his pallid way is as different from the street-wise community around him as the adolescent Laura from her sniggering schoolmates. By dint of coming to her rescue when she is prostrated by Schilsky's sudden flight from sexual thraldom, Guest becomes Louise's second string. Her capricious demands on his time and energy destroy whatever slight chance he may have had of distinguishing himself. The more he slides into failure, the more striking the contrast between him and the absent genius, who still holds first place in Louise's thoughts and feelings, until he becomes for her a mere sexual instrument.

> . . . she brought to bear on their intercourse all her own hard-won knowledge, and all her arts. She drew from her store of experience those trifling, yet weighty details, which, once she has learned them, a woman never forgets . . . she took advantage of the circumstances in which they found themselves, utilising to the full the stimulus of strange times and places: she fired the excitement that lurked in a surreptitious embrace and surrender, under all the dangers of a possible surprise . . . Her devices were never-ending. Not that they were necessary; for he was helpless in her hands when she assumed the mastery. But she could not afford to omit one of the means to her end, for she had herself to lash as well as him.

The degeneration of their relationship runs its full course, until jealousy and hatred are its only vital forms. When Guest's integrity is almost completely derelict, he uncovers a depth of depravity in Louise's character which disgusts him so uncontrollably that he bashes her, only to expiate this new degradation in her bed. The *coup de grace* comes in the form of Schilsky's return to Leipzig. Louise moves toward him as if

Guest's long agony had never happened.

In order to dispel any lingering hope that great art is not made of such material, Richardson adds a bitterly ironical epilogue. Guest's suicide is two-years-old gossip. Schilsky, the vulgar voluptuary and kept man, is an avant-garde composer whose works rejoice in names like *Uber die Letzten Dinge*, and Louise Dufrayer is his lawful wife. At their heels trots another devotee, like Guest, a piano student, who flushes with awareness when Mrs Schilsky's robe brushes his hand.

The product of all the frenzied human endeavour that was Leipzig, with its exhausted, mad and debauched sacrifices to high art, is the genius, Schilsky, distinguished from other mortals not so much by native talent, which remains an unknown quantity, as by selfishness, ambition, libidinousness and lack of scruple. Richardson does not indicate whether his great works are trumpery or the real thing because when all is said and done, it cannot be said to matter. What she was later to call gloom is in fact artistic nihilism, and it is that rather than the knowing about loveless sex which makes *Maurice Guest* a profoundly shocking novel.

Maurice Guest is Richardson's Emma Bovary, but if we cannot care as much for Guest as we do for Bovary, the explanation lies not only in the comparative unwieldiness of Richardson's prose. It may be a part of her masculine posture that she is committed to supplying proliferating details and supporting scenery and sub-plots which contrast with Flaubert's apparently effortless government of emphasis and attention, but she is also far less interested in her hero than Flaubert was in Emma Bovary. Far too much of her energy is monopolised by her anti-heroine, whose behaviour is, on the face of it, inexcusable. Louise is drawn too fully to support any hypothesis that the pseudonymous author was the male original of Maurice Guest, for every twist of her ungovernable feelings is faithfully conveyed, while Guest's male vulnerability remains an idea, rather than a force in the novel. The author actually stands in the relationship of a female confidante to Louise, in something the same way as undeclared female lovers have stood to heterosexual women, for example, Ida Baker to Katherine Mansfield. Richardson was very well aware of the impossibility of ascribing her own understanding of Louise to Guest, and repeatedly steps outside his field of awareness to describe Louise's motivation, thereby creating an uncomfortable tension between the *intimismo* of the Louise story and the Zolaësque exposé of the Leipzig music establishment. There is also a clue in one of the parallel sub-plots in the character of Joanna, whose whole life was regulated by her love for her charming younger sister, until she betrayed her by conducting a clandestine affair with Schilsky.

The themes which emerge in *Maurice Guest* strangled in circumstantial detail are also dealt with in *The Getting of Wisdom*, which is as fresh and loose-limbed in style as the earlier book is clogged and crabbed. Because of this lightness of touch, *The Getting of Wisdom* has been called a light novel, when it is in fact profound, but so gracefully and unself-consciously so that it makes *Maurice Guest* seem pretentious and overdrawn. In the shorter novel, every stroke is subordinated to the main design, the enactment (rather than description) of the implacable destruction of a child's innocence. *Maurice Guest*, for all its outspokenness about sex and perversion, is a nineteenth-century novel; in *The Getting of Wisdom* we are suddenly aware that a tenth of the twentieth is almost over. Richardson herself thought that economy of effect and informality of style would prove to be ephemeral modernities rather than her one true claim to immortality, and tended all her life to undervalue *The Getting of Wisdom*, saying that her whole intention had been merely to raise a laugh. The laugh she gets, as Samuel Beckett might have said, is the only true laugh, the genuine laugh mirthless. *The Getting of Wisdom* is a tragedy of the absurd. Its stage is the stage of the absurd, bare, spare, peopled by nobodies. Their apparently inconsequential exchanges are disturbing because they stir our deepest fears, the fears of the inevitability of loss. Thus, in the true absurd fashion, the novel affirms what it appears to deny, our inescapable responsibility for each other, beyond any notion of deserving, which alone makes the whole worth more than the sum of its parts.

Laura Tweedle Rambotham's journey from up-country to Melbourne is every bit as momentous as Maurice Guest's pilgrimage to Leipzig, but it means more to the reader who makes the journey with her, as we do not with Guest, from a paradisaical home which is more garden than house, where the animals named by Laura eat from her hand. The brashness of the provincial capital strikes as harshly upon the reader as it does upon Laura, and so we are committed to her from the outset. We view her weaknesses with the same kind of ruefulness as we view our own. At the end of the second chapter, she is a fully defined character (as Guest never becomes), the sort of skinny, pale, intense girl for whom puberty is still far distant at twelve years old. She is the difficult eldest child of an impecunious gentlewoman, replete with inappropriate notions of refinement, who might do well, if only most of the time she were not listening to a different drummer, bursting with unanswerable questions which she dare not ask. The reader passes with her from the blinding light of the Australian outdoors to the penumbra of fake gentility which engulfs the Ladies' College. The interplay of dazzle and twilight is finely managed throughout the novel. In her red hat and her purple dress, Laura is a child of the light who gropes through the shadowless gloom where her sparkle is to be exchanged for polish, coming hard up against the problems that others have ignored, returning only occasionally to the realm of light where she gulps sustenance before plunging once more.

Laura's version of Guest's fantasies of moving audiences to tears has been developed by dint of weaving fantastic tales for her younger siblings. In a wider world she expects to find opportunities for further ranging; instead, she learns the hard way, that she has to compress herself into a smaller compass, to mitigate the brilliance of her effects and to ingratiate where she intended to astonish. Mediocrity dashes over her like the sea and for long periods she is quite submerged, while the combined pressures for conformity weigh her down, coming perilously close to exhausting her energy. The only outward sign of this Herculean struggle is a depressingly familiar one, a 'Fair' school report, which will have as its outcome a problematic career, about which the author gives no comforting reassurances. It is not as memorable a story as the suicide of a young music student, but in its very ordinariness it is more dreadful.

Laura's intensity is the cause of most of her suffering, and it will also be her way of transcending it. Her anguish at the rudeness and coldness of her reception at the Ladies' College causes her to capitulate at once, but her own passionate nature and innate sensitivity persist in disrupting the completeness of her capitulation. So she sniggers with the bigger girls, cringes to the staff, and is callous toward her juniors, but underdoes, overdoes and forgets to do all of these things constantly. The power and spontaneity of her feelings repeatedly confound her attempts at manipulation of the people around her, so that although a willing enough hypocrite, she makes but a poor one. However fervent her wish to cram herself into the common mould, she is too volatile to stay in it. The reader follows this sickening zig-zag, as Laura courts first one group and then another only to be eventually repulsed, wondering all the time whether her personality will survive, and finding the only hope in her clear-eyed satirical view of the very people with whom she is currying favour.

Richardson herself retold her experiences at the Presbyterian Ladies' College (or P.L.C. as the school is mostly known) in her account of herself when young, but the recapitulation only goes to show how the unselfconsciousness of the novel written thirty years before saves it from her rather pompous notions of importance, which lead to odd mistakes of taste. Her conscious preference was for grandeur, even the spurious grandeur of Hummel (for whose music her fingers were to remain too spidery) and the evanescent thrill of Longfellow, whom she preferred to Tennyson and, by implication, to other poets much greater than either. In these rather distorted notions, we may see the true reflection of Richardson's provincialism, for in a country which is utterly philistine, people who are genuinely excited by the arts tend to distrust any art form which seems close to ordinary life and to adopt paranoid, overblown concepts of the artistic personality. Richardson's adoption of Handel as her middle name reflects the kind of taste which found a performance of the *Messiah* a more mean-ingful and rewarding experience than any work of Mozart. Her own understanding of her achievement in *The Getting of Wisdom* reflects this same wrong-headedness. It is almost as if the clear-eyed, passionate child who was almost suffocated by educational authoritarianism sneaked out of her while her back was turned and wrote a perfect novel that the self-conscious adult had no power to understand.

'I persist in thinking of it as a little book,' she wrote in 1931, 'though modern writers who give such short measure don't agree with me.' H. G. Wells, quite rightly, thought the book a masterpiece and it is one of the ironies of art that Richardson could not understand why he should. The concept of infinite riches in a little room is beyond one bred up on bombast.

Given the lack of grandiosity in Richardson's intent, as she whiled away a wet summer in the Bavarian mountains by writing *The Getting of Wisdom*, it must nevertheless not be supposed for an instant that she was not carefully constructing a finished novel, but merely recounting some personal experiences. Her own career at the Presbyterian Ladies' College was markedly different from that of Laura Rambotham. Ethel Richardson won first-class honours in Latin, English and History, and the Senior Pianoforte Scholarship, and was the school tennis champion. It would be confusing the horse with the cart to point out that she suppresses these facts and gives a misleading account of her school career, for she is not engaged in writing a reminiscence. *The Getting of Wisdom* has its own artistic logic, characterised in this instance as in no other instance of her writing, as a fine control of emphasis and exact calculation of mood. It is the imperious operation of artistic tact which causes her to hold the soft pedal down in telling the story of Laura's love affair with Evelyn—not that she held it down as successfully as she later imagined. The dreadful pain of adolescent infatuation grinds in every line, the more effectively because Richardson does not do for Laura what she had done for Maurice Guest, namely, explain and expound the nature of the feeling. Because of her posture of detachment, the abandonment of this small, passionate soul is more touching than all Guest's operatic miseries. The cynical reader might suspect that voluptuous Evelyn kept her 'Byronic scrap of humanity' by her to feed her own sensual narcissism, because Richardson does not leap in and close the gap. The situation remains true to the amorphous and terrible emotional life of adolescents. The equally significant possibility also survives, that either Laura or Evelyn or both ought to have been lovers of women, if only such a possibility had been psychologically acceptable.

Sexual tension tightens every page of *The Getting of Wisdom*, if not as subtly as it does every page of a novel by Jane Austen, yet with a stimulating degree of restraint. The mistresses of the school, except for poor Miss Chapman, the only born teacher among them, are all living on the edges of heterosexual fulfillment, which they may be supposed to have missed, while the older students, 'whose ripe, bursting forms told their own tale', are obsessed by their eventual sexual function and invariably talk boys and smut, from which Laura would instinctively recoil if only she were not so desperately eager to be accepted. Then there are the crushes, poor little Chinky's for Laura, which effectively ruins her young life and leaves Laura disgracefully cold, and Laura's for Evelyn, which almost squeezes her heart dry on its first encounter. The intensity of the emotional life of schoolgirls has inspired other novels, most notably perhaps, *Olivia* by 'Olivia', who was actually Dorothy Bussy, the translator of Gide into English. There is an important difference however, between the hothouse where Madame Julie, Bussy's version of the remarkable Madeleine Souvestre, forced her young women to intellectual and affective maturity and the dreary suburban seminary where middle-class non-conformist Laura was sent to school. Laura's was not the stimulating environment offered to upper-class girls at Les Ruches (called Les Avons in Bussy's novel) where her sensitivity would have flourished under the delicate attentions of elegant, sophisticated, worldly and cultivated women. Mrs Gurley is a common martinet and her subordinates are simply representatives of the limited, empty-headed world beyond the school. The leitmotif of their banal exchanges chimes regularly through the schoolgirl chatter; whether it is Miss Zielinsky sniffling over Ouida, Miss Snodgrass sneering at her because she is a foreigner, Miss Day snapping and barking, or Mrs Gurley oppressing Miss Chapman, their behaviour serves to remind us that women who taught in the 1880's did so because they had no choice. They were almost always of a lower social class than most of their students, untrained, perfunctory and dissatisfied. The only person who makes any contribution to Laura's intellectual development is the visiting teacher, Miss Hicks, who does so by accident as she is rating another pupil. It is to Laura's credit that she decides that she does not want a 'real woman's brain: vague, slippery, inexact, interested only in the personal aspect of a thing', which is incapable alike of concentration or intellectual curiosity. However, she is given no further help in transcending the sex of her brain, nor is the justice of Miss Hicks's anti-feminist statement ever queried. After meeting Miss Hicks on page 75, we hear the last of her on page 78. Thereafter the teaching at P.L.C. is represented by remarks which are either unkind, unnecessary, irrelevant or all three.

Henry Handel Richardson pretended to be amazed when P.L.C. refused to admit her as a guest when she passed by in 1912, on her trip to gather background material for her *magnum opus*, *The Fortunes of Richard Mahony*. In vain she insisted that her damning portrait of private schooling for girls was meant merely to amuse. She herself had hated her brief experience as an unwilling schoolteacher, and her first hero, Maurice Guest, was a runaway schoolteacher. Her attitude towards the whole question was far more rancorous than light-hearted, and justly so. Her contemptuous treatment of the school where she had done so well cannot be dismissed as a mere comic device, for the school is the instrument whereon the soul of Laura Rambotham is strung out for the torture, and although she is a little girl, her suffering is not less important for that. It takes a peculiarly sadistic sense of humour to grin cheerfully at the picture of the new girl going from one teacher to another trying earnestly to find out what she should be doing, only to be rebuffed sarcastically, apathetically and downright rudely by first one and then another, to the accompaniment of dutiful titters from her wretched peers.

In later life, Richardson was wont to make extraordinary

claims for Laura Rambotham, calling her 'a girl with a difference', 'a writer in the making' whom 'the taint of her calling' marked off from the rest of her schoolmates. If *The Getting of Wisdom* is a *Bildungsroman* about the making of an artist it is clearly inferior to *A Portrait of the Artist as a Young Man*, which appeared seven years later, and even to *A Portrait of the Artist as a Young Dog*, for the concept of art which it develops is entirely superficial. Nevertheless in 1940, Richardson was to claim in an article which she wrote for the *Virginia Quarterly Review*, that Laura, 'by dint of sad experience . . . discovered, unaided, the craft of realistic fiction'. In fact, Laura was aided by the boarders' Literary Society, which gave her very good advice and forced her to take it by that most effective of means, peer-group pressure. She already knew what was required, for the recipe was the same as that which she had unwittingly used in her lies about the curate: she had invented what could have happened and simply had not. All she had to do was to transfer her skill at libel to the field of declared fiction, and all she learned was how to tell a likely story, at a time when such narrative had lost its hold upon English fiction. If we are to understand the greatness of *The Getting of Wisdom*, we must realise that Laura is potentially any twelve-year-old girl, as unique in her undeveloped potential as all other little girls. Because she comes from a fatherless household in a small town she comes late into the socialisation process. Like a little wild creature brought into a parlour, she dashes herself against the obstacles to her self-realisation set up by Godmother and Mrs Gurley, and most cunningly, by her peers. Ultimately the tale is a hopeful one, for we leave Laura wary and toughened, but still full of growing.

Richardson did not continue in her modern, concentrated, ironic vein. By 1912, she had finished the first draft of the first volume of a trilogy, *The Fortunes of Richard Mahony*, considered by most people to be her most important, because it is her most ambitious work. To be sure, there is wonderful writing in the trilogy, but the canvas that it sketches remains unfilled; her foreground characters are carefully delineated in a convention that was lifeless by the turn of the century, and her central character, based upon her father, cannot carry the weight she places on his shoulders. Richardson's Australian epic remains her chief claim to fame, because the Australians, who are the only people who study it, share the common misconception that breadth equals profundity, especially when it is accompanied by seriousness of tone and turgidity of style. Richardson herself looked back on *The Getting of Wisdom* through the glass of her study of the artist as tormented freak of nature, *The Young Cosima*, published in 1939. Nevertheless, despite the fact that the great lady herself would disagree, the enduring truth is that *The Getting of Wisdom* is Richardson's only great book, precisely because the subject is like the rest of us, ordinary, and therefore deeply important.

Germaine Greer, 1980

TO MY
UNNAMED
LITTLE COLLABORATOR

Wisdom is the principal thing;
therefore get wisdom: and with
all thy getting get understanding.

Proverbs, iv, 7

Chapter One

THE four children were lying on the grass.

'. . . and the Prince went further and further into the forest,' said the elder girl, 'till he came to a beautiful glade – a glade, you know, is a place in the forest that is open and green and lovely. And there he saw a lady, a beautiful lady, in a long white dress that hung down to her ankles, with a golden belt and a golden crown. She was lying on the sward – a sward, you know, is grass as smooth as velvet, just like green velvet – and the Prince saw the marks of travel on her garments. The bottom of the lovely silk dress was all dirty—'

'Wondrous Fair, if you don't mind you'll make that sheet dirty, too,' said Pin.

'Shut up, will you!' answered her sister who, carried away by her narrative, had approached her boots to some linen that was bleaching.

'Yes, but you know Sarah'll be awfly cross if she has to wash it again,' said Pin, who was practical.

'You'll put me out altogether,' cried Laura angrily. – 'Well, as I said, the edge of her robe was all muddy – no, I don't think I will say that; it sounds prettier if it's clean. So it hung in long, straight beautiful folds to her ankles, and the Prince saw two little feet in golden sandals peeping out from under the hem of the silken gown, and—'

'But what about the marks of travel?' asked Leppie.

'Donkey! haven't I said they weren't there? If I say they

weren't, then they weren't. She hadn't travelled at all.'

'Oh, parrakeets!' cried little Frank.

Four pairs of eyes went up to the bright green flock that was passing over the garden.

'Now you've all interrupted, and I shan't tell any more,' said Laura in a proud voice.

'Oh, yes, please do, Wondrous Fair! Tell what happened next,' begged Pin and Leppie.

'No, not another word. You can only think of sheets and parrakeets.'

'Please, Wondrous Fair,' begged little Frank.

'No, I can't now. – Another thing: I don't mind if you call me Laura to-day, as it's the last day.'

She lay back on the grass, her hands clasped under her head. A voice was heard, loud, imperative.

'Laura, I want you. Come here.'

'That's mother calling,' said Pin.

Laura kicked her heels. The two little boys laughed approval.

'Go on, Laura,' coaxed Pin. 'Mother'll be angry. I'll come, too.'

Laura raised herself with a grumble. 'It's to try on that horrid dress.'

In very fact Mother was standing, already somewhat impatient, with the dress in her hand. Laura wriggled out of the one she had on, and stood stiffly and ungraciously, with her arms held like pokers from her sides, while Mother on her knees arranged the length.

'Don't put on a face like that, miss!' she said sharply on seeing Laura's air. 'Do you think I'm making it for my own pleasure?' She had sewn at it all day, and was hot and tired.

'It's too short,' said Laura, looking down.

'It's nothing of the kind,' said Mother, with her mouth full of pins.

'It is, it's much too short.'

Mother gave her a slight shake. 'Don't you contradict *me*! Do you want to tell me I don't know what length you're to wear your dresses?'

'I won't wear it at all if you don't make it longer,' said Laura defiantly.

Pin's chubby, featureless little face lengthened with apprehension.

'Do let her have it just a tiny bit longer, mother dear, dear!' she pleaded.

'Now, Pin, what have you got to do with it I'd like to know!' said Mother, on the verge of losing her temper over the back folds, which *would* not hang.

'I'm going to school to-morrow, and it's a shame,' said Laura in the low, passionate tone that never failed to exasperate Mother, so different was it from her own hearty fashion of venting displeasure. Pin began to sniff, in sheer nervous anxiety.

'Very well then, I won't do another stitch to it!' and Mother, now angry in earnest, got up and bounced out of the room.

'Laura, how can you?' said Pin, dissolving. 'It's only you who make her so cross.'

'I don't care,' said Laura rebelliously, though she was not far off tears herself. 'It *is* a shame. All the other girls will have dresses down to the tops of their boots, and they'll laugh at me, and call me a baby;' and touched by the thought of what lay before her, she, too, began to sniffle. She did not fail, however, to roll the dress up and to throw it into a corner of the room. She also kicked the ewer, which fell over and flooded the floor. Pin cried more loudly, and ran to fetch Sarah.

Laura returned to the garden. The two little boys came up to her; but she waved them back.

'Let me alone, children. I want to think.'

She stood in a becoming attitude by the garden-gate, her brothers hovering in the background. – Then Mother called once more.

'Laura, where are you?'

'Here, mother. What is it?'

'Did you knock this jug over or did Pin?'

'I did, mother.'

'Did you do it on purpose?'

'Yes.'

'Come here to me.'

She went, with lagging steps. But Mother's anger had passed: she was at work on the dress again, and by squinting her eyes Laura could see that a piece was being added to the skirt. She was penitent at once; and when Mother in a sorry voice said: 'I'm ashamed of you, Laura. And on your last day, too,' her throat grew narrow.

'I didn't mean it, mother.'

'If only you would ask properly for things, you would get them.'

Laura knew this, knew indeed that, did she coax, Mother could refuse her nothing. But coaxing came hard to her; something within her forbade it. Sarah called her 'high-stomached', to the delight of the other children and her own indignation; she had explained to them again and again what Sarah really meant.

On leaving the house she went straight to the flower-beds: she would give Mother, who liked flowers very well but had no time to gather them, a bouquet the size of a cabbage. Pin and the boys were summoned to help her, and when their hands were full, Laura led the way to a secluded part of the garden on the farther side of the detached brick kitchen. In this strip, which was filled with greenery, little sun fell: two thick fir trees and a monstrous blue-gum stood there; high bushes screened the fence; jessamine climbed the wall of the house and encircled the bedroom windows; and on the damp and shady ground only violets grew. Yet, with the love children bear to the limited and compact, the four had chosen their own little plots here rather than in the big garden at the back of the house; and many were the times they had all begun anew to dig and to rake. But if Laura's energy did not fizzle out as quickly as usual – she was the model for the rest – Mother was sure to discover that it was too cramped and dark for them in there, and send Sarah to drive them off.

Here, safely screened from sight, Laura sat on a bench and made up her bouquet. When it was finished – red and white in the centre with a darker border, the whole surrounded by a ring of violet leaves – she looked about for something to tie it up with. Sarah, applied to, was busy ironing, and had no string in the kitchen, so Pin ran to get a reel of cotton. But while she was away Laura had an idea. Bidding Leppie hold the flowers tight in both his sticky little hands, she climbed in at her bedroom window, or rather, by lying on the sill with her legs waving in the air, she managed to grab, without losing her balance, a pair of scissors from the chest of drawers. With these between her teeth she emerged, to the excited interest of the boys who watched her open-mouthed.

Laura had dark curls, Pin fair, and both wore them flapping at their backs, the only difference being that Laura, who was now twelve years old, had for the past year been allowed to bind hers together with a ribbon, while Pin's bobbed as they chose. Every morning early, Mother brushed and twisted, with a kind of grim pride, these silky ringlets round her finger. Although the five odd minutes the curling occupied were durance vile to Laura, the child was proud of her hair in her own way; and when in the street she heard someone say: 'Look – what pretty curls!' she would give her head a toss and send them all a-rippling. In addition to this, there was a crowning glory connected with them: one hot December morning, when they had been tangled and Mother had kept her standing too long, she had fainted, pulling the whole dressing-table

down about her ears; and ever since, she had been marked off
in some mysterious fashion from the other children. Mother
would not let her go out at midday in summer: Sarah would
say: 'Let that be, can't you!' did she try to lift something that
was too heavy for her; and the younger children were to be
quelled by a threat to faint on the spot, if they did not do as she
wished. 'Laura's faint' had become a byword in the family;
and Laura herself held it for so important a fact in her life that
she had more than once begun a friendship with the words:
'Have you ever fainted? I have.'

From among these long, glossy curls, she now cut one of the
longest and most spiral, cut it off close to the root, and with it
bound the flowers together. Mother should see that she did
know how to give up something she cared for, and was not
as selfish as she was usually supposed to be.

'Oh...h...h!' said both little boys in a breath, then doubled
up in noisy mirth. Laura was constantly doing something to
set their young blood in amazement: they looked upon her as
the personification of all that was startling and unexpected.
But Pin, returning with the reel of thread, opened her eyes in
a different way.

'Oh, Laura ... !' she began, tearful at once.

'Now, res'vor!' retorted Laura scornfully – 'res'vor' was
Sarah's name for Pin, on account of her perpetual wateriness.
'Be a cry-baby, do.' But she was not damped; she was lost in
the pleasure of self-sacrifice.

Pin looked after her as she danced on, then moved submis-
sively in her wake to be near at hand should intercession be
needed. Laura was so unsuspecting, and Mother would be so
cross. In her dim, childish way Pin longed to see these, her two
nearest, at peace; she understood them both so well, and they
had little or no understanding for each other. – So she crept
to the house at her sister's heels.

Laura did not go indoors; hiding against the wall of the

flagged verandah, she threw her bouquet in at the window, meaning it to fall on Mother's lap.

But Mother had dropped her needle, and was just lifting her face, flushed with stooping, when the flowers hit her a thwack on the head. She groped again, impatiently, to find what had struck her, recognised the peace-offering, and thought of the surprise cake that was to go into Laura's box on the morrow. Then she saw the curl, and her face darkened. Was there ever such a tiresome child? What in all the world would she do next?

'Laura, come here, directly!'

Laura had moved away; she was not expecting recognition. If Mother were pleased she would call Pin to put the flowers in water for her, and that would be the end of it. The idea of a word of thanks would have made Laura feel uncomfortable. Now, however, at the tone of Mother's voice, her mouth set stubbornly. She went indoors as bidden, but was already up in arms again.

'You're a very naughty girl indeed!' began Mother as soon she appeared. 'How dare you cut off your hair? Upon my word, if it weren't your last night I'd send you to bed without any supper!' – an unheard-of threat on the part of Mother, who punished her childen in any way but that of denying them their food. 'It's a very good thing you're leaving home to-morrow, for you'd soon be setting the others at defiance, too, and I should have four naughty children on my hands instead of one. – But I'd be ashamed to go to school such a fright if I were you. Turn round at once and let me see you!'

Laura turned, with a sinking heart. Pin cried softly in a corner.

'She thought it would please you, mother,' she sobbed.

'I *will* not have you interfering, Pin, when I'm speaking to Laura. She's old enough by now to know what I like and what I don't,' said Mother, who was vexed at the thought of the

child going among strangers thus disfigured. – 'And now get
away, and don't let me see you again. You're a perfect sight.'

'Oh, Laura, you do look funny!' said Leppie and Frank in
weak chorus, as she passed them in the passage.

'Well, you've made a guy of yourself this time, Miss Laura,
and no mistake!' said Sarah, who had heard the above.

Laura went into her own room and locked the door, a thing
Mother did not allow. Then she threw herself on the bed and
cried. Mother had not understood in the least; and she had made
herself a sight into the bargain. She refused to open the door,
though one after another rattled the handle, and Sarah threatened to turn the hose in at the window. So they left her alone,
and she spent the evening in watery dudgeon on her pillow.
But before she undressed for the night she stealthily made a
chink and took in the slice of cake Pin had left on the door-mat.
Her natural buoyancy of spirit was beginning to reassert itself.
By brushing her hair well to one side she could cover up the gap,
she found; and after all, there was something rather pleasant
in knowing that you were misunderstood. It made you feel
different from everyone else.

Mother – sewing hard after even the busy Sarah had retired –
Mother smiled a stern little smile of amusement to herself; and
before locking up for the night put the dark curl safely away.

Chapter Two

LAURA, sleeping flat on her stomach, was roused next morning by Pin who said:

'Wake up, Wondrous Fair, mother wants to speak to you. She says you can get into bed in my place, before you dress.' – Pin slept warm and cosy at Mother's side.

Laura rose on her elbow and looked at her sister: Pin was standing in the doorway holding her nightgown to her, in such a way as to expose all of her thin little legs.

'Come on,' urged Pin. 'Sarah's going to give me my bath while you're with mother.'

'Go away, Pin,' said Laura snappily. 'I told you yesterday you could say Laura, and . . . and you're more like a spider than ever.'

'Spider' was another nickname for Pin, owed to her rotund little body and mere sticks of legs – she was 'all belly' as Sarah put it – and the mere mention of it made Pin fly; for she was very touchy about her legs.

As soon as the door closed behind her, Laura sprang out of bed and, waiting neither to wash herself not to say her prayers, began to pull on her clothes, confusing strings and buttons in her haste, and quite forgetting that on this eventful morning she had meant to dress herself with more than ordinary care. She was just lacing her shoes when Sarah looked in.

'Why, Miss Laura, don't you know your ma wants you?'

'It's too late. I'm dressed now,' said Laura darkly.

9

Sarah shook her head. 'Missis'll be fine an' angry. An' you needn't 'ave 'ad a row on your last day.'

Laura stole out of the door and ran down the garden to the summer-house. This, the size of a goodly room, was formed of a single dense, hairy-leafed tree, round the trunk of which a seat was built. Here she cowered, her elbows on her knees, her chin in her hands. Her face wore the stiff expression that went by the name of 'Laura's sulks'; but her eyes were big, and as watchful as those of a scared animal. If Sarah came to fetch her she would hold on to the seat with both hands. But even if she had to yield to Sarah's greater strength – well, at least she was up and dressed. Not like the last time – about a week ago – Mother had tried this kind of thing. Then, she had been caught unawares. She had gone into Pin's warm place, curious and un-suspecting, and thereupon Mother had begun to talk seriously to her, and not with her usual directness. She had reminded Laura that she was growing up apace and would soon be a woman; had told her that she must now begin to give up childish habits, and learn to behave in a modest and womanly way – all disagreeable, disturbing things, which Laura did not in the least want to hear. When it became clear to her what it was about, she had thrown back the bedclothes and escaped from the room. And since then she had been careful never to be long alone with Mother.

But now half an hour went by and no one came to fetch her: her grim little face relaxed. She felt very hungry, too, and when at length she heard Pin calling, she jumped up and betrayed her hiding-place.

'Laura! Laura, where are you? Mother says to come to breakfast and not be silly. The coach'll be here in an hour.'

Taking hands the sisters ran to the house.

In the passage, Sarah was busy roping a battered tin box. With their own hands the little boys had been allowed to paste on this a big sheet of notepaper, which bore, in Mother's writing, the words:

Miss Laura Tweedle Rambotham
The Ladies' College
Melbourne.

Mother herself was standing at the breakfast-table cutting sandwiches.

'Come and eat your breakfast, child,' was all she said at the moment. 'The tea's quite cold.'

Laura sat down and fell to with appetite, but also with a side-glance at the generous pile of bread and meat growing under Mother's hands.

'I shall never eat all that,' she said ungraciously; it galled her still to be considered a greedy child with an insatiable stomach.

'I know better than you do what you'll eat,' said Mother. 'You'll be hungry enough by this evening I can tell you, not getting any dinner.'

Pin's face fell at this prospect. 'Oh, mother, won't she really get any dinner?' she asked: and to her soft little heart going to school began to seem one of the blackest experiences life held.

'Why, she'll be in the train, stupid, 'ow can she?' said Sarah. 'Do you think trains give you dinners?'

'Oh, mother, please cut ever such a lot!' begged Pin, sniffing valiantly.

Laura began to feel somewhat moved herself at this solicitude, and choked down a lump in her throat with a gulp of tea. But when Pin had gone with Sarah to pick some nectarines, Mother's face grew stern, and Laura's emotion passed.

'I feel more troubled about you than I can say, Laura. I don't know how you'll ever get on in life – you're so disobedient and self-willed. It would serve you very well right, I'm sure, for not coming this morning, if I didn't give you a penny of pocket-money to take to school.'

Laura had heard this threat before, and thought it wiser not to reply. Gobbling up the rest of her breakfast she slipped away.

With the other children at her heels she made a round of the garden, bidding good-bye to things and places. There were the two summer-houses in which she had played house; in which she had cooked and eaten and slept. There was the tall fir tree with the rung-like branches by which she had been accustomed to climb to the very tree-top; there was the wilderness of bamboo and cane where she had been Crusoe; the ancient, broad-leaved cactus on which she had scratched their names and drawn their portraits; here, the high aloe that had such a mysterious charm for you, because you never knew when the hundred years might expire and the aloe burst into flower. Here again was the old fig tree with the rounded, polished boughs, from which, seated as in a cradle, she had played Juliet to Pin's Romeo, and vice versa – but oftenest Juliet: for though Laura greatly preferred to be the ardent lover at the foot, Pin was but a poor climber, and, as she clung trembling to her branch, needed so much prompting in her lines – even then to repeat them with such feeble emphasis – that Laura invariably lost patience with her and the love-scene ended in a squabble. Passing behind a wooden fence which was a tangle of passion-flower, she opened the door of the fowl-house, and out strutted the mother-hen followed by her pretty brood. Laura had given each of the chicks a name, and she now took Napoleon and Garibaldi up in her hand and laid her cheek against their downy breasts, the younger children following her movements in respectful silence. Between the bars of the rabbit hutch she thrust enough greenstuff to last the two little occupants for days; and everywhere she went she was accompanied by a legless magpie, which, in spite of its infirmity, hopped cheerily and quickly on its stumps. Laura had rescued it and reared it; it followed her like a dog; and she was only less devoted to it than she had been to a native bear which died under her hands.

'Now listen, children,' she said as she rose from her knees before the hutch. 'If you don't look well after Maggy and the bunnies, I don't know what I'll do. The chicks'll be all right. Sarah'll take care of them, 'cause of the eggs. But Maggy and the bunnies don't have eggs, and if they're not fed, or if Frank treads on Maggy again, then they'll die. Now if you let them die, I don't know what I'll do to you! Yes, I do: I'll send the devil to you at night when the room's dark, before you go to sleep. – So there!'

'How can you if you're not here?' asked Leppie.

Pin, however, who believed in ghosts and apparitions with all her fearful little heart, promised tremulously never, never to forget; but Laura was not satisfied until each of them in turn had repeated, in a low voice, with the appropriate gestures, the sacred secret, and forbidden formula:

> Is my finger wet?
> Is my finger dry?
> God'll strike me dead,
> If I tell a lie.

Then Sarah's voice was heard calling, and the boys went out into the road to watch for the coach. Laura's dressing proved a lengthy business, and was accomplished amid bustle, and scolding, and little peace-making words from Pin; for in her hurry that morning Laura had forgotten to put on the clean linen Mother had laid beside the bed, and consequently had now to strip to the skin.

The boys announced the coming of the coach with shrill cries, and simultaneously the rumble of wheels was heard. Sarah came from the kitchen drying her hands, and Pin began to cry.

'Now, shut up, res'vor!' said Sarah roughly: her own eyes were moist. 'You don't see Miss Laura be such a silly-billy. Anyone 'ud think you was goin', not 'er.'

The ramshackle old vehicle, one of Cobb's Royal Mail Coaches, big-bodied, lumbering, scarlet, pulled by two stout horses, drew up before the door, and the driver climbed down from his seat.

'Now good day to you, ma'am, good day, miss' – this to Sarah who, picking up the box, handed it to him to be strapped on under the apron. 'Well, well, and so the little girl's goin' to school, is she? My, but time flies! Well do I remember the day, ma'am, when I drove you all across for the first time. These children wasn't big enough then to git up and down be thimselves. Now I warrant you they can – just look at 'em, will you? – But my! Ain't you ashamed of yourself' – he spoke to Pin – 'pipin' your eye like that? Why, you'll flood the road, if you don't hould on. – Yes, yes, ma'am, bless you, I'li look after her, and put her inter the train wid me own han's. Don't you be oneasy. The Lord he cares for the widder and the orphun, and if He don't, why Patrick O'Donnell does.'

This was O'Donnell's standing joke; he uttered it with a loud chuckle. While speaking he had let down the steps and helped the three children up – they were to ride with Laura to the outskirts of the township. The little boys giggled excitedly at his assertion that the horses would not be equal to the weight. Only Pin wept on, in undiminished grief.

'Now, Miss Laura.'

'Now, Laura. Good-bye, darling. And do try and be good. And be sure you write once a week. And tell me everything. Whether you are happy – and if you get enough to eat – and if you have enough blankets on your bed. And remember always to change your boots if you get your feet wet. And don't lean out of the window in the train.'

For some time past Laura had had need of all her self-control, not to cry before the children. As the hour drew near it had grown harder and harder; while dressing, she had resorted to counting the number of times the profile of a Roman emperor appeared in the flowers on the wallpaper. Now the worst moment of all was come – the moment of good-bye. She did not look at Pin, but she heard her tireless, snuffly weeping, and set her own lips tight.

'Yes, mother . . . no, mother,' she answered shortly, 'I'll be all right. Good-bye.' She could not, however, restrain a kind of dry sob, which jumped up her throat.

When she was in the coach Sarah, whom she had forgotten, climbed up to kiss her; and there was some joking between O'Donnell and the servant while the steps were being folded and put away. Laura did not smile; her thin little face was very pale. Mother's heart went out to her in a pity which she did not know how to express.

'Don't forget your sandwiches. And when you're alone, feel in the pocket of your ulster and you'll find something nice. Good-bye, darling.'

'Good-bye . . . good-bye.'

The driver had mounted to his seat, he unwound the reins, cried 'Get up!' to the two burly horses, the vehicle was set in motion and trundled down the main street. Until it turned the corner by the Shire Gardens, Laura let her handkerchief fly from the window. Sarah waved hers; then wiped her eyes and lustily blew her nose. Mother only sighed.

'It was all she could do to keep up,' she said as much to herself as to Sarah. 'I do hope she'll be all right. She seems such a child to be sending off like this. Yet what else could I do? To a State School, I've always said it, my children shall never go – not if I have to beg the money to send them elsewhere.'

But she sighed again, in spite of the energy of her words, and stood gazing at the place where the coach had disappeared. She was still a comparatively young woman, and straight of body; but trouble, poverty and night-watches had scored many lines on her forehead.

'Don't you worry,' said Sarah. 'Miss Laura'll be all right. She's just a bit too clever – brains for two, that's what it is. An' children *will* grow up an' get big . . . an' change their feathers.' She spoke absently, drawing her metaphor from a brood of chickens which had strayed across the road, and was now trying to mount the wooden verandah – 'Shooh! Get away with you!'

'I know that. But Laura— The other children have never given me a moment's worry. But Laura's different. I seem to get less and less able to manage her. If only her father had been alive to help!'

'I'm sure no father livin' could do more than you for those blessed children,' said Sarah with impatience. 'You think of nothin' else. It 'ud be a great deal better if you took more care o' yourself. You sit up nights an' don't get no proper sleep, slavin' away at that blessed embroid'ry an' stuff, so as Miss Laura can get off to school an' to 'er books. An' then you want to worry over 'er as well. – She'll be all right. Miss Laura's like peas. You've got to get 'em outer the pod – they're in there sure enough. An' b'sides I guess school'll knock all the nonsense out of 'er.'

'Oh, I hope they won't be too hard on her,' said Mother in quick alarm. – 'Shut the side gate, will you. Those children have left it open again. – And, Sarah, I think we'll turn out the drawing-room.'

Sarah grunted to herself as she went to close the gate. This had not entered into her scheme of work for the day, and her cooking was still undone. But she did not gainsay her mistress, as she otherwise would have made no scruple of doing; for she knew that nothing was more helpful to the latter in a crisis than hard, manual work. Besides, Sarah herself had a sneaking weakness for what she called 'dra'in'-room days'. For the drawing-room was the storehouse of what treasures had remained over from a past prosperity. It was crowded with bric-à-brac and ornament; and as her mistress took these objects up one by one, to dust and polish them, she would, if she were in a good humour, tell Sarah where and how they had been bought, or describe the places they had originally come from: so that Sarah, pausing broom in hand to listen, had with time gathered some vague ideas of a country like 'Inja', for example, whence came the little silver 'pagody', and the expressionless brass god who squatted vacantly and at ease.

Chapter Three

As long as the coach rolled down the main street Laura sat bolt upright at the window. In fancy she heard people telling one another that this was little Miss Rambotham going to school. She was particularly glad that just as they went past the Commercial Hotel, Miss Perrotet, the landlord's red-haired daughter, should put her fuzzy head out of the window; for Miss Perrotet had also been to boarding-school, and thought very highly of herself in consequence, though it had only been for a year, to finish. At the National Bank the manager's wife waved a friendly hand to the children, and at the Royal Mail Hotel where they drew up for passengers or commissions, Mrs Paget, the stout landlady, came out, smoothing down her black satin apron.

'Well, I'm sure I wonder your ma likes sendin' you off so alone.'

The ride had comforted Pin a little; but when they had passed the chief stores and the flour-mill, and were come to a part of the road where the houses were fewer, her tears broke out afresh. The very last house was left behind, the high machinery of the claims came into view, the watery flats where Chinese were for ever rocking washdirt in cradles; and O'Donnell dismounted and opened the door. He lifted the three out one by one, shaking his head in humorous dismay at Pin, and as little Frank showed sighs of beginning, too, by puckering up his face and doubling up his body, the kindly man

18

tried to make them laugh by asking if he had the stomach-ache. Laura had one more glimpse of the children standing hand in hand – even in her trouble Pin did not forget her charges – then a sharp bend in the road hid them from her sight.

She was alone in the capacious body of the coach, alone, and the proud excitement of parting was over. The staunchly repressed tears welled up with a gush, and flinging herself down across the seat she cried bitterly. It was not a childishly irresponsible grief like Pin's: it was more passionate, and went deeper; and her overloaded feelings were soon relieved. But as she was not used to crying, she missed the moment at which she might have checked herself, and went on shedding tears after they had become a luxury.

'Why, goodness gracious, what's this?' cried a loud, cheerful and astonished voice, and a fat, rosy face beamed in on Laura. 'Why, here's a little girl in here, cryin' fit to break 'er heart. Come, come, my dear, what's the matter? Don't cry like that, now don't.'

The coach had stopped, the door opened and a stout woman climbed in, bearing a big basket, and followed by a young man with straw-coloured whiskers. Laura sat up like a dart and pulled her hat straight, crimson with mortification at being discovered in such a plight. She had instantly curbed her tears, but she could not disguise the fact that she had red eyes and a swollen nose – that she was in short what Sarah called 'all bunged up'. She made no reply to the newcomer's exclamations, but sat clutching her handkerchief and staring out of the window. The woman's good-natured curiosity, however, was not to be done.

'You poor little thing, you!' she persisted. 'Wherever are you goin', my dear, so alone?'

'I'm going to boarding-school,' said Laura, and shot a glance at the couple opposite.

'To boardin'-school? Peter! D'you hear? – Why, whatever's

your ma thinkin' of to send such a little chick as you to boardin'-school? ... and so alone, too.'

Laura's face took on a curious air of dignity.

'I'm not so very little,' she answered; and went on to explain, in phrases which she had heard so often that she knew them by heart: 'Only small for my age. I was twelve in spring. And I have to go to school, because I've learnt all I can at home.'

This failed to impress the woman.

'Snakes alive! – that's young enough in all conscience. And such a delicate little creature, too. Just like that one o' Sam MacFarlane's that popped off last Christmas – isn't she, Peter?'

Peter, who avoided looking at Laura, sheepishly mumbled something about like enough she was.

'And who *is* your ma, my dear? What's your name?' continued her interrogator.

Laura replied politely; but there was a reserve in her manner which, together with the name she gave, told enough: the widow, Laura's mother, had the reputation of being very 'stuck-up', and of bringing up her children in the same way.

The woman did not press Laura further, she whispered something behind her hand to Peter, then searching in her basket found a large, red apple, which she held out with an encouraging nod and smile.

'Here, my dear. Here's something for you. Don't cry any more, don't now. It'll be all right.'

Laura, who was well aware that she had not shed a tear since the couple entered the coach, coloured deeply, and made a movement, half shy, half unwilling, to put her hands behind her.

'Oh no, thank you,' she said in extreme embarrassment, not wishing to hurt the giver's feelings. 'Mother doesn't care for us to take things from strangers.'

'Bless her soul!' cried the stout woman in amaze. 'It's only an apple! Now, my dear, just you take it, and make your mind easy. Your ma wouldn't have nothin' against it to-day, I'm sure o' that – goin' away so far and all so alone like this. – It's sweet and juicy.'

'It's Melb'm you'll be boun' for I dessay?' said the yellow-haired Peter so suddenly that Laura started.

She confirmed this, and let her solemn eyes rest on him, wondering why he was so red and fidgety and uncomfortable. The woman said: 'Tch, tch, tch!' at the length of the journey Laura was undertaking, and Peter, growing still redder, volunteered another remark.

'I was nigh to bein' in Melb'm once meself,' he said.

'Aye, and he can't never forget it, the silly loon,' threw in the woman, but so good-naturedly that it was impossible, Laura felt, for Peter to take offence.

She gazed at the pair, speculating upon the relation they stood in to each other. She had obediently put out her hand for the apple, and now sat holding it, without attempting to eat it. It had not been Mother's precepts alone that had weighed with her in declining it; she was mortified at the idea of being bribed, as it were, to be good, just as though she were Pin or one of the little boys. It was a punishment on her for having been so babyish as to cry; had she not been caught in the act, the woman would never have ventured to be so familiar. – The very large-ness and rosiness of the fruit made it hateful to her, and she turned over in her mind how she could get rid of it.

As the coach bumped along, her fellow-passengers sat back and shut their eyes. The road was shadeless; beneath the horses' feet a thick red dust rose like smoke. The grass by the wayside, under the scattered gum trees or round the big black boulders that dotted the hillocks, was burnt to straw. In time, Laura also grew drowsy, and she was just falling into a doze when, with a jerk, the coach pulled up at the 'Halfway House'. Here

her companions alighted, and there were more nods and smiles
from the woman.

'You eat it, my dear. I'm sure your ma won't say nothin','
was her last remark as she pushed the swing-door and vanished
into the house, followed by Peter.

Then the driver's pleasant face appeared at the window of
the coach. In one hand he held a glass, in the other a bottle of
lemonade.

'Here, little woman, have a drink. It's warm work ridin'.'

Now this was quite different from the matter of the apple.
Laura's throat was parched with dust and tears. She accepted
the offer gratefully, thinking as she drank how envious Pin
would be, could she see her drinking bottle-lemonade.

Then the jolting and rumbling began anew. No one else
got in, and when they had passed the only two landmarks she
knew – the hut of the leprous Chinese and the market garden
of Ah Chow, who twice a week jaunted at a half-trot to the
township with his hanging baskets, to supply people with
vegetables – when they had passed these, Laura fell asleep. She
wakened with a start to find that the coach had halted to apply
the brakes, at the top of the precipitous hill that led down to the
railway township. In a two-wheeled buggy this was an
exciting descent; but the coach jammed on both its brakes,
moved like a snail, and seemed hardly able to crawl.

At the foot of the hill the little town lay sluggish in the sun.
Although it was close on midday, but few people were astir
in the streets; for the place had long since ceased to be an
important mining centre: the chief claims were worked out;
and the coming of the railway had been powerless to give it the
impetus to a new life. It was always like this in these streets
of low, verandahed, red-brick houses, always dull and sleepy,
and such animation as there was, was invariably to be found
before the doors of the many public-houses.

At one of these the coach stopped and unloaded its goods,

for an interminable time. People came and looked in at the window at Laura, and she was beginning to feel alarmed lest O'Donnell, who had gone inside, had forgotten all about her having to catch the train, when out he came, wiping his lips.

'Now for the livin' luggage!' he said with a wink, and Laura drew back in confusion from the laughter of a group of larrikins round the door.

It was indeed high time at the station; no sooner was her box dislodged and her ticket taken than the train steamed in. O'Donnell recommended her to the guard's care; she shook hands with him and thanked him, and had just been locked into a carriage by herself when he came running down the platform again, holding in his hand, for everyone to see, the apple, which Laura believed she had safely hidden under the cushions of the coach. Red to the roots of her hair she had to receive it, before a number of heads put out to see what the matter was, and she was even forced to thank O'Donnell into the bargain. Then the guard came along once more, and told her he would let no one get in beside her: she need not be afraid.

'Yes. And will you please tell me when we come to Melbourne.'

Directly the train was clear of the station, she lowered a window and, taking aim at a telegraph post, threw the apple from her with all her might. Then she hung out of the window, as far out as she could, till her hat was nearly carried off. This was the first railway journey she had made by herself, and there was an intoxicating sense of freedom in being locked in, alone, within the narrow compass of the compartment. She was at liberty to do everything that had previously been forbidden her: she walked up and down the carriage, jumped from one seat to another, then lay flat on her back singing to herself, and watching the telegraph poles fly past the windows, and the wires mount and descend. – But now came a station and, though the train did not stop, she sat up, in order that people might see she was travelling alone.

She grew hungry and attacked her lunch, and it turned out that Mother had not provided too much after all. When she had finished, had brushed herself clean of crumbs and handled, till her finger-tips were sore, the pompous half-crown she had found in her pocket, she fell to thinking of them at home, and of what they would now be doing. It was between two and three o'clock: the sun would be full on the flagstones of the back verandah; inch by inch Pin and Leppie would be driven away to find a cooler spot for their afternoon game, while little Frank slept, and Sarah splashed the dinner-dishes in the brick-floored kitchen. Mother sat sewing, and she would still be sitting there, still sewing, when the shadow of the fir tree, which at noon was shrunken like a dwarf, had stretched to giant size, and the children had opened the front gate to play in the shade of the public footpath. – At the thought of these shadows, of all the familiar things she would not see again for months to come, Laura's eyelids began to smart.

They had flashed through several stations; now they stopped; and her mind was diverted by the noïse and bustle. As the train swung into motion again, she fell into a pleasanter line of thought. She painted to herself, for the hundredth time, the new life towards which she was journeying, and, as always, in the brightest colours.

She had arrived at school, and in a spacious apartment, which was a kind of glorified Mother's drawing-room, was being introduced to a bevy of girls. They clustered round, urgent to make the acquaintance of the newcomer, who gave her hand to each with an easy grace and an appropriate word. They were too well-bred to cast a glance at her clothes, which, however she might embellish them in fancy, Laura knew were not what they ought to be: her ulster was some years old, and so short that it did not cover the flounce of her dress, and this dress, and her hat with it, were Mother's taste, and consequently, Laura felt sure, nobody else's. But her new companions saw that she wore these clothes with an elegance that made up for their shortcomings; and she heard them whisper: 'Isn't she pretty? What black eyes! What lovely curls!' But she was not proud, and by her ladylike manners soon made them feel at home with her, even though they stood agape at her cleverness: none of *them* could claim to have absorbed the knowledge of a whole house. With one of her admirers she had soon formed a friendship that was the wonder of all who saw it: in deep respect the others drew back, forming a kind of allée, down which, with linked arms, the two friends sauntered, blind to everything but themselves. – And having embarked thus upon her sea of dreams, Laura set sail and was speedily borne away.

'Next station you'll be there, little girl.'

She sprang up and looked about her, with vacant eyes. This had been the last stoppage, and the train was passing through the flats. In less than two minutes she had collected her belongings, tidied her hair and put on her gloves.

Some time afterwards they steamed in alongside a gravelled platform, among the stones of which a few grass-blades grew. This was Melbourne. At the nearer end of the platform stood two ladies, one stout and elderly in bonnet and mantle, with glasses mounted on a black stick, and shortsighted, peering eyes; the other stout and comely, too, but young, with a fat, laughing face and rosy cheeks. Laura descried them a long way off; and, as the carriage swept past them, they also saw her, eager and prominent at her window. Both stared at her, and the younger lady said something, and laughed. Laura instantly connected the remark, and the amusement it caused the speaker, with the showy red lining of her hat, at which she believed their eyes had been directed. She also realised, when it was too late, that her greeting had been childish, unnecessarily effusive; for the ladies had responded only by nods. Here were two thrusts to parry at once, and Laura's cheeks tingled. But she did not cease to smile, and she was still wearing this weak little smile, which did its best to seem easy and unconcerned, when she alighted from the train.

Chapter Four

THE elderly lady was Laura's godmother; she lived at Prahran, and it was at her house that Laura would sometimes spend a monthly holiday. Godmother was good to them all in a brusque, sharp-tongued fashion; but Pin was her especial favourite and she made no secret of it. Her companion on the platform was a cousin of Laura's, of at least twice Laura's age, who invariably struck awe into the children by her loud and ironic manner of speech. She was an independent, manly person, in spite of her plump roundnesses; she lived by herself in lodgings, and earned her own living as a clerk in an office.

The first greetings over, Godmother's attention was entirely taken up by Laura's box: after this had been picked out from among the other luggage, grave doubts were expressed whether it could be got on to the back seat of the pony-carriage, to which it was conveyed by a porter and the boy. Laura stood shyly by and waited, while Cousin Grace kept up the conversation by putting abrupt and embarrassing questions.

'How's your ma?' she demanded rather than asked, in the slangy and jocular tone she employed. 'I guess she'll be thanking her stars she's got rid of you;' at which Laura smiled uncertainly, not being sure whether Cousin Grace spoke in jest or earnest.

'I suppose you think no end of yourself going to boarding-school?' continued the latter.

'Oh no, not at all,' protested Laura with due modesty; and

27

as both at question and answer Cousin Grace laughed boisterously, Laura was glad to hear Godmother calling: 'Come, jump in. The ponies won't stand.'

Godmother was driving herself – a low basket-carriage, harnessed to two buff-coloured ponies. Laura sat with her back to them. Godmother flapped the reins and said: 'Get up!' but she was still fretted about the box, which was being held on behind by the boy. An inch larger, she asserted, and it would have had to be left behind. Laura eyed its battered sides uneasily. Godmother might remember, she thought, that it contained her whole wardrobe; and she wondered how many of Godmother's own ample gowns could be compressed into so small a space.

'All my clothes are inside,' she explained; 'that I shall need for months.'

'Ah, I expect your poor mother has sat up sewing herself to death, that you may be as well dressed as the rest of them,' said Godmother, and heaved a doleful sigh. But Cousin Grace laughed the wide laugh that displayed a mouthful of great healthy teeth.

'What? All your clothes in there?' she cried. 'I say! You couldn't be a queen if you hadn't more togs than that.'

'Oh, I know,' Laura hastened to reply, and grew very red. 'Queens need a lot more clothes than I've got.'

'Tut, tut!' said Godmother: she did not understand the allusion, which referred to a former ambition of Laura's. 'Don't talk such nonsense to the child.'

She drove very badly, and they went by quiet by-streets to escape the main traffic: the pony-chaise wobbled at random from one side of the road to the other, obstacles looming up only just in time for Godmother to see them. The ponies shook and tossed their heads at the constant sawing of the bits, and Laura had to be continually ducking, to keep out of the way of the reins. She let the unfamiliar streets go past her in a kind of dream; and there was silence for a time, broken only by Godmother's expostulations with the ponies, till Cousin Grace, growing tired of playing her bright eyes first on this, then on that, brought them back to Laura and studied her up and down.

'I say, who on earth trimmed your hat?' she asked almost at once.

'Mother,' answered Laura bravely, while the colour mounted to her cheeks again.

'Well, I guess she made up her mind you shouldn't get lost as long as you wore it,' went on her cousin with disconcerting candour. 'It makes you look just like a great big red double dahlia.'

'Let the child be. She looks well enough,' threw in God-mother in her snappish way. But Laura was sure that she, too, disapproved; and felt more than she heard the muttered remark about 'Jane always having had a taste for something gay.'

'Oh, I like the colour very much. I chose it myself,' said Laura, and looked straight at the two faces before her. But her lips twitched. She would have liked to snatch the hat from her head, to throw it in front of the ponies and hear them trample it under their hoofs. She had never wanted the scarlet lining of the big, upturned brim; in a dislike to being conspicuous which was incomprehensible to Mother, she had implored the latter to 'leave it plain'. But Mother had said: 'Nonsense!' and 'Hold your tongue!' and 'I know better,' – with this result.

Oh yes, she saw well enough how Godmother signed with her eyes to Cousin Grace to say no more; but she pretended not to notice, and for the remainder of the drive nobody spoke. They went past long lines of grey houses, joined one to another and built exactly alike; past large, fenced-in public parks where all kinds of odd, unfamiliar trees grew, with branches that ran right down their trunks, and bushy leaves. The broad streets were hilly; the wind, coming in puffs, met them with clouds of gritty white dust. They had just, with bent heads, their hands at their hats, passed through one of these miniature whirlwinds, when turning a corner they suddenly drew up, and the boy sprang to the ponies' heads. Laura, who had not been expecting the end so soon, saw only a tall wooden fence; but Cousin Grace looked higher, gave a stagey shudder and cried: 'Oh my eye Betty Martin! Aren't I glad it isn't me that's going to school! It looks just like a prison.'

It certainly was an imposing building viewed from within, when the paling-gate had closed behind them. To Laura, who came from a township of one-storeyed brick or weatherboard houses, it seemed vast in its breadth and height, appalling in its sombre greyness. Between Godmother and Cousin Grace she walked up an asphalted path, and mounted the steps that led to a massive stone portico. The bell Godmother rang made no answering sound, but after a very few seconds the door swung back, and a slender maidservant in cap and apron stood before them. She smiled at them pleasantly, as, in Chinaman-fashion, they crossed the threshold; then, inclining her head at a murmured word from Godmother, she vanished as lightly as she had come, and they sat and looked about them. They were in a plainly furnished but very lofty waiting-room. There were two large windows. The venetian blinds had not been lowered, and the afternoon sun, beating in, displayed a shabby patch on the carpet. It showed up, too, a coating of dust that had gathered on the desk-like, central table. There was the faint, distinctive smell of strange furniture. But what impressed Laura most was the stillness. No street noises pierced the massy walls, but neither did the faintest echo of all that might be taking place in the great building itself reach their ears: they sat aloof, shut off, as it were, from the living world. And this feeling soon grew downright oppressive: it must be like this to be dead, thought Laura to herself; and inconsequently remembered a quarter of an hour she had once spent in a dentist's ante-room: there as here the same soundless vacancy, the same anguished expectancy. Now, as then, her heart began to thump so furiously that she was afraid the others would hear it. But they, too, were subdued; though Cousin Grace tittered continually you heard only a gentle wheezing, and even Godmother expressed the hope that they would not be kept waiting long, under her breath. But minute after minute went by; there they sat and nothing happened. It began to seem as if they might sit on for ever.

All of a sudden, from out the spacious halls of which they had caught a glimpse on arriving, brisk steps began to come towards them over the oilcloth – at first as a mere tapping in the distance, then rapidly gaining in weight and decision. Laura's palpitations reached their extreme limit – another second and they might have burst her chest. Cousin Grace ceased to giggle; the door opened with a peculiar flourish; and all three rose to their feet.

The person who entered was a very stately lady; she wore a cap with black ribbons. With the door-handle still in her hand she made a slight obeisance, in which her whole body joined, afterwards to become more erect than before. Having introduced herself to Godmother as Mrs Gurley, the Lady Superintendent of the institution, she drew up a chair, let herself down upon it, and began to converse with an air of ineffable condescension.

While she talked Laura examined her, with a child's thirst for detail. Mrs Gurley was large and generous of form, and she carried her head in such a haughty fashion that it made her look taller than she really was. She had a high colour, her black hair was touched with grey, her upper teeth were prominent. She wore gold eyeglasses, many rings, a long gold chain, which hung from an immense cameo brooch at her throat, and a black apron with white flowers on it, one point of which was pinned to her ample bosom. The fact that Laura had just such an apron in her box went only a very little way towards reviving her spirits; for altogether Mrs Gurley was the most impressive person she had ever set eyes on. Beside her, God-mother was nothing but a plump, shortsighted fidgety lady.

Particularly awe-inspiring was Mrs Gurley when she listened to another speaking. She held her head a little to one side, her teeth met her underlip and her be-ringed hands toyed incessantly with the long gold chain, in a manner which seemed to denote that she set little value on what was being said. Awful, too, was the habit she had of suddenly lowering her head and looking at you over the tops of her glasses: when she did this, and when her teeth came down on her lip, you would have liked to shrink to the size of a mouse. Godmother, it was true, was not afraid of her; but Cousin Grace was hushed at last; and as for Laura herself, she consciously wore a fixed little simper, which was meant to put it beyond doubt that butter would not melt in her mouth.

Godmother now asked if she might say a few words in private, and the two ladies left the room. As the door closed behind them Cousin Grace began to be audible again.

'Oh, snakes!' she giggled, and her double chin spread itself. 'There's a Tartar for you! Don't I thank my stars it's not me that's being shunted off here! She'll give you what-for.'

'I don't think so. I think she's very nice,' said Laura staunchly, out of an instinct that made her chary of showing fear, or pain, or grief. But her heart began to bound again, for the moment in which she would be left alone.

'You see!' said Cousin Grace. 'It'll be bread and water for a week, if you can't do *amare* first go-off – not to mention the deponents.'

'What's *amare*?' asked Laura anxiously, and her eyes grew so big that they seemed to fill her face.

But Cousin Grace only laughed till it seemed probable that

she would burst her bodice; and Laura blushed, aware that she had compromised herself anew.

There followed a long and nervous pause.

'I bet Godmother's asking her not to wallop you too often,' the tease had just begun afresh, when the opening of the door forced her to swallow her sentence in the middle.

Godmother would not sit down; so the dreaded moment had come.

'Now, Laura. Be a good girl and learn well, and be a comfort to your mother. – Not that there's much need to urge her to her books,' Godmother interrupted herself, turning to Mrs Gurley. 'The trouble her dear mother has always had has been to keep her from them.'

Laura glowed with pleasure. Now at least the awful personage would know that she was clever, and loved to learn. But Mrs Gurley smiled the chilliest thinkable smile of acknowledgment, and did not reply a word.

She escorted the other to the front door, and held it open for them to pass out. Then, however, her pretence of affability faded clean away: turning her head just so far that she could look down her nose at her own shoulder, she said: 'Follow me!' – in a tone Mother would not have used even to Sarah. Feeling inexpressibly small Laura was about to obey, when a painful thought struck her.

'Oh please, I had a box – with my clothes in it!' she cried. 'Oh, I hope they haven't forgotten and taken it away again.'

But she might as well have spoken to the hatstand: Mrs Gurley had sailed off, and was actually approaching a turn in the hall before Laura made haste to follow her and to keep further anxiety about her box to herself. They went past one staircase, round a bend into shadows as black as if, outside, no sun were shining, and began to ascend another flight of stairs, which was the widest Laura had ever seen. The banisters were as thick as your arm, and on each side of the stair-carpeting the space was broad enough for two to walk abreast: what a splendid game of trains you could have played there! On the other hand the landing windows were so high up that only a giant could have seen out of them.

These things occurred to Laura mechanically. What really occupied her, as she trudged behind, was how she could please this hard-faced woman and make her like her; for the desire to please, to be liked by all the world, was the strongest her young soul knew. And there must be a way, for Godmother had found it without difficulty.

She took two steps at once, to get nearer to the portly back in front of her.

'What a *very* large place this is!' she said in an insinuating voice.

She hoped the admiration, thus subtly expressed in the form of surprise, would flatter Mrs Gurley, as a kind of co-proprietor; but it was evident that it did nothing of the sort: the latter seemed to have gone deaf and dumb, and marched on up the stairs, her hands clasped at her waist, her eyes fixed ahead, like a walking stone-statue.

On the top floor she led the way to a room at the end of a long passage. There were four beds in this room, a washhand-stand, a chest of drawers, and a wall cupboard. But at first sight Laura had eyes only for the familiar object that stood at the foot of one of the beds.

'Oh, *there's* my box!' she cried. 'Someone must have brought it up.'

It was unroped; she had simply to hand over the key. Mrs Gurley went down on her knees before it, opened the lid, and began to pass the contents to Laura, directing her where to lay and hang them. Overawed by such complaisance, Laura moved nimbly about the room shaking and unfolding, taking care to be back at the box to the minute so as not to keep Mrs Gurley waiting. And her promptness was rewarded; the stern face seemed to relax. At the mere hint of this, Laura grew warm through and through; and as she could neither control her feelings nor keep them to herself, she rushed to an extreme and overshot the mark.

'I've got an apron like that. I think they're so pretty,' she said cordially, pointing to the one Mrs Gurley wore.

The latter abruptly stopped her work, and, resting her hands on the sides of the box, gave Laura one of the dreaded looks over her glasses, looked at her from top to toe, and as though she were only now beginning to see her. There was a pause, a momentary suspension of the breath, which Laura soon learned to expect before a rebuke.

'Little gels,' said Mrs Gurley – and even in the midst of her confusion Laura could not but be struck by the pronunciation of this word. 'Little gels – are required – to wear white aprons – when they come here!' – a break after each few words, as well as an emphatic head-shake, accentuated their severity. 'And I should like to know, if your mother, has never taught you, that it is very rude, to point, and also to remark, on what people wear.'

Laura went scarlet: if there was one thing she, Mother, all of them prided themselves on, it was the good manners that had been instilled into them since their infancy. – The rough reproof seemed to scorch her.

She went to and fro more timidly than before. Then, however, something happened which held a ray of hope.

'Why, what is this?' asked Mrs Gurley freezingly, and held up to view – with the tips of her fingers, Laura thought – a small, black Prayer Book. 'Pray, are you not a dissenter?' – For the College was nonconformist.

'Well . . . no, I'm not,' said Laura, in a tone of intense apology. Here, at last, was her chance. 'But it really doesn't matter a bit. I can go to another church quite well. I even think I'd rather. For a change. And the service isn't so long, at least so I've heard – except the sermon,' she added truthfully.

Had she denied religion altogether, the look Mrs Gurley bent on her could not have been more annihilating.

'There is – unfortunately! – no occasion, for you to do anything of the kind,' she retorted. 'I myself, am an Episcopalian, and I expect those gels, who belong to the Church of England, to attend it, with me.'

The unpacking at an end, Mrs Gurley rose, smoothed down her apron, and was just on the point of turning away, when on the bed opposite Laura's she espied an under-garment, lying wantonly across the counterpane. At this blot on the orderliness of the room she seemed to swell like a turkey-cock, seemed literally to grow before Laura's eyes as, striding to the door, she commanded an invisible someone to send Lilith Gordon to her '*di*-rectly!'

There was an awful pause; Laura did not dare to raise her head; she even said a little prayer. Mrs Gurley stood working at her chain, and tapping her foot – like a beast waiting for its prey, thought the child. And at last a hurried step was heard in the corridor, the door opened and a girl came in, high-coloured and scant of breath. Laura darted one glance at Mrs Gurley's face, then looked away and studied the pattern of a quilt, trying not to hear what was said. Her throat swelled, grew hard and dry with pity for the culprit. But Lilith Gordon – a girl with sandy eyebrows, a turned-up nose, a thick plait of red-gold hair, and a figure so fully developed that Laura mentally dubbed it a 'lady's figure', and put its owner down for years older than herself – Lilith Gordon neither fell on her knees nor sank through the floor. Her lashes were lowered, in a kind of dog-like submission, and her face had gone very red when Laura ventured to look at her again; but that was all. And Mrs Gurley having swept Jove-like from the room, this bold girl actually set her finger to her nose and muttered: 'Old Brimstone Beast!' As she passed Laura, too, she put out her tongue and said: 'Now then, goggle-eyes, what have *you* got to stare at?'

Laura was deeply hurt: she had gazed at Lilith out of the purest sympathy. And now, as she stood waiting for Mrs Gurley, who seemed to have forgotten her, the strangeness of things, and the general unfriendliness of the people struck home with full force. The late afternoon sun was shining in, in an unfamiliar way; outside were strange streets, strange noises, a strange white dust, the expanse of a big, strange city. She felt unspeakably far away now, from the small, snug domain of home. Here, nobody wanted her . . . she was alone among strangers, who did not even like her . . . she had already, without meaning it, offended two of them.

Another second, and the shameful tears might have found their way out. But at this moment there was a kind of preparatory boom in the distance, and the next, a great bell clanged through the house, pealing on and on, long after one's ears were rasped by the din. It was followed by an exodus from the rooms round about; there was a sound of voices and of feet. Mrs Gurley ceased to give orders in the passage, and returning, bade Laura put on a pinafore and follow her.

They descended the broad staircase. At a door just at the foot, Mrs Gurley paused and smoothed her already faultless bands of hair; then turned the handle and opened the door, with the majestic swing Laura had that day once before observed.

Chapter Five

FIFTY-FIVE heads turned as if by clockwork, and fifty-five pairs of eyes were levelled at the small girl in the white apron who meekly followed Mrs Gurley down the length of the dining-room. Laura crimsoned under the unexpected ordeal, and tried to fix her attention on the flouncing of Mrs Gurley's dress. The room seemed hundreds of feet long, and not a single person at the tea-tables but took stock of her. The girls made no scruple of leaning backwards and forwards, behind and before their neighbours, in order to see her better, and even the governesses were not above having a look. All were standing. On Mrs Gurley assigning Laura a place at her own right hand, Laura covered herself with confusion by taking her seat at once, before grace had been said, and before the fifty-five had drawn in their chairs with the noise of a cavalry brigade on charge. She stood up again immediately, but it was too late; an audible titter whizzed round the table: the new girl had sat down. For minutes after, Laura was lost in the pattern on her plate; and not till tongues were loosened and dishes being passed, did she venture to steal a glance round.

There were four tables, with a governess at the head and foot of each to pour out tea. It was more of a hall than a room, and had high, church-like windows down one side. At both ends were scores of pigeon-holes. There was a piano in it and a fireplace; it had pale blue walls, and only strips of carpet on the floor. At present it was darkish, for the windows did not catch the sun.

Laura was roused by a voice at her side; turning, she found her neighbour offering her a plate of bread.

'No, thank you,' she said impulsively; for the bread was cut in chunks, and did not look inviting.

But the girl nudged her on the sly. 'You'd better take some,' she whispered.

Laura then saw that there was nothing else. But she saw, too, the smiles and signs that again flew round: the new girl had said no.

Humbly she accepted the butter and the cup of tea which were passed to her in turn, and as humbly ate the piece of rather stale bread. She felt forlornly miserable under the fire of all these unkind eyes, which took a delight in marking her slips: at the smallest further mischance she might disgrace herself by bursting out crying. Just at this moment, however, something impelled her to look up. Her vis-à-vis, whom she had as yet scarcely noticed, was staring hard. And now, to her great surprise, this girl winked at her, winked slowly and deliberately with the right eye. Laura was so discomposed that she looked away again at once, and some seconds elapsed before she was brave enough to take another peep. The wink was repeated.

It was a black-haired girl this time, a girl with small blue eyes, a pale, freckled skin, and large white teeth. What most impressed Laura, though, was her extraordinary gravity: she chewed away with a face as solemn as a parson's; and then, just when you were least expecting it, came the wink. Laura was fascinated: she lay in wait for it beforehand and was doubtful whether to feel offended by it or to laugh at it. But at least it made her forget her mishaps, and did away with the temptation to cry.

When, however, Mrs Gurley had given the signal, and the fifty-five had pushed back their chairs and set them to the table again with the same racket as before, Laura's position was a painful one. Everybody pushed, and talked, and laughed, in a hurry to leave the hall, and no one took any notice of her except to stare. After some indecision, she followed the rest through a door. Here she found herself on a verandah facing the grounds of the school. There was a long bench, on which several people were sitting: she took a modest seat at one end. Two of the younger governesses looked at her and laughed, and made a remark. She saw her room-mate, Lilith Gordon, arm in arm with a couple of companions. The winker of the tea-table turned out to be a girl of her own age, but of a broader make; she had fat legs, which were encased in thickly-ribbed black stockings. As she passed the bench she left the friend she was with, to come up to Laura and dig her in the ribs.

'*Didn't* she like her bread and butter, poor little thing?' she said.

Laura shrank from the dig, which was rough; but she could not help smiling shyly at the girl, who looked good-natured. If only she had stayed and talked to her! But she was off and away, her arm round a comrade's neck.

Besides herself, there was now only an elderly governess left, who was reading. She, Laura, in her solitude, was conspicuous to every eye. But at this juncture up came two rather rollicking older girls, one of whom was fair, with a red complexion. As soon as their loud voices had driven the governess away, the smaller of the two, who had a pronounced squint, turned to Laura.

'Hallo, you kid,' she said, 'what's *your* name?'

Laura artlessly replied. She was dumbfounded by the storm of merriment that followed. Maria Morell, the fat girl, went purple, and had to be thumped on the back by her friend.

'Oh, my!' she gasped, when she had got her breath. 'Oh, my ... hold me, someone, or I shall split! Oh, golly! Laura ... Tweedle ... Rambotham – Laura ... Tweedle ... Rambotham! ...' her voice tailed off again. 'Gosh! Was there ever such a name?'

She laughed till she could laugh no more, rocking backwards and forwards and from side to side; while her companion proceeded to make further inquiries.

'Where do you come from?' the squint demanded of Laura, in a business-like way.

Laura named the township, quaveringly.

'What's your father?'

'He's dead,' answered the child.

'Well, but I suppose he was alive once wasn't he, duffer? What was he before he was dead?'

'A barrister.'

'What did he die of?'

'Consumption.'

'How many servants do you keep?'

'One.'

'How much have you got a year?'

'I don't know.'

'How old are you?'

'Twelve and a quarter.'

'Who made your dress?'

'Mother.'

'Oh, I say, hang it, that's enough. Stop teasing the kid,' said Maria Morell, when the laughter caused by the last admission had died away. But the squint spied a friend, ran to her, and there was a great deal of whispering and sniggering. Presently the pair came sauntering up and sat down; and after some artificial humming and hawing the newcomer began to talk, in a loud and fussy manner, about certain acquaintances of hers called Tweedledum and Tweedledee. Both the fat girl and the squint 'split' with laughter. Laura sat with her hands locked one inside the other; there was no escape for her, for she did not know where to go. But when the third girl put the regulation question: 'What's your name and what's your father?' she turned on her, with the courage of despair.

'What's yours?' she retorted hotly, at the same time not at all sure how the big girl might revenge herself.

To her relief, the others burst out laughing at their friend's bafflement.

'That's one for you, Kate Horner,' said Maria with a chuckle. 'Not bad for the kid. – Come on, Kid, will you have a walk round the garden?'

'Oh yes, *please*,' said Laura, reddening with pleasure; and there she was, arm in arm with her fat saviour, promenading the grounds like any other of the fifty-five.

She assumed, as well as she could, an air of feeling at her ease; even in the presence of the cold and curious looks that met her. The fat girl was protective, and Laura felt too grateful to her to take it amiss that every now and then she threw back her head and laughed anew, at the remembrance of Laura's patronymics; or that she still exchanged jokes about them with the other couple, when they met.

But by this time half an hour had slipped away, and the girls were fast disappearing. Maria Morell loitered till the last minute, then said, she, too, must be off to 'stew'. Everyone was hastening across the verandah laden with books, and disappearing down a corridor. Left alone, Laura made her way back to the dining-hall. Here some of the very young boarders were preparing their lessons, watched over by a junior governess. Laura lingered for a little, to see if no order were forthcoming, then diffidently approached the table and asked the governess if she would please tell her what to do.

'I'm sure *I* don't know,' answered that lady, disinclined for responsibility. 'You'd better ask Miss Chapman. Here, Maggie, show her where the study is.'

Laura followed the little girl over the verandah and down the corridor. At the end, the child pointed to a door, and on opening this Laura found herself in a very large brightly lighted room, where the boarders sat at two long tables with their books before them. Every head was raised at her entrance. In great embarrassment, she threaded her way to the more authoritative-looking of the governesses in charge, and proffered her request. It was not understood, and she had to repeat it.

'I'm sure I don't know,' said Miss Day in her turn: she had stiff, black, wavy hair, a vivid colour, and a big, thick nose which made her profile resemble that of a horse. 'Can't you twiddle your thumbs for a bit? – Oh well, if you're so desperately anxious for an occupation, you'd better ask Miss Chapman.'

The girls in the immediate neighbourhood laughed noise-lessly, in a bounden-duty kind of way, at their superior's pleasantry, and Laura, feeling as though she had been hit, crossed to the other table. Miss Chapman, the head governess, was neither so hard-looking nor so brilliant as Miss Day. She even eyed Laura somewhat uneasily, meanwhile toying with a long gold chain, after the manner of the Lady Superintendent.

'Didn't Mrs Gurley tell you what to do?' she queried. 'I should think it likely she would. Oh well, if she didn't, I suppose you'd better bring your things downstairs. Yes ... and ask Miss Zielinski to give you a shelf.'

Miss Zielinski – she was the governess in the dining-hall – said: 'Oh, very well,' in the rather whiny voice that seemed natural to her, and went on reading.

'Please, I don't think I know my way,' ventured Laura.

'Follow your nose and you'll find it!' said Miss Zielinski without looking up, and was forthwith wrapt in her novel again.

Once more Laura climbed the wide staircase: it was but dimly lighted, and the passages were in darkness. After a few false moves she found her room, saw that her box had been taken away, her books left lying on a chair. But instead of picking them up, she threw herself on her bed and buried her face in the pillow. She did not dare to cry, for fear of making her eyes red, but she hugged the cool linen to her cheeks.

'I hate them all,' she said passionately, speaking aloud to herself. 'Oh, *how* I hate them!' – and wild schemes of vengeance flashed through her young mind. She did not even halt at poison or the knife: a big cake, sent by Mother, of which she invited all alike to partake, and into which she inserted a fatal poison, so that the whole school died like rabbits; or a nightly stabbing, a creeping from bed to bed in the dark, her penknife open in her hand...

But she had not lain thus for more than a very few minutes when steps came along the passage; and she had only just time to spring to her feet before one of the little girls appeared at the door.

'You're to come down at once.'

'Don't you know you're not *allowed* to stay upstairs?' asked Miss Zielinski crossly. 'What were you doing?' And as Laura did not reply: 'What was she doing, Jessie?'

'I don't know,' said the child. 'She was just standing there.' And all the little girls laughed, after the manner of their elders.

Before Laura had finished arranging her belongings on the shelves that were assigned to her, some of the older girls began to drop in from the study. One unceremoniously turned over her books, which were lying on the table.

'Let's see what the kid's got.'

Now Laura was proud of her collection: it really made a great show; for a daughter of Godmother's had once attended the College, and her equipment had been handed down to Laura.

'Why, you don't mean to say a kid like you's in the Second Principia already?' said a big girl, and held up, incredulously, Smith's black and red boards. 'Wherever did *you* learn Latin?'

In the reediest of voices Laura was forced to confess that she had never learnt Latin at all.

The girl eyed her in dubious amaze, then burst out laughing. 'Oh, I say!' she called to a friend. 'Here's a rum go. Here's this kid brings the Second Principia with her and doesn't know the First.'

Several others crowded round; and all found this divergence from the norm, from the traditional method of purchasing each book new and as it was needed, highly ridiculous. Laura, on her knees before her shelf, pretended to be busy; but she could not see what she was doing, for the mist that gathered in her eyes.

Just at this moment, however, in marched Maria Morell. 'Here, I say, stop that!' she cried. 'You're teasing that kid again. I won't have it. Here, come on, Kid – Laura Tweedledum – come and sit by me for supper.'

For the second time, Laura was thankful to the fat girl. But, as ill-luck would have it, Miss Chapman chanced to let her eyes stray in their direction; and having fingered her chain indecisively for a little, said: 'It seems a pity, doesn't it, Miss Day, that that nice little girl should get in with that vulgar set?'

Miss Chapman liked to have her opinions confirmed. But this was a weakness Miss Day did not pamper; herself strong-minded, she could afford to disregard Miss Chapman's foibles. So she went on with her book, and ignored the question. But Miss Zielinski, who lost no opportunity of making herself agreeable to those over her, said with foreign emphasis: 'Yes, indeed it does.'

So Laura was summoned and made to sit down at the end of the room, close to the governesses and beside the very big girls – girls of eighteen and nineteen, who seemed older still to her, with their figures, and waists, and skirts that touched the ground.

Instinctively she felt that they resented her proximity. The biggest of all, a pleasant-faced girl with a kind smile, said on seeing her downcast air: 'Poor little thing! Never mind.' But when they talked among themselves they lowered their voices, and cast stealthy glances at her, to see if she were listening.

Supper over, three chairs were set out in an exposed position; the big bell in the passage was lightly touched; everyone fetched a hymn-book, one with music in it being handed to Miss Chapman at the piano. The door opened to admit first Mrs Gurley, then the Principal and his wife – a tall, fair gentleman in a long coat, and a sweet-faced lady, who wore a rose in her velvet dress.

'Let us sing in the hundred and fifty-seventh hymn,' said the gentleman, who had a Grecian profile and a drooping, sandy moustache; and when Miss Chapman had played through the tune, the fifty-five, the governesses, the lady and gentleman rose to their feet and sang, with halting emphasis, of the Redeemer and His mercy, to Miss Chapman's accompaniment, which was as indecisive as her manner, the left hand dragging lamely along after the right.

'Let us read in the third chapter of the Second Epistle of Paul to the Thessalonians.'

Everyone laid her hymn-book on the table and sat down to listen to Paul's words, which the sandy gentleman read to a continual nervous movement of the left leg.

'Let us pray.'

Obeying the word, the fifty-five rose, faced about, and knelt to their chairs. It was an extempore prayer, and a long one, and Laura did not hear much of it; for the two big girls on her right kept up throughout a running conversation. Also, when it was about half over she was startled to hear Miss Zielinski say, in a shrill whisper: 'Heavens! There's that mouse again,' and audibly draw her skirts round her. Even Miss Chapman, praying to her piano-chair some distance off, had heard, and turned her head to frown rebuke.

The prayer at an end, Mr and Mrs Strachey bowed vaguely in several directions, shook hands with the governesses, and left the room. This was the signal for two of the teachers to advance with open Bibles.

'Here, little one, have you learned your verse?' whispered Laura's pleasant neighbour.

Laura knew nothing of it; but the big girl lent her a Bible, and, since it was not a hard verse and every girl repeated it, it was quickly learned.

I wisdom dwell with prudence and find out knowledge of witty inventions.

Told off in batches, they filed up the stairs. On the first landing stood Miss Day, watching with lynx-eyes to see that no books or eatables were smuggled to the bedrooms. In a strident voice she exhorted the noisy to silence, and the loiterers to haste.

Laura sped to her room. She was fortunate enough to find it still empty. Tossing off her clothes, she gabbled ardently through her own prayers, drew the blankets up over her head, and pretended to be asleep. Soon the lights were out and all was quiet. Then, with her face burrowed deep, so that not a sound could escape, she gave free play to her tears.

Chapter Six

My dear mother

I sent you a postcard did you get it. I told you I got here all right
and liked it very much. I could not write a long letter before I had no
time and we are only alowed to write letters two evenings a week
Tuesday and Friday. When we have done our lessons for next day
we say please may I write now and Miss Chapman says have you
done everything and if we say we have she says yes and if you sit
at Miss Days table Miss Day says it. And sometimes we haven't
but we say so. I sit up by Miss Chapman and she can see everything
I do and at tea and dinner and breakfast I sit beside Mrs Gurley.
Another girl in my class sits opposite and one sits beside me and we
would rather sit somewhere else. I dont care for Mrs Gurley much
she is very fat and never smiles and never listens to what you say
unless she scolds you and I think Miss Chapman is afraid of her to.
Miss Day is not afraid of anybody. I am in the first class. I am in the
College and under that is the school. Only very little girls are in the
school they go to bed at half past eight and do their lessons in the
dining hall. I do mine in the study and go to bed with the big girls.
They wear dresses down to the ground. Lilith Gordon is a girl in my
class she is in my room to she is only as old as me and she wears stays
and has a beautiful figgure. All the girls wear stays. Please send me
some I have no waste. A governess sleeps in our room and she has no
teeth. She takes them out every night and puts them in water when
the light is out. Lilith Gordon and the other girl say goodnight to her
after she has taken them off then she cant talk propperly and we want

48

to hear her. I think she knows for she is very cross. I don't learn latin yet till I go into the second class my sums are very hard. For supper there is only bread and butter and water if we don't have cake and jam of our own. Please send me some strawberry jam and another cake. Tell Sarah there are three servants to wait at dinner they have white aprons and a cap on their heads. They say will you take beef miss

I remain

your loving daughter

Laura.

Dear Pin

I am very busy I will write you a letter. You would not like being here I think you should always stop at home you will never get as far as long division. Mrs Gurley is an awful old beast all the girls call her that. You WOULD *be frightened of her. In the afternoon after school we walk two and two and you ask a girl to walk with you and if you dont you have to walk with Miss Chapman. Miss Chapman and Miss Day walks behind and they watch to see you dont laugh at boys. Some girls write letters to them and say they will meet them up behind a tree in the corner of the garden a paling is lose and the boys put letters in. I think boys are silly but Maria Morell says they are tip top that means awfully jolly. She writes a letter to boys every week she takes it to church and drops it coming out and he picks it up and puts an answer through the fence. We put our letters on the mantlepiece in the dining hall and Mrs Gurley or Miss Chapman read the adress to see we dont write to boys. They are shut up she cant read the inside. I hope you dont cry so much at school no one cries. Now Miss Chapman says it is time to stop*

I remain

your afectionate sister

Laura.

P.S. I took the red lineing out of my hat.

Warrenega
Sunday.

My dear Laura

    We were very glad to get your letters which came this morning. Your postcard written the day after you arrived at the College told us little or nothing. However Godmother was good enough to write us an account of your arrival so that we were not quite without news of you. I hope you remembered to thank her for driving in all that way to meet you and take you to school which was very good of her. I am glad to hear you are settling down and feeling happy and I hope you will work hard and distinguish yourself so that I may be proud of you. But there are several things in your letters I do not like. Did you really think I shouldnt read what you wrote to Pin. You are a very foolish girl if you did. Pin the silly child tried to hide it away because she knew it would make me cross but I insisted on her showing it to me and I am ashamed of you for writing such nonsense to her. Maria Morell must be a very vulgar minded girl to use the expressions she does. I hope my little girl will try to only associate with nice minded girls. I didnt sent you to school to get nasty ideas put into your head but to learn your lessons well and get on. If you write such vulgar silly things again I shall complain to Mrs Gurley or Mr Strachey about the tone of the College and what goes on behind their backs. I think it is very rude of you too to call Mrs Gurley names. Also about the poor governess who has to wear false teeth. Wait till all your own teeth are gone and then see how you will like it. I do want you to have nice feelings and not grow rough and rude. There is evidently a very bad tone among some of the girls and you must be careful in choosing your friends. I am sorry to hear you are only in the lowest class. It would have pleased me better if you had got into the second but I always told you you were lazy about your sums – you can do them well enough if you like. You dont need stays. I have never worn them myself and I dont intend you to either. Your own muscles are quite strong enough to bear the weight of your back. Bread and water is not much of a supper for you to go to bed on. I will send you another cake soon and some jam and I hope you will share it with the other girls. Now try and be sensible and industrious and make nice friends and then I shant have to scold you

your loving mother
J.T.R.

P.S. Another thing in your letter I dont like. You say you tell your governess you have finished your lessons when you have not done so. That is telling an untruth and I hope you are not going to be led away by the examples of bad girls. I have always brought you children up to be straightforward and I am astonished at you beginning fibbing as soon as you get away from home. Fibbing soon leads to something worse.

P.P.S. You must have written your letter in a great hurry for your spelling is anything but perfect. You are a very naughty girl to meddle with your hat. Pin has written a letter which I enclose though her spelling is worse than ever.

Daer Laura

mother says you are a very sily girl to rite such sily letters I think you are sily to I shood be fritened of Mrs Girly I dont want to go to Skool I wood rather stop with mother and be a cumfert to her I think it is nauty to drop letters in Cherch and verry sily to rite to Boys boys are so sily Sarah sends her luv she says she wood not ware a cap on her hed not for annything she says She wood just as soon ware a ring thrugh her nose.

I remain
your luving sister
Pin.

Dear mother

please please dont write to Mrs Gurley about the Tone in the College or not to Mr Strachey either. I will never be so silly again. I am sorry my letters were so silly I wont do it again. Please dont write to them about it. I dont go much with Maria Morell now I think she

she is vulger to. I know two nice girls now in my own class their names are Inez and Bertha they are very nice and not at all vulger. Maria Morell is fat and has a red face she is much older than me and I dont care for her now. Please dont write to Mrs Gurley I will never call her names again. I had to write my letter quickly because when I have done my lessons it is nearly time for supper. I am sorry my spelling was wrong I will take more pains next time I will learn hard and get on and soon I will be in the second class. I did not mean I said I had done my lessons when I had not done them the other girls say it and I think it is very wrong of them. Please dont write to Mrs Gurley I will try and be good and sensible and not do it again if you only wont write.

I remain
your afectionate daughter
Laura.

P.S. I can do my sums better now.

Warrenega

My dear Laura

My letter evidently gave you a good fright and I am not sorry to hear it for I think you deserved it for being such a foolish girl. I hope you will keep your promise and not do it again. Of course I dont mean that you are not to tell me everything that happens at school but I want you to only have nice thoughts and feelings and grow into a wise and sensible girl. I am not going to write a long letter today. This is only a line to comfort you and let you know that I shall not write to Mrs Gurley or Mr Strachey as long as I see that you are being a good girl and getting on well with your lessons. I do want you to remember that you are a lady though you are poor and must behave in a ladylike way. You dont tell me what the food at the College is like and whether you have blankets enough on your bed at night. Do try and remember to answer the questions I ask you. Sarah is busy washing today and the children are helping her by sitting with their arms in the tubs. I am to tell you from Pin *that Maggy is moulting badly and has not eaten much since you left which is just three weeks today*

your loving
Mother.

Friday

My dear mother

I was so glad to get your letter I am so glad you will not write to Mrs Gurley this time and I will promise to be very good and try to remember everything you tell me. I am sorry I forgot to answer the questions I have two blankets on my bed and it is enough. The food is very nice for dinner for tea we have to eat a lot of bread and butter I dont care for bread much. Sometimes we have jam but we are not alowed to eat butter and jam together. A lot of girls get up at six and go down to practice they dont dress and have their bath they just put on their dressing gowns on top of their night gowns. I dont go down now till seven I make my own bed. We have prayers in the morning and the evening and prayers again when the day scholers come. I do my sums better now I think I shall soon be in the second class. Pins spelling was dreadfull and she is nearly nine now and is such a baby the girls would laugh at her.

I remain
your afectionate daughter
Laura.

P.S. I parssed a long sentence without any mistakes.

Chapter Seven

THE mornings were beginning to grow dark and chilly: fires were laid overnight in the outer classrooms; and the junior governess who was on early duty, having pealed the six-o'clock bell, flitted like a grey wraith from room to room and from one gas-jet to another, among stretched, sleeping forms. And the few minutes' grace at an end, it was a cold, unwilling pack that threw off coverlets and jumped out of bed, to tie on petticoats and snuggle into dressing-gowns and shawls; for the first approach of cooler weather was keenly felt, after the summer heat. The governess blew on speedily chilblained fingers, in making her rounds of the verandahs to see that each of the twenty pianos was rightly occupied; and, as winter crept on, its chief outward sign an occasional thin white spread of frost, which vanished before the mighty sun of ten o'clock, she sometimes took the occupancy for granted, and skipped an exposed room.

At eight, the boarders assembled in the dining-hall for prayers and breakfast. After this meal it was Mrs Gurley's custom to drink a glass of hot water. While she sipped, she gave audience, meting out rebukes and crushing complaints – were any bold enough to offer them – standing erect behind her chair at the head of the table, supported by one or more of the staff. To suit the season she was draped in a shawl of crimson wool, which reached to the flounce of her skirt, and was borne by her portly shoulders with the grace of a past day. Beneath the shawl, her dresses were built, year in, year out, on the same plan: cut in one piece, buttoning right down the front, they fitted her like an eelskin, rigidly outlining her majestic proportions, and always short enough to show a pair of surprisingly small, well-shod feet. Thus she stood, sipping her water, and boring with her hard, unflagging eye every girl that presented herself to it. Most shrank noiselessly away as soon as breakfast was over; for, unless one was very firm indeed in the conviction of one's own innocence, to be beneath this eye was apt to induce a disagreeable sense of guilt. In the case of Mrs Gurley, familiarity had never been known to breed contempt. She was possessed of what was little short of genius, for ruling through fear; and no more fitting overseer could have been set at the head of these half-hundred girls, of all ages and degrees: gentle and common; ruly and unruly, children hardly out of the nursery, and girls well over the brink of womanhood, whose ripe, bursting forms told their own tale; the daughters of poor ministers at reduced fees; and the spoilt heiresses of wealthy wool-brokers and squatters, whose dowries would mount to many thousands of pounds. – Mrs Gurley was equal to them all.

In a very short time, there was no more persistent shrinker from the ice of this gaze than little Laura. In the presence of Mrs Gurley the child had a difficulty in getting her breath. Her first week of school life had been one unbroken succession of snubs and reprimands. For this, the undue familiarity of her manner was to blame: she was all too slow to grasp – being of an impulsive disposition and not naturally shy – that it was indecorous to accost Mrs Gurley off-hand, to treat her, indeed, in any way as if she were an ordinary mortal. The climax had come one morning – it still made Laura's cheeks burn to remember it. She had not been able to master her French lesson for that day, and seeing Mrs Gurley chatting to a governess had gone thoughtlessly up to her and tapped her on the arm.

'Mrs Gurley, please, do you think it would matter very much if I only took half this verb today? It's *coudre*, and means to sew, you know, and it's *so* hard. I don't seem to be able to get it into my head.'

Before the words were out of her mouth, she saw that she had made a terrible mistake. Mrs Gurley's face, which had been smiling, froze to stone. She looked at her arm as though the hand had bitten her, and Laura's sudden shrinking did not move her, to whom seldom anyone addressed a word un-bidden.

'How *dare* you interrupt me – when I am speaking!' – she hissed, punctuating her words with the ominous head-shakes and pauses. 'The first thing, miss, for you to do, will be, to take a course of lessons, in manners. Your present ones, may have done well enough, in the outhouse, to which you have evidently belonged. They will not do, here, in the company of your betters.'

Above the child's head the two ladies smiled significantly at each other, assured that, after this, there would be no further want of respect; but Laura did not see them. The iron of the thrust went deep down into her soul: no one had ever yet cast a slur upon her home. Retreating to a lavatory she cried herself nearly sick, making her eyes so red that she was late for prayers in trying to wash them white. Since that day, she had never of her own free will approached Mrs Gurley again, and even avoided those places where she was likely to be found. This was why one morning, some three weeks later, on discovering that she had forgotten one of her lesson-books, she hesitated long before re-entering the dining-hall. The governesses still clustered round their chief, and the pupils were not expected to return. But it was past nine o'clock; in a minute the public prayer-bell would ring, which united boarders, several hundred day-scholars, resident and visiting teachers in the largest class-room; and Laura did not know her

English lesson. So she stole in, cautiously dodging behind the group, in a twitter lest the dreaded eyes should turn her way.

It was Miss Day who spied her and demanded an explanation.

'Such carelessness! You girls would forget your heads if they weren't screwed on,' retorted the governess, in the dry, violent manner that made her universally disliked.

Thankful to escape with this, Laura picked out her book and hurried from the room.

But the thoughts of the group had been drawn to her.

'The greatest little oddity we've had here for some time,' pronounced Miss Day, pouting her full bust in decisive fashion.

'She is, indeed,' agreed Miss Zielinski.

'I don't know what sort of a place she comes from, I'm sure,' continued the former: 'but it must be the end of creation. She's utterly no idea of what's what, and as for her clothes, they're fit for a Punch and Judy show.'

'She's had no training either – stupid, I call her,' chimed in one of the younger governesses, whose name was Miss Snodgrass. 'She doesn't know the simplest things, and her spelling is awful. And yet, do you know, at history the other day, she wanted to hold forth about how London looked in Elizabeth's reign – when she didn't know a single one of the dates!'

'She can say some poetry,' said Miss Zielinski. 'And she's read Scott.'

One and all shook their heads at this, and Mrs Gurley went on shaking hers and smiling grimly. 'Ah! the way gels are brought up nowadays,' she said. 'There was no such thing in my time. We were made to learn what would be of some use and help to us afterwards.'

Elderly Miss Chapman twiddled her chain. 'I hope I did right, Mrs Gurley. She had one week's early practice, but she looked so white all day after it that I haven't put her down for it again. I hope I did right?'

'Oh, well, we don't want to have them ill, you know,' replied Mrs Gurley, in the rather irresponsive tone she adopted towards Miss Chapman. 'As long as it isn't mere laziness.'

'I don't think she's lazy,' said Miss Chapman. 'At least she takes great pains with her lessons at night.'

This was true. Laura tried her utmost, with an industry born of despair. For the comforting assurance of speedy promotion, which she had given Mother, had no root in fact. These early weeks only served to reduce, bit by bit, her belief in her own knowledge. How slender this was, and of how little use to her in her new state, she did not dare to confess even to herself. Her disillusionment had begun the day after her arrival, when Dr Pughson, the Headmaster, to whom she had gone to be examined in arithmetic, flung up hands of comical dismay at her befogged attempts to solve the mysteries of long division. An upper class was taking a lesson in Euclid, and in the intervals between her mazy reckonings she had stolen glances at the master. A tiny little nose was as if squashed flat on his face, above a grotesquely expressive mouth, which displayed every one of a splendid set of teeth. He had small, short-sighted, red-rimmed eyes, and curly hair which did not stop growing at his ears, but went on curling, closely cropped, down the sides of his face. He taught at the top of his voice, thumped the blackboard with a pointer, was biting at the expense of a pupil who confused the angle BFC with the angle BFG, a moment later to volley forth a broad Irish joke which convulsed the class. He bewitched Laura; she forgot her sums in the delight of watching him; and this made her learning seem a little scantier than it actually was; for she had to wind up in a great hurry. He pounced down upon her; the class laughed anew at his playful horror; and yet again at the remark that it was evident she had never had many pennies to spend, or she would know better what to do with the figures that represented them. – In these words

Laura scented a reference to Mother's small income, and grew as red as fire.

In the lowest class in the College she sat bottom, for a week or more: what she did know, she knew in such an awkward form that she might as well have known nothing. And after a few efforts to better her condition she grew cautious, and hesitated discreetly before returning one of those ingenuous answers which, in the beginning, had made her the merry-andrew of the class. She could for instance, read a French story-book without skipping very many words; but she had never heard a syllable of the language spoken, and her first attempts at pronunciation caused even Miss Zielinski to sit back in her chair and laugh till the tears ran down her face. History Laura knew in a vague, pictorial way: she and Pin had enacted many a striking scene in the garden – such as 'Not Angles but Angels,' or, did the pump-drain overflow, Canute and his silly courtiers – and she also had out-of-the-way scraps of information about the characters of some of the monarchs, or, as the governess had complained, about the state of London at a certain period; but she had never troubled her head with dates. Now they rose before her, a hard, dry, black line from 1066 on, accompanied, not only by the kings who were the cause of them, but by dull laws, and their duller repeals. Her lessons in English alone gave her a mild pleasure: she enjoyed taking a sentence to pieces to see how it was made. She was fond of words, too, for their own sake, and once, when Miss Snodgrass had occasion to use the term 'eleemosynary', Laura was so enchanted by it that she sought to share her enthusiasm with her neighbour. This girl went crimson from trying to stifle her laughter.

'What *is* the matter with you girls down there?' cried Miss Snodgrass. 'Carrie Isaacs, what are you laughing like that for?'

'It's Laura Rambotham, Miss Snodgrass. She's so funny,' spluttered the girl.

'What are you doing, Laura?'

Laura did not answer. The girl spoke for her.

'She said – hee, hee! – she said it was blue.'

'Blue? What's blue?' snapped Miss Snodgrass.

'That word. She said it was so beautiful . . . and that it was blue.'

'I didn't. Grey-blue, I said,' murmured Laura her cheeks aflame.

The class rocked; even Miss Snodgrass herself had to join in the laugh while she hushed and reproved. And sometimes after this, when a particularly long or odd word occurred in the lesson, she would turn to Laura and say jocosely: 'Now, Laura, come on, tell us what colour that is. Red and yellow, don't you think?'

But these were 'Tom Fool's colours'; and Laura kept a wise silence.

One day at geography, the pupils were required to copy the outline of the map of England. Laura, about to begin, found to her dismay that she had lost her pencil. To confess the loss meant one of the hard, public rebukes from which she shrank. And so, while the others drew, heads and backs bent low over their desks, she fidgeted and sought – on her lap, the bench, the floor.

'What on earth's the matter?' asked her neighbour crossly; it was the black-haired boarder who had winked at Laura the first evening at tea; her name was Bertha Ramsey. 'I can't draw a stroke if you shake like that.'

'I've lost my pencil.'

The girl considered Laura for a moment, then pushed the lid from a box of long, beautifully sharpened drawing-pencils. 'Here, you can have one of these.'

Laura eyed the well-filled box admiringly, and modestly selected the shortest pencil. Bertha Ramsay, having finished her map, leaned back in her seat.

'And next time you feel inclined to boo-hoo at the tea-table, hold on to your eyebrows and sing Rule Britannia. – *Did* it want its mummy, poor ickle sing?'

Here Bertha's chum, a girl called Inez, chimed in from the other side.

'It's all very well for you,' she said to Bertha, in a deep, slow voice. 'You're a weekly boarder.'

Laura had the wish to be very pleasant, in return for the pencil. So she drew a sigh, and said, with over-emphasis: 'How nice for your mother to have you home every week!'

Bertha only laughed at this, in a teasing way: 'Yes, isn't it?' But Inez leaned across behind her and gave Laura a poke.

'Shut up!' she telegraphed.

'Who's talking down there?' came the governess's cry. 'Here you, the new girl, Laura what's-your-name, come up to the map.'

A huge map of England had been slung over an easel; Laura was required to take the pointer and show where Stafford lay. With the long stick in her hand, she stood stupid and confused. In this exigency, it did not help her that she knew, from hear-say, just how England looked; that she could see, in fancy, its ever-green grass, thick hedges, and spreading trees; its never-dry rivers; its hoary old cathedrals; its fogs, and sea-mists, and over-populous cities. She stood face to face with the most puzzling map in the world – a map seared and scored with boundary-lines, black and bristling with names. She could not have laid her finger on London at this moment, and as for Stafford, it might have been in the moon.

While the class straggled along the verandah at the end of the hour, Inez came up to Laura's side.

'I say, you shouldn't have said that about her mother.' She nodded mysteriously.

'Why not?' asked Laura, and coloured at the thought that she had again, without knowing it, been guilty of a *faux pas*.

Inez looked round to see that Bertha was not within hearing, then put her lips to Laura's ear.

'She drinks.'

Laura gaped incredulous at the girl, her young eyes full of horror. From actual experience, she hardly knew what drunkenness meant; she had hitherto associated it only with the lowest class of Irish agricultural labourer, or with those dreadful white women who lived, by choice, in Chinese Camps. That there could exist a mother who drank was unthinkable . . . outside the bounds of nature.

'Oh, how awful!' she gasped, and turned pale with excitement.

Inez could not help giggling at the effect produced by her words – the new girl was a 'rum stick' and no mistake – but as Laura's consternation persisted, she veered about.

'Oh, well, I don't know for certain if that's it. But there's something awfully queer about her.'

'Oh, *how* do you know?' asked her breathless listener, mastered by a morbid curiosity.

'I've been there – at Vaucluse – from a Saturday till Monday. She came in to lunch, and she only talked to herself, not to us. She tried to eat mustard with her pudding too, and her meat was cut up in little pieces for her. I guess if she'd had a knife she'd have cut our throats.'

'Oh!' was all Laura could get out.

'I was so frightened my mother said I shouldn't go again.'

'Oh, I hope she won't ask me. What shall I do if she does?'

'Look out, here she comes! Don't say a word. Bertha's awfully ashamed of it,' said Inez, and Laura had just time to give a hasty promise.

'Hullo, you two, what are you gassing about?' cried Bertha, and dealt out a couple of her rough and friendly punches. – 'I say, who's on for a race up the garden?'

They raced, all three, with flying plaits and curls, much

kicking-up of long black legs, and a frank display of frills and tuckers. Laura won; for Inez's wind gave out half way, and Bertha was heavy of foot. Leaning against the palings Laura watched the latter come puffing up to join her – Bertha with the shameful secret in the background, of a mother who was not like other mothers.

Chapter Eight

LAURA had been, for some six weeks or more, a listless and unsuccessful pupil, when one morning she received an invitation from Godmother to spend the coming monthly holiday – from Saturday till Monday – at Prahran. The month before, she had been one of the few girls who had nowhere to go; she had been forced to pretend that she liked staying in, did it in fact by preference. – Now her spirits rose.

Marina, Godmother's younger daughter, from whom Laura inherited her school-books, was to call for her. By a little after nine o'clock on Saturday morning, Laura had finished her weekly mending, tidied her bedroom, and was ready dressed even to her gloves. It was a cool, crisp day; and her heart beat high with expectation.

From the dining-hall, it was not possible to hear the ringing of the front-door bell; but each time either of the maids entered with a summons, Laura half rose from her chair, sure that her turn had come at last. But it was half-past nine, then ten, then half-past; it struck eleven, the best of the day was passing, and still Marina did not come. Only two girls besides herself remained. Then respectively an aunt and a mother were announced, and these two departed. Laura alone was left: she had to bear the disgrace of Miss Day observing: 'Well, it looks as if *your* friends had forgotten all about you, Laura.'

Humiliated beyond measure, Laura had thoughts of tearing off her hat and jacket and declaring that she felt too ill to go out. But at last, when she was almost sick with suspense. Mary put her tidy head in once more.

'Miss Rambotham has been called for.'

Laura was on her feet before the words were spoken. She sped to the reception-room.

Marina, a short, sleek-haired, soberly dressed girl of about twenty, had Godmother's brisk, matter-of-fact manner.

She offered Laura her cheek to kiss. 'Well, I suppose you're ready now?'

Laura forgave her the past two hours. 'Yes, quite, thank you,' she answered.

They went down the asphalted path and through the garden-gate, and turned to walk townwards. For the first time since her arrival Laura was free again – a prisoner at large. Round them stretched the broad white streets of East Melbourne; at their side was the thick, exotic greenery of the Fitzroy Gardens; on the brow of the hill rose the massive proportions of the Roman Catholic Cathedral. – Laura could have danced, as she walked at Marina's side.

After a few queries, however, as to how she liked school and how she was getting on with her lessons, Marina fell to contemplating a strip of paper that she held in her hand. Laura gathered that her companion had combined the task of calling for her with a morning's shopping, and that she had only worked half through her list of commissions before arriving at the College. At the next corner they got on to the outside car of a cable-tramway, and were carried into town. Here Marina entered a co-operative grocery store, where she was going to give an order for a quarter's supplies. She was her mother's housekeeper, and had an incredible knowledge of groceries, as well as a severely practical mind: she stuck her finger-nail into butter, tasted cheeses off the blade of a knife, ran her hands through currants, nibbled biscuits, discussed brands of burgundy and desiccated soups – Laura meanwhile looking on, from a high, uncomfortable chair, with a some-what hungry envy. When everything, down to pepper and salt, had been remembered, Marina filled in a cheque, and was just about to turn away when she recollected an affair of some empty cases, which she wished to send back. Another ten minutes' parley ensued; she had to see the manager, and was closeted with him in his office, so that by the time they emerged into the street again a full hour had gone by.

'Getting hungry?' she inquired of Laura.

'A little. But I can wait,' answered Laura politely.

'That's right,' said Marina, off whose own appetite the edge had no doubt been taken by her various nibblings. 'Now there's only the chemist.'

They rode to another street, entered a druggist's, and the same thing on a smaller scale was repeated, except that here Marina did no tasting, but for a stray gelatine or jujube. By the time the shop door closed behind them, Laura could almost have eaten liquorice powder. It was two o'clock, and she was faint with hunger.

'We'll be home in plenty of time,' said Marina, consulting a neat watch. 'Dinner's not till three today, because of father.'

Again a tramway jerked them forward. Some half mile from their destination, Marina rose.

'We'll get out here. I have to call at the butcher's.'

At a quarter to three, it was a very white-faced, exhausted little girl that followed her companion into the house.

'Well, I guess you'll have a fine healthy appetite for dinner,' said Marina, as she showed her where to hang up her hat and wash her hands.

Godmother was equally optimistic. From the sofa of the morning-room, where she sat knitting, she said: 'Well, you've had a fine morning's gadding about I must say! How are you? And how's your dear mother?'

'Quite well, thank you.'

Godmother scratched her head with a spare needle, and the attention she had had for Laura evaporated. 'I hope, Marina, you told Graves about those empty jam-jars he didn't take back last time?'

Marina, without lifting her eyes from a letter she was reading, returned: 'Indeed I didn't. He made such a rumpus about the sugar-boxes that I thought I'd try to sell them to Petersen instead.'

Godmother grunted, but did not question Marina's decision. 'And what news have you from your dear mother?' she asked again, without looking at Laura – just as she never looked at the stocking she held, but always over the top of it.

Here, however, the dinner-bell rang, and Laura, spared the task of giving more superfluous information, followed the two ladies to the dining-room. The other members of the family were waiting at the table. Godmother's husband – he was a lawyer – was a morose, black-bearded man who, for the most part, kept his eyes fixed on his plate. Laura had heard it said that he and Godmother did not get on well together; she supposed this meant that they did not care to talk to each other, for they never exchanged a direct word: if they had to communicate, it was done by means of a third person. There was the elder daughter, Georgina, dumpier and still brusquer than Marina; the eldest son, a bank-clerk, who was something of a dandy, and did not waste civility on little girls; and lastly there were two boys, slightly younger than Laura, black-haired, pug-nosed, pugnacious little creatures, who stood in awe of their father, and were all the wilder when not under his eye.

Godmother mumbled a blessing; and the soup was eaten in silence.

During the meat course, the bank-clerk complained in extreme displeasure of the way the laundress had of late dressed his collars – these were so high that, as Laura was not slow to notice, he had to look straight down the two sides of his nose to see his plate – and announced that he would not be home for tea, as he had an appointment to meet some 'chappies' at five, and in the evening was going to take a lady friend to Brock's Fireworks. These particulars were received without comment. As the family plied its pudding-spoons, Georgina in her turn made a statement.

'Joey's coming to take me driving at four.'

It looked as if this remark, too, would founder on the general indifference. Then Marina said warningly, as if recalling her parent's thoughts: 'Mother!'

Awakened, Godmother jerked out: 'Indeed and I hope if you go you'll take the boys with you!'

'Indeed and I don't see why we should!'

'Very well, then, you'll stop at home. If Joey doesn't choose to come to the point—'

'Now hold your tongue, mother!'

'I'll do nothing of the sort.'

'Crikey!' said the younger boy, Erwin, in a low voice. 'Joey's got to take us riding.'

'If you and Joey can't get yourselves properly engaged,' snapped Godmother, 'then you shan't go driving without the boys, and that's the end of it.'

Like dogs barking at one another, thought Laura, listening to the loveless bandying of words – she was unused to the snappishness of the Irish manner, which sounds so much worse than it is meant to be: and she was chilled anew by it when, over the telephone, she heard Georgy holding a heated conversation with Joey.

He was a fat young man, with hanging cheeks, small eyes, and a lazy, lopsided walk.

'Hello – here's a little girl! What's *her* name? – Say, this kiddy can come along too.'

As it had leaked out that Marina's afternoon would be spent

between the shelves of her storeroom, preparing for the incoming goods, Laura gratefully accepted the offer.

They drove to Marlborough Tower. With their backs to the horse sat the two boys, mercilessly alert for any display of fondness on the part of the lovers; sat Laura, with her straight, inquisitive black eyes. Hence Joey and Georgy were silent, since, except to declare their feelings, they had nothing to say to each other.

The Tower reached, the mare was hitched up and the ascent of the light wooden erection began. It was a blowy day.

'Boys first!' commanded Joey. 'Cos o' the petticuts.' – His speech was as lazy as his walk.

He himself led the way, followed by Erwin and Marmaduke, and Laura, at Georgy's bidding, went next. She clasped her bits of skirts anxiously to her knees, for she was just as averse to the frills and flounces that lay beneath being seen by Georgy, as by any of the male members of the party. Georgy came last, and, though no one was below her, so tightly wound about was she that she could hardly advance her legs from one step to another. Joey looked approval; but the boys sniggered, and kept it up till Georgy, having gained the platform, threatened them with a 'clout on the head'.

On the return journey a dispute arose between the lovers: it related to the shortest road home, waxed hot, and was rapidly taking on the dimensions of a quarrel, when the piebald mare shied at a traction-engine and tried to bolt. Joey gripped the reins, and passed his free arm round Georgy's waist.

'Don't be frightened, darling.'

Though the low chaise rocked from side to side and there seemed a likelihood of it capsizing, the two boys squirmed with laughter, and dealt out sundry nudges, kicks and pokes, all of which were received by Laura, sitting between them. She herself turned red – with embarrassment. At the same time she wondered why Joey should believe George was afraid; there was no sign of it in Georgy's manner; she sat stolid and un-moved. Besides she, Laura, was only a little girl, and felt no fear. – She also asked herself why Joey should suddenly grow concerned about Georgy, when, a moment before, they had been so rude to each other. – These were interesting specula-tions, and, the chaise having ceased to sway, Laura grew meditative.

In the evening Godmother had a visitor, and Laura sat in a low chair, listening to the ladies' talk. It was dull work: for, much as she liked to consider herself 'almost grown up', she yet detested the conversation of 'real grown-ups' with a child's heartiness. She was glad when nine o'clock struck and Marina, lighting a candle, told her to go to bed.

The next day was Sunday. Between breakfast and church-time yawned two long hours. Georgy went to a Bible-class; Marina was busy with orders for the dinner.

It was a bookless house – like most Australian houses of its kind: in Marina's bedroom alone stood a small bookcase containing school and Sunday school prizes. Laura was very fond of reading, and as she dressed that morning had cast longing looks at these volumes, had evenly shyly fingered the glass doors. But they were locked. Breakfast over, she ap-proached Marina on the subject. The latter produced the key, but only after some haggling, for her idea of books was to keep the gilt on their covers untarnished.

'Well, at any rate it must be a Sunday book,' she said ungraciously.

She drew out *The Giant Cities of Bashan and Syria's Holy Places*, and with this Laura retired to the drawing-room, where Godmother was already settled for the day, with a suitable magazine. When the bells began to clang the young people, primly hatted, their prayer-books in their hands, walked to the neighbouring church. There Laura sat once more between the boys, Marina and Georgy stationed like sentinels at the ends of the pew, ready to pounce down on their brothers if necessary, to confiscate animals and eatables, or to rap impish knuckles with a Bible. It was a spacious church; the pew was in a side aisle; one could see neither reading-desk nor pulpit; and the words of the sermon seemed to come from a great way off.

After dinner, Laura and the boys were dispatched to the garden, to stroll about in Sunday fashion. Here no elder person being present, the natural feelings of the trio came out: the distaste of a quiet little girl for rough boys and their pranks; the resentful indignation of the boys at having their steps dogged by a sneak and a tell-tale. As soon as they had rounded the tennis-court and were out of sight of the house, Erwin and Marmaduke clambered over the palings and dropped into the street, vowing a mysterious vengeance on Laura if she went indoors without them. The child sat down on the edge of the lawn under a mulberry tree and propped her chin on her hands. She was too timid to return to the house and brave things out; she was also afraid of someone coming into the garden and finding her alone, and of her then being forced to 'tell'; for most of all she feared the boys, and their vague, rude threats. So she sat and waited . . . and waited. The shadows on the grass changed their shapes before her eyes; distant chapel-bells tinkled their quarter of an hour and were still again; the blighting torpor of a Sunday afternoon lay over the world. Would to-morrow ever come? She counted on her fingers the hours that had still to crawl by before she could get back to school – counted twice over to be sure of them – and all but yawned her head off, with ennui. But time passed, and passed, and nothing happened. She was on the verge of tears, when two black heads bobbed up above the fence, the boys scrambled over, red and breathless, and hurried her into tea.

She wakened next morning at daybreak, so eager was she to set out. But Marina had a hundred and one odd jobs to do before she was ready to start, and it struck half-past nine as the two of them neared the College. Child-like, Laura felt no special gratitude for the heavy pot of mulberry jam Marina bore on her arm; but at sight of the stern, grey, stone building she could have danced with joy; and on the front door swinging to behind her, she drew a deep sigh of relief.

Chapter Nine

FROM this moment on – the moment when Mary the maid's pleasant smile saluted her – Laura's opinion of life at school suffered a change. She was glad to be back – that was the first point: just as an adventurous sheep is glad to regain the cover of the flock. Learning might be hard; the governesses mercilessly secure in their own wisdom; but here she was at least a person of some consequence, instead of as at Godmother's a mere negligible null.

Of her unlucky essay at holiday-making she wrote home guardedly: the most tell-tale sentence in her letter was that in which she said she would rather not go to Godmother's again in the meantime. But there was such a lack of warmth in her account of the visit that mother made this, together with the above remark, the text for a scolding.

'You're a very ungrateful girl,' she wrote, 'to forget all God-mother has done for you. If it hadn't been for her supplying you with books and things I couldn't have sent you to school at all. And I hope when you grow up you'll be as much of a help to me as Marina is to her mother. I'd much rather have you good and useful than clever and I think for a child of your age you see things with very sharp unkind eyes. Try and only think nice things about people and not be always spying out their faults. Then you'll have plenty of friends and be liked wherever you go.'

Laura took the statement about the goodness and cleverness with a grain of salt: she knew better. Mother thought it the proper thing to say, and she would certainly have preferred the two qualities combined; but, had she been forced to choose between them, there was small doubt how her choice would have fallen out. And if, for instance, Laura confessed that her teachers did not regard her as even passably intelligent, there would be a nice to-do. Mother's ambitions knew no bounds; and, wounded in these, she was quite capable of writing post-haste to Mrs Gurley or Mr Strachey, complaining of their want of insight, and bringing forward a string of embarrassing proofs. So, leaving Mother to her pleasing illusions, Laura settled down again to her rôle of dunce, now, though, with more equanimity than before. School was really not a bad place after all – this had for some time been her growing conviction, and the visit to Godmother seemed to bring it to a head.

About this time, too, a couple of pieces of good fortune came her way.

The first: she was privileged to be third in the friendship between Inez and Bertha – a favour of which she availed herself eagerly, though the three were as different from one another as three little girls could be. Bertha was a good-natured romp, hard-fisted, thick of leg, and of a plodding but ineffectual industry. Inez, on the other hand, was so pretty that Laura never tired of looking at her: she had a pale skin, hazel eyes, brown hair with a yellow light in it, and a Greek nose. Her mouth was very small; her nostrils were mere tiny slits; and so lazy was she that she seldom more than half opened her eyes. Both girls were well over fourteen, and very fully developed: compared with them, Laura was like nothing so much as a skinny young colt.

She was so grateful to them for tolerating her that she never took up a stand of real equality with them: proud and sensitive, she was always ready to draw back and admit their prior rights to each other; hence the friendship did not advance to intimacy.

But such as it was, it was very comforting; she no longer needed to sit alone in recess; she could link arms and walk the garden with complacency; and many were the supercilious glances she now threw at Maria Morell and that clique; for her new friends belonged socially to the best set in the school.

In another way, too, their company made things easier for her: neither of them aimed high; and both were well content with the lowly places they occupied in the class. And so Laura, who was still, in her young confusion, unequal to discovering what was wanted of her, grew comforted by the presence and support of her friends, and unmindful of higher opinion; and Miss Chapman, in supervising evening lessons, remarked with genuine regret that little Laura was growing perky and lazy.

Her second piece of good luck was of quite a different nature.

Miss Hicks, the visiting governess for geography, had a gift for saying biting things that really bit. She bore Inez a peculiar grudge; for she believed that certain faculties slumbered behind the Grecian profile, and that only the girl's ingrained sloth prevented them.

One day she lost patience with this sluggish pupil.

'I'll tell you what it is, Inez,' she said; 'you're blessed with a real woman's brain: vague, slippery, inexact, interested only in the personal aspect of a thing. You can't concentrate your thoughts, and, worst of all, you've no curiosity – about anything that really matters. You take all the great facts of existence on trust – just as a hen does – and I've no doubt you'll go on contentedly till the end of your days, without ever knowing why the ocean has tides, and what causes the seasons. – It makes me ashamed to belong to the same sex.'

Inez's classmates tittered furiously, let the sarcasm glide over them, unhit by its truth. Inez herself, indeed, was inclined to consider the governess's taunt a compliment, as proving that she was incapable of a vulgar inquisitiveness. But Laura, though she laughed docilely with the rest, could not forget the incident – words in any case had a way of sticking to her memory – and what Miss Hicks had said often came back to her, in the days that followed. And then, all of a sudden, just as if an invisible hand had opened the door to an inner chamber, a light broke on her. Vague, slippery, inexact, interested only in the personal – every word struck home. Had Miss Hicks set out to describe *her*, in particular, she could not have done it more accurately. It was but too true: until now, she, Laura, had been satisfied to know things in a slipslop, razzle-dazzle way, to know them anyhow, as it best suited herself. She had never set to work to master a subject, to make it her own in every detail. Bits of it, picturesque scraps, striking features – what Miss Hicks no doubt meant by the personal – were all that had attracted her. – Oh, and she, too, had no intelligent curiosity. She could not say that she had ever teased her brains with considering why the earth went round the sun and not the sun round the earth. Honestly speaking, it made no difference to her that the globe was indented like an orange, and not the perfect round you began by believing it to be. – But if this were so, if she were forced to make these galling admissions, then it was clear that her vaunted cleverness had never existed, except in Mother's imagination. Or, at any rate, it had crumbled to pieces like a lump of earth, under the hard, heavy hand of Miss Hicks. Laura felt humiliated, and could not understand her companions treating the matter so airily. She did not want to have a woman's brain, thank you; not one of that sort; and she smarted for the whole class.

Straightway she set to work to sharpen her wits, to follow the strait road. At first with some stumbling, of course, and frequent backslidings. Intellectual curiosity could not, she discovered, be awakened to order; and she often caught herself napping. Thus though she speedily became one of the most troublesome askers-why, her desire for information was apt

to exhaust itself in putting the question, and she would forget
to listen to the answer. Besides, for the life of her she could
not drum up more interest in, say, the course of the Gulf
Stream, or the formation of a plateau, than in the fact that, when
Nelly Bristow spoke, little bubbles came out of her mouth,
and that she needed to swallow twice as often as other people;
or that when Miss Hicks grew angry her voice had a way of
failing, at the crucial moment, and flattening out to nothing –
just as if one struck tin after brass. No, it was indeed difficult
for Laura to invert the value of these things. – In another
direction she did better. By dint of close attention, of pondering
both the questions asked by Miss Hicks, and the replies made
by the cleverest pupils, she began to see more clearly where
true knowledge lay. It was facts that were wanted of her; facts
that were the real test of learning; facts she was expected to
know. Stories, pictures of things, would not help her an inch
along the road. Thus, it was not the least use in the world to
her to have seen the snowy top of Mount Kosciusko stand out
against a dark blue evening sky, and to know its shape to a
tittlekin. On the other hand, it mattered tremendously that
this mountain was 7308 and not 7309 feet high: that piece of
information was valuable, was of genuine use to you; for it
was worth your place in the class.

Thus did Laura apply herself to reach the school ideal, thus
force herself to drive hard nails of fact into her vagrant thoughts.
And with success. For she had, it turned out, a retentive memory, and to her joy learning by heart came easy to her – as easy
as to the most brilliant scholars in the form. From now on she
gave this talent full play, memorising even pages of the history-
book in her zeal; and before many weeks had passed, in all
lessons except those in arithmetic – you could not, alas! get
sums by rote – she was separated from Inez and Bertha by the
width of the class.

But neither her taste of friendship and its comforts, nor the abrupt change for the better in her class-fortunes, could counterbalance Laura's luckless knack of putting her foot in it. This she continued to do, in season and out of season. And not with the authorities alone.

There was, for instance, that unfortunate evening when she was one of the batch of girls invited to Mrs Strachey's drawing-room. Laura, ignorant of what it meant to be blasée, had received her note of invitation with a thrill, had even enjoyed writing, in her best hand, the prescribed formula of acceptance. But she was alone in this; by the majority of her companions these weekly parties were frankly hated, the chief reason being that every guest was expected to take a piece of music with her. Even the totally unfit had to show what they could do. And the fact that cream-tarts were served for supper was not held to square accounts.

'It's all very well for you,' grumbled Laura's room-mate, Lilith Gordon, as she lathered her thick white arms and neck before dressing. 'You're a new girl; you probably won't be asked.'

Laura did not give the matter a second thought: hastily selecting a volume of music, she followed the rest of the white dresses into the passage. The senior girl tapped at the drawing-room door. It was opened by no other than the Principal himself.

In the girls' eyes, Mr Strachey stood over six feet in his stocking-soles. He had also a most arrogant way of looking down his nose, and of tugging, intolerantly, at his long, drooping moustache. There was little need for him to assume the frigid contemptuousness of Mrs Gurley's manner: his mere presence, the very unseeingness of his gaze, inspired awe. Tales ran of his wrath, were it roused; but few had experienced it. He quelled the high spirits of these young colonials by his dignified air of detachment.

Now, however, he stood there affable and smiling, endeavouring to put a handful of awkward girls at their ease. But neither his nor Mrs Strachey's efforts availed. It was impossible for the pupils to throw off, at will, the crippling fear that governed their relations with the Principal. To them, his amiability resembled the antics of an uncertain-tempered elephant, with which you could never feel safe. – Besides on this occasion it was a young batch, and of particularly mixed stations. And so a dozen girls, from twelve to fifteen years old, sat on the extreme edges of their chairs, and replied to what was said to them, with dry throats.

Though the youngest of the party, Laura was the least embarrassed: she had never known a nursery, but had mixed with her elders since her babyhood. And she was not of a shy disposition; indeed, she still had to be reminded daily that shyness was expected of her. So she sat and looked about her. It was an interesting room in which she found herself. Low bookshelves, three shelves high, ran round the walls, and on the top shelf were many outlandish objects. What an evening it would have been had Mr Strachey invited them to examine these ornaments, or to handle the books, instead of having to pick up a title here and there by chance. – From the shelves, her eyes strayed to the pictures on the walls; one, in particular, struck her fancy. It hung over the mantelpiece, and was a man's head seen in profile, with a long hooked nose, and wearing a kind of peaked cap. But that was not all: behind this head were other profiles of the same face, and seeming to come out of clouds. Laura stared hard, but could make nothing of it. – And meanwhile her companions were rising with sickly smiles, to seat themselves, red as turkey-cocks' combs, on the piano stool, where with cold, stiff fingers they stumbled through the movement of a sonata or sonatina.

It was Lilith Gordon who broke the chain by offering to sing. The diversion was welcomed by Mrs Strachey, and Lilith went to the piano. But her nervousness was such that she broke down half-way in the little prelude to the ballad.

Mrs Strachey came to the rescue. 'It's so difficult, is it not, to accompany oneself?' she said kindly. 'Perhaps one of the others would play for you?'

No one moved.

'Do any of you know the song?'

Two or three ungraciously admitted the knowledge, but none volunteered.

It was here Laura chimed in. 'I could play it,' she said; and coloured at the sound of her own voice.

Mrs Strachey looked doubtfully at the thin little girl. 'Do you know it, dear? You're too young for singing, I think.'

'No, I don't know it. But I could play it from sight. It's quite easy.'

Everyone looked disbelieving, especially the unhappy singer.

'I've played much harder things than that,' continued Laura.

'Well, perhaps you might try,' said Mrs Strachey, with the ingrained distrust of the unmusical.

Laura rose and went to the piano, where she conducted the song to a successful ending.

Mrs Strachey looked relieved. 'Very nice indeed.' And to Laura: 'Did you say you didn't know it, dear?'

'No, I never saw it before.'

Again the lady looked doubtful. 'Well, perhaps you would play us something yourself now?'

Laura had no objection; she had played to people before her fingers were long enough to cover the octave. She took the volume of Thalberg she had brought with her, selected 'Home, Sweet Home', and pranced in.

Her audience kept utter silence; but, had she been a little sharper, she would have grasped that it was the silence of amazement. After the prim sonatinas that had gone before, Thalberg's florid ornaments had a shameless sound. Her performance, moreover, was a startling one; the forte pedal was held down throughout; the big chords were crashed and banged with all the strength a pair of twelve-year-old arms could put into them; and wrong notes were freely scattered. Still, rhythm and melody were well marked, and there was no mistaking the agility of the small fingers.

Dead silence, too, greeted the conclusion of the piece. Several girls were very red, from trying not to laugh. The Principal tugged at his moustache, in abstracted fashion.

Laura had reached her seat again before Mrs Strachey said undecidedly: 'Thank you, dear. Did you . . . hm . . . learn that piece here?'

Laura saw nothing wrong. 'Oh, no, at home,' she answered. 'I wouldn't care to play the things I learn here, to people. They're so dull.'

A girl emitted a faint squeak. But a half turn of Mrs Strachey's head subdued her. 'Oh, I hope you will soon get to like classical music also,' said the lady gravely, and in all good faith. 'We prefer it, you know, to any other.'

'Do you mean things like the *Air in G with Variations*? I'm afraid I never shall. There's no tune in them.'

Music was as fatal to Laura's equilibrium as wine would have been. Finding herself next Mr Strachey, she now turned to him and said, with what she believed to be ease of manner: 'Mr Strachey, will you please tell me what that picture is, hanging over the mantelpiece? I've been looking at it ever since I came in, but I can't make it out. Are those ghosts, those things behind the man, or what?'

It took Mr Strachey a minute to recover from his astonishment. He stroked hard, and the look he bent on Laura was not encouraging.

'It seems to be all the same face,' continued the child, her eyes on the picture.

'That,' said Mr Strachey, with extreme deliberation: 'that is the portrait, by a great painter, of a great poet – Dante Alighieri.'

'Oh, Dante, is it?' said Laura showily – she had once heard the name. 'Oh, yes, of course, I know now. He wrote a book, didn't he, called *Faust*? I saw it over there by the door. – What lovely books!'

But here Mr Strachey abruptly changed his seat, and Laura's thirst for information was left unquenched.

The evening passed, and she was in blessed ignorance of anything being amiss, till the next morning after breakfast she was bidden to Mrs Gurley.

A quarter of an hour later, on her emerging from that lady's private sitting-room, her eyes were mere swollen slits in her face. Instead, however, of sponging them in cold water and bravely joining her friends, Laura was still foolish enough to hide and have her cry out. So that when the bell rang, she was obliged to go in to public prayers looking a prodigious fright, and thereby advertising to the curious what had taken place.

Mrs Gurley had crushed and humiliated her. Laura learnt that she had been guilty of a gross impertinence, in profaning the ears of the Principal and Mrs Strachey with Thalberg's music, and that all the pieces she had brought with her from home would now be taken from her. Secondly, Mr Strachey had been so unpleasantly impressed by the boldness of her behaviour, that she would not be invited to the drawing-room again for some time to come.

The matter of the music touched Laura little: if they preferred their dull old exercises to what she had offered them, so much the worse for them. But the reproach cast on her manners stung her even more deeply than it had done when she was still the raw little newcomer: for she had been pluming herself of late that she was now 'quite the thing'.

And yet, painful as was this fresh overthrow of her pride, it was neither the worst not the most lasting result of the incident. That concerned her schoolfellows. By the following morning the tale of her doings was known to everyone. It was circulated in the first place, no doubt, by Lilith Gordon, who bore her a grudge for her offer to accompany the song: had Laura not put herself forward in this objectionable way, Lilith might have escaped singing altogether. Lilith also resented her having shown that she could do it – and this feeling was generally shared. It evidenced a want of good-fellowship, and made you very glad the little prig had afterwards come to grief: if you had abilities that others had not, you concealed them, instead of parading them under people's noses.

In short, Laura had committed a twofold breach of school etiquette. No one of course vouchsafed to explain this to her; these things one did not put into words, things you were expected to know without telling. Hence, she never more than half understood what she had done. She only saw disapproval painted on faces that had hitherto been neutral, and from one or two quarters got what was unmistakably the cold shoulder. – Her little beginnings at popularity had somehow received a setback, and through her own foolish behaviour.

Chapter Ten

THE lesson went home; Laura began to model herself more and more on those around her; to grasp that the unpardonable sin is to vary from the common mould.

In August, after the midwinter holidays, she was promoted to the second class; she began Latin; and as a reward was allowed by Mother to wear her dresses an inch below her knees. She became a quick, adaptable pupil, with a parrot-like memory, and at the end of the school year delighted Mother's heart with a couple of highly gilt volumes, of negligible contents.

At home, during those first holidays, she gave her sister and brothers cold creeps down their spines, with her stories of the great doings that took place at school; and none of her class-mates would have recognised in this arrant drawer-of-the-long-bow, the unlucky little blunderbuss of the early days.

On her return, Laura's circle of friends was enlarged. The morning after her arrival, on entering the dining-hall, she found a new girl standing shy and awkward before the fireplace. This was the daughter of a millionaire squatter named Macnamara; and the report of her father's wealth had preceded her. Yet here she now had to hang about, alone, unhappy, the target of all eyes. It might be supposed that Laura would feel some sympathy for her, having so recently undergone the same experience herself. But that was not her way. She rejoiced, in barbarian fashion, that this girl, older than she by about a year, and of a higher social standing, should have to endure a like ordeal. Staring heartlessly, she accentuated her part of old girl knowing all the ropes, and was so inclined to show off that she let herself in for a snub from Miss Snodgrass.

Tilly Macnamara joined Laura's class, and the two were soon good friends.

Tilly was a short, plump girl, with white teeth, rather boyish hands, and the blue-grey eyes predominant in Australia. She was usually dressed in silk, and she never wore an apron to protect the front of her frock. Naturally, too, she had a bottomless supply of pocket-money: if a subscription were raised, she gave ten shillings where others gave one; and on the Saturday holidays she flung about with half-crowns as Laura would have been afraid to do with pennies.

For the latter with her tiny dole, which had to last so and so long, since no more was forthcoming, it was a difficult task to move gracefully among companions none of whom knew what it meant to be really poor. Many trivial mortifications were the result; and countless small subterfuges had to be resorted to, to prevent it leaking out just how paltry her allowance was.

But the question of money was, after all, trifling, compared with the infinitely more important one of dress.

With regard to dress, Laura's troubles were manifold. It was not only that here, too, by reason of Mother's straitened means, she was forced to remain an outsider: that, in itself, she would have borne lightly; for, as little girls go, she was indifferent to finery. Had she had a couple of new frocks a year, in which she could have been neat and unremarkable, she would have been more than content. But, from her babyhood on, Laura – Pin with her – had lamented the fact that children could not go about clad in sacks, mercifully indistinguishable one from another. For they were the daughters of an imaginative mother, and, balked in other outlets, this imagination had wreaked itself on their clothing. All her short life long, Laura had suffered under a home-made, picturesque style of dress; and she had resented, with a violence even Mother did not gauge, this use of her young body as a peg on which to hang fantastic garments. After her tenth birthday she was, she thanked goodness, considered too old for the quaint shapes beneath which Pin still groaned; but there remained the matter of colour for Mother to sin against, and in this she seemed to grow more intemperate year by year. Herself dressed always in the soberest browns and blacks, she liked to see her young flock gay as Paradise birds, lighting up a drab world; and when Mother liked a thing, she was not given to consulting the wishes of little people. Those were awful times when she went, say, to Melbourne, and bought as a bargain a whole roll of cloth of an impossible colour, which had to be utilised to the last inch; or when she unearthed, from an old trunk, some antiquated garment to be cut up and reshaped – a Paisley shawl, a puce ball-dress, even an old pair of green rep curtains.

It was thus a heavy blow to Laura to find, on going home, that Mother had already bought her new spring dress. In one respect all was well: it had been made by the local dressmaker, and consequently had not the home-made cut that Laura abhorred. But the colour! Her heart fell to the pit of her stomach the moment she set eyes on it, and only with difficulty did she restrain her tears. – Mother had chosen a vivid purple, of a crude, old-fashioned shade.

Now, quite apart from her personal feelings, Laura had come to know very exactly, during the few months she had been at school, the views held by her companions on the subject of colour. No matter how sumptuous or how simple the material of which the dress was made, it must be dark, or of a delicate tint. Brilliancy was a sign of vulgarity, and put the wearer outside the better circles. Hence, at this critical juncture, when Laura was striving to ape her fellows in all vital matters,

the unpropitious advent of the purple threatened to undo
her.

After her first dismayed inspection, she retreated to the
bottom of the garden to give vent to her feelings.

'I shall never be able to wear it,' she moaned. 'Oh, how *could*
she buy such a thing? And I needed a new dress so awfully,
awfully much.'

'It isn't really so bad, Laura,' pleaded Pin. 'It'll look darker,
I'm sure, if you've got it on – and if you don't go out in the sun.'

'You haven't got to wear it. It was piggish of you, Pin,
perfectly piggish! You *might* have watched what she was
buying.'

'I did, Laura!' asseverated Pin, on the brink of tears. 'There
was a nice dark brown and I said take that, you would like it
better, and she said hold your tongue, and did I think she was
going to dress you as if you were your own grandmother.'

This dress hung for weeks in the most private corner of
Laura's school wardrobe. Her companions had all returned
with new outfits, and on the first assemblage for church there
was a great mustering of one another, both by girls and teachers.
Laura was the only one to descend in the dress she had worn
throughout the winter. Her heart was sore with bitterness, and
when the handful of Episcopalians were marching to St
Stephen's-on-the-Hill, she strove to soothe her own wound.

'I can't think why my dress hasn't come,' she said gratuitously, out of this hurt, with an oblique glance to see how her
partner took the remark: it was the good-natured Maria
Morell, who was resplendent in velvet and feathers. 'I expect
that stupid dressmaker couldn't get it done in time. I've waited
for it all the week.'

'What a sell!' said Maria, but with mediocre interest; for she
had cocked her eye at a harmless-looking youth, who was doing
his best not to blush on passing the line of girls. – 'I say, do look
at that toff making eyes. Isn't he a nanny-goat?'

On several subsequent Sundays, Laura fingered, in an agony of indecision, the pleasing stuff of the dress, and ruefully considered its modish cut. Once, no one being present, she even took it out of the wardrobe. But the merciless spring sunshine seemed to make the purple shoot fire, to let loose a host of other colours it in as well, and, with a shudder, she re-hung it on its peg.

But the evil day came. After a holiday at Godmother's, she received a hot letter from Mother. Godmother had complained of her looking 'dowdy', and Mother was exceedingly cross. Laura was ordered to spend the coming Saturday as well at Prahran, and in her new dress, under penalty of a correspondence with Mrs Gurley. There was no going against an order of this kind, and with death at her heart Laura prepared to obey. On the fatal morning she dawdled as long as possible over her mending, thus postponing dressing to go out till the others had vacated the bedroom; where, in order not to be forced to see herself, she kept her eyes half shut, and turned the looking-glass hind-before. Although it was a warm day, she hung a cloak over her shoulders. But her arms peeped out of the loose sleeves, and at least a foot of skirt was visible. As she walked along the corridor and down the stairs, she seemed to smudge the place with colour, and, directly she entered the dining-hall, comet-like she drew all eyes upon her. Astonished titterings followed in her wake; even the teachers goggled her, afterwards to put their heads together. In the reception-room Marina remarked at once: 'Hullo! – is *this* the new dress your mother wrote us about?'

Outside, things were no better; the very tram-conductors were fascinated by it; and every passer-by was a fresh object of dread: Laura waited, her heart a-thump, for the moment when he should raise his eyes and, with a start of attention, become aware of the screaming colour. At Godmother's all the faces disapproved: Georgina said, 'What a guy!' when she thought

Laura was out of earshot; but the boys stated their opinion openly as soon as they had her to themselves.

'Oh, golly! Like a parrot – ain't she?'

'This way to the purple parrot – this way! Step up, ladies and gentlemen! A penny the whole show!'

That evening, she tore the dress from her back and, hanging it up inside the cloak, vowed that, come what might, she would never put it on again. A day or two later, on unexpectedly entering her bedroom, she found Lilith Gordon and another girl at her wardrobe. They grew very red, and hurried giggling from the room, but Laura had seen what they were looking at. After this, she tied the dress up with string and brown paper and hid it in a drawer, under her nightgowns. When she went home at Christmas it went with her, still in the parcel, and then there was a stormy scene. But Laura was stubborn: rather than wear the dress, she would not go back to the College at all. Mother's heart had been softened by the prizes; Laura seized the occasion, and extracted a promise that she should be allowed in future to choose her own frocks. – And so the purple dress was passed on to Pin, who detested it with equal heartiness, but, living under Mother's eye, had not the spirit to fight against it.

'Got anything new in the way of clothes?' asked Lilith Gordon as she and Laura undressed for bed a night or two after their return.

'Yes, one,' said Laura shortly. – For she thought Lilith winked at the third girl, a publican's daughter from Clunes.

'Another like the last? Or have you gone in for yellow ochre this time?'

Laura flamed in silence.

'Great Scott, what a colour that was! Fit for an Easter Fair – Miss Day said so.'

'It wasn't mine,' retorted Laura passionately. 'It . . . it belonged to a girl I knew who died – and her mother gave it to me as a remembrance of her – but I didn't care for it.'

'I shouldn't think you did. – But I say, does your mother let you wear other people's clothes? What a rummy thing to do!'

She went out of the room – no doubt to spread this piece of gossip further. Laura looked daggers after her. She was angry enough with Lilith for having goaded her to the lie, but much angrier with herself for its blundering ineffectualness. It was not likely she had been believed, and if she were, well, it made matters worse instead of better: people would conclude that she lived on charity. Always when unexpectedly required to stand on the defensive, she said or did something foolish. That morning, for instance, a similar thing had happened – it had rankled all day in her mind. On looking through the washing, Miss Day had exclaimed in horror at the way in which her stockings were mended.

'Whoever did it? They've been done since you left here. *I* would never have passed such darns.'

Laura crimsoned. 'Those? Oh, an old nurse we've got at home. We've had her for years and years – but her eyesight's going now.'

Miss Day sniffed audibly. 'So I should think. To cobble like that!'

They were Mother's darns, hastily made, late at night, and with all Mother's genial impatience at useful sewing as opposed to beautiful. Laura's intention had been to shield Mother from criticism, as well as to spare Miss Day's feelings. But to have done it so clumsily as this! To have had to wince under Miss Day's scepticism! It was only a wonder the governess had not there and then taxed her with the fib. For who believed in old nurses nowadays? They were a stock property, borrowed on the spur of the moment from readings in *The Family Herald*, from Tennyson's *Lady Clare*. Why on earth had such a far-fetched excuse leapt to her tongue? Why could she not have said Sarah, the servant, the maid-of-all-work? Then Miss

Day would have had no chance to sniff, and she, Laura, could have believed herself believed, instead of having to fret over her own stupidity. – But what she would like more than anything to know was, why the mending of the stockings at home should *not* be Sarah's work? Why must it just be Mother – her mother alone – who made herself so disagreeably conspicuous, and not merely by darning the stockings, but, what was a still greater grievance, by not even darning them well?

Chapter Eleven

IT was an odd thing, all the same, how easy it was to be friends with Lilith Gordon: though she did not belong to Laura's set, though Laura did not even like her, and though she had had ample proof that Lilith was double-faced, not to be trusted. Yet, in the months that followed the affair of the purple dress, Laura grew more intimate with the plump, sandy-haired girl than with either Bertha, or Inez, or Tilly. Or, to put it more exactly, she was continually having lapses into intimacy, and repenting them when it was too late. In one way Lilith was responsible for this: she could make herself very pleasant when she chose, seem to be your friend through thick and thin, thus luring you on to unbosom yourself; and afterwards she would go away and laugh over what you had told her, with other girls. And Laura was peculiarly helpless under such circumstances: if it was done with tact, and with a certain assumed warmth of manner, anyone could make a cat's paw of her.

That Lilith and she undressed for bed together had also something to do with their intimacy: this half-hour when one's hair was unbound and replaited, and fat and thin arms wielded the brush, was the time of all others for confidences. The governess who occupied the fourth bed did not come upstairs till ten o'clock; the publican's daughter, a lazy girl, was usually half asleep before the other two had their clothes off.

It was in the course of one of these confidential chats that Laura did a very foolish thing. In a moment of weakness, she gratuitously gave away the secret that Mother supported her family by the work of her hands.

The two girls were sitting on the side of Lilith's bed. Laura had a day of mishaps behind her – that partly, no doubt, accounted for her self-indulgence. But, in addition, her companion had just told her, unasked, that she thought her 'very pretty'. It was not in Laura's nature to let this pass: she was never at ease under an obligation; she had to pay the coin back in kind.

'Embroidery? What sort? However does she do it?' – Lilith's interest was on tiptoe at once – a false and slimy interest, the victim afterwards told herself.

'Oh, my mother's awfully clever. It's just lovely, too, what she does – all in silk – and ever so many different colours. She made a piano-cover once, and got fifty pounds for it.'

'How perfectly splendid!'

'But that was only a lucky chance . . . that she got that to do. She mostly does children's dresses and cloaks and things like that.'

'But she's not a dressmaker, is she?'

'A dressmaker? I should think not indeed! They're sent up, all ready to work, from the biggest shops in town.'

'I say! – she must be clever.'

'She is; she can do anything. She makes the patterns up all out of her own head.' – And filled with pride in Mother's accomplishments and Lilith's appreciation of them, Laura fell asleep that night without a qualm.

It was the next evening. Several of the boarders who had finished preparing their lessons were loitering in the dining-hall, Laura and Lilith among them. In the group was a girl called Lucy, young but very saucy; for she lived at Toorak, and came of one of the best families in Melbourne. She was not as old as Laura by two years, but was already feared and respected for the fine scorn of her opinions.

Lilith Gordon had bragged: 'My uncle's promised me a gold watch and chain when I pass matric.'

Lucy of Toorak laughed: her nose came down, and her mouth went up at the corners. 'Do you think you ever will?'

'G. o. k. and He won't tell. But I'll probably get the watch all the same.'

'Where does your uncle hang out?'

'Brisbane.'

'Sure he can afford to buy it?'

'Of course he can.'

'What is he?'

Lilith was unlucky enough to hesitate, ever so slightly. 'Oh, he's got plenty of money,' she asserted.

'She doesn't like to say what he is!'

'I don't care whether I say it or not.'

'A butcher, p'raps, or an undertaker?'

'A butcher! He's got the biggest newspaper in Brisbane!'

'A newspaper! Great Scott! Her uncle keeps a newspaper!'

There was a burst of laughter from those standing round.

Lilith was scarlet now. 'It's nothing to be ashamed of,' she said angrily.

But Lucy of Toorak could not recover from her amusement. 'An uncle who keeps a newspaper! A newspaper! Well, I'm glad none of *my* uncles are so rummy. – I say, does he leave it at front doors himself in the morning?'

Laura had at first looked passively on, well pleased to see another than herself the butt of young Lucy's wit. But at this stage of her existence she was too intent on currying favour, to side with any but the stronger party. And so she joined in the boisterous mirth Lilith's admission and Lucy's reception of it excited, and flung her gibes with the rest.

She was pulled up short by a hissing in her ear. 'If you say one word more, I'll tell about the embroidery!'

Laura went pale with fright: she had been in good spirits

that day, and had quite forgotten her silly confidence of the
night before. Now, the jeer that was on the tip of her tongue
hung fire. She could not all at once obliterate her smile – that
would have been noticeable; but it grew weaker, stiffer and
more unnatural, then gradually faded away, leaving her with a
very solemn little face.

From this night on, Lilith Gordon represented a powder-
mine, which might explode at any minute. – And she herself
had laid the train!

From the outset, Laura had been accepted, socially, by even
the most exclusive, as one of themselves; and this, in spite of
her niggardly allowance, her ridiculous clothes. For the child
had race in her: in a well-set head, in good hands and feet and
ears. Her nose, too, had a very pronounced droop, which
could stand only for blue blood, or a Hebraic ancestor – and
Jews were not received as boarders in the school. Now, loud
as money made itself in this young community, effectual as it
was in cloaking shortcomings, it did not go all the way:
inherited instincts and traditions were not so easily subdued.
Just some of the wealthiest too, were aware that their ante-
cedents would not stand a close scrutiny; and thus a mighty
respect was engendered in them for those who had nothing
to fear. Moreover, directly you got away from the vastly
rich, class distinctions were observed with an exactitude such
as can only obtain in an exceedingly mixed society. The three
professions alone were sacrosanct. The calling of architect, for
example, or of civil engineer, was, if a fortune had not been
accumulated, utterly without prestige; trade, any connection
with trade – the merest bowing acquaintance with buying and
selling – was a taint that nothing could remove; and those girls
who were related to shopkeepers, or, more awful still, to
publicans, would rather have bitten their tongues off than have
owned to the disgrace.

Yet Laura knew very well that good birth and an aristocratic appearance would not avail her, did the damaging fact leak out that Mother worked for her living. Work in itself was bad enough – how greatly to be envied were those whose fathers did nothing more active than live on their money! But the additional circumstance of Mother being a woman made things ten times worse: ladies did not work; someone always left them enough to live on, and if he didn't, well, then he, too, shared the ignominy. So Laura went in fear and trembling lest the truth should come to light – in that case, she would be a pariah indeed – went in hourly dread of Lilith betraying her. Nothing, however, happened – at least as far as she could discover – and she sought to propitiate Lilith in every possible way. For the time being, though, anxiety turned her into a porcupine, ready to erect her quills at a touch. She was ever on the look-out for an allusion to her mother's position, and for the slight that was bound to accompany it.

Even the governesses noticed the change in her.

Three of them sat one evening round the fire in Mrs Gurley's sitting-room, with their feet on the fender. The girls had gone to bed; it was Mrs Gurley's night off, and as Miss Day was also on leave, the three who were left could draw in more closely than usual. Miss Snodgrass had made the bread into toast – in spite of Miss Chapman's quakings lest Mrs Gurley should notice the smell when she came in – and, as they munched, Miss Snodgrass related how she had just confiscated a book Laura Rambotham was trying to smuggle upstairs, and how it had turned out that it belonged, not to Laura herself, but to Lilith Gordon.

'She was like a little spitfire about it all the same. A most objectionable child, I call her. It was only yesterday I wanted to look at some embroidery on her apron – a rather pretty new stitch – and do you think she'd let me see it? She jerked it away and glared at me as if she would have liked to eat me. I could have boxed her ears.'

'I never have any trouble with Laura. I don't think you know how to manage her,' said Miss Chapman, and executed a little manœuvre. She had poor teeth; and, having awaited a moment when Miss Snodgrass's sharp eyes were elsewhere engaged, she surreptitiously dropped the crusts of the toast into her handkerchief.

'I'd be sorry to treat her as you do,' said Miss Snodgrass, and yawned. 'Girls need to be made to sit up nowadays.'

She yawned again, and gazing round the room for fresh food for talk, caught Miss Zielinski with her eye. 'Hullo, Ziely, what are you deep in?' She put her arm round the other's neck, and unceremoniously laid hold of her book. 'You naughty girl, you're at Ouida again! Always got your nose stuck in some trashy novel.'

'*Do* let me alone,' said Miss Zielinski pettishly, holding fast to the book; but she did not raise her eyes, for they were wet.

'You know you'll count the washing all wrong again to-morrow, your head'll be so full of that stuff.'

'Yes, it's time to go, girls; to-morrow's Saturday.' And Miss Chapman sighed; for, on a Saturday morning between six and eight o'clock, fifty-five lots of washing had to be sorted out and arranged in piles.

'Holy Moses, what a life!' ejaculated Miss Snodgrass, and yawned again, in a kind of furious desperation. 'I swear I'll marry the first man that asks me, to get away from it. – As long as he has money enough to keep me decently.'

'You would soon wish yourself back, if you had no more feeling for him that that,' reproved Miss Chapman.

'Catch me! Not even if he had a hump, or kept a mistress, or was over eighty. Oh dear, oh dear!' – she stretched herself so violently that her bones cracked; to resume, in a tone of ordinary conversation: 'I do wish I knew whether to put a brown wing or a green one in that blessed hat of mine.'

Miss Chapman's face straightened out from its shocked

expression. 'Your hat? Why do you want to change it? It's very nice as it is.'

'My dear Miss Chapman, it's at least six months out of date. – Ziely, you're crying!'

'I'm not,' said Miss Zielinski weakly, caught in the act of blowing her nose.

'How on earth can you cry over a book? As if it were true!'

'I thank God I haven't such a cold heart as you.'

'And I thank God I'm not a romantic idiot. But your name's not Thekla for nothing I suppose.'

'My name's as good as yours. And I won't be looked down on because my father was once a German.'

' "Mr Kayser, do you vant to buy a dawg?" ' hummed Miss Snodgrass.

'Girls, girls!' admonished Miss Chapman. 'How you two do bicker. – There, that's Mrs Gurley now! And it's long past ten.'

At the creaking of the front door both juniors rose, gathered their belongings together, and hurried from the room. But it was a false alarm; and having picked up some crumbs and set the chairs in order, Miss Chapman resumed her seat. As she waited, she looked about her and wondered, with a sigh, whether it would ever be her good fortune to call this cheery little room her own. It was only at moments like the present that she could indulge such a dream. Did Mrs Gurley stand before her, majestic in bonnet and mantle, as in a minute or two she would, or draped in her great shawl, thoughts of this kind sank to their proper level, and Miss Chapman knew them for what they were worth. But sitting alone by night, her chin in her hand, her eyes on the dying fire, around her the eerie stillness of the great house, her ambition did not seem wholly out of reach; and, giving rein to her fancy, she could picture herself sweeping through halls and rooms, issuing orders that it was the business of others to fulfil, could even think out a few changes that should be made, were she head of the staff.

But the insertion of Mrs Gurley's key in the lock, the sound of her foot on the oilcloth, was enough to waken a sense of guilt in Miss Chapman, and make her start to her feet – the drab, elderly, apologetic governess once more.

Chapter Twelve

YOU might regulate your outward habit to the last button of what you were expected to wear; you might conceal the tiny flaws and shuffle over the big improprieties in your home life, which were likely to damage your value in the eyes of your companions; you might, in brief, march in the strictest order along the narrow road laid down for you by these young lawgivers, keeping perfect step and time with them: yet of what use were all your pains, if you could not marshal your thoughts and feelings – the very realest part of you – in rank and file as well? . . . if these persisted in escaping control? – Such was the question which, about this time, began to present itself to Laura's mind.

It first took form on the day Miss Blount, the secretary, popped her head in at the door and announced: 'At half-past three, Class Two to Number One.'

Class Two was taking a lesson in elocution: that is to say, Mr Repton, the visiting-master for this branch of study, was reading aloud, in a sonorous voice, a chapter of *Handy Andy*. He underlined his points heavily, and his hearers, like the self-conscious, emotionally shy young colonials they were, felt half amused by, half superior to the histrionic display. They lounged in easy, ungraceful postures while he read, reclining one against another, or sprawling forward over the desks, their heads on their arms. It was the first hour after dinner, when one's thoughts were sleepy and stupid, and Mr Repton was not a pattern

disciplinarian; but the general abandonment of attitude had
another ground as well. It had to do with the shape of the
master's legs. These were the object of an enthusiastic admiration. They were generally admitted to be the handsomest
in the school, and those girls were thought lucky who could
get the best view of them beneath the desk. Moreover, the
rumour ran that Mr Repton had once been an actor – his very
curly hair no doubt lent weight to the report – and Class Two
was fond of picturing the comely limbs in the tights of a
Hamlet or Othello. It also, of course, invented for him a lurid
life outside the College walls – notwithstanding the fact that
he and his sonsy wife sat opposite the boarders in church every
Sunday morning, the embodiment of the virtuous commonplace; and whenever he looked at a pupil, every time he singled
one of them out for special notice, he was believed to have
an ulterior motive, his words were construed into meaning
something they should not mean: so that the poor man was
often genuinely puzzled by the reception of his friendly
overtures. – Such was Class Two's youthful contribution to
the romance of school life.

On this particular day, however, the sudden, short snap
of the secretary's announcement that, instead of dispersing at
half-past three, the entire school was to reassemble, galvanised
the class. Glances of mingled apprehension and excitement
flew round; eyes telegraphed vigorous messages; and there
was little attention left for well-shaped members, or for the
antics of Handy Andy under his mother's bed.

But when the hour came, and all classes were moving in the
same direction, verandahs and corridors one seething mass of
girls, it was the excitement that prevailed. For any break was
welcome in the uniformity of the days; and the nervous
tension now felt was no more disagreeable, at bottom, than
was the pleasant trepidation experienced of old by those who
went to be present at a hanging.

In the course of the past weeks a number of petty thefts had been committed. Day-scholars who left small sums of money in their jacket pockets would find, on returning to the cloakrooms, that these had been pilfered. For a time, the losses were borne in silence, because of the reluctance inherent in young girls to making a fuss. But when shillings began to vanish in the same fashion, and once even half-a-crown was missing, it was recognised that the thing must be put a stop to; and one bolder than the rest, and with a stronger sense of public morality, lodged a complaint. Investigations were made, a trap was set, and the thief discovered. – The school was now assembled to see justice done.

The great room was fuller even than at morning prayers; for then there was always an unpunctual minority. A crowd of girls who had not been able to find seats was massed together at the further end. As at prayers, visiting and resident teachers stood in a line, with their backs to the high windows; they were ranged in order of precedence, topped by Dr Pughson, who stood next Mr Strachey's desk. All alike wore blank, stern faces.

In one of the rows of desks for two – blackened, ink-scored, dusty desks, with eternally dry ink-wells – sat Laura and Tilly, behind them Inez and Bertha. The cheeks of the four were flushed. But, while the others only whispered and wondered, Laura was on the tiptoe of expectation. She could not get her breath properly, and her hands and feet were cold. Twisting her fingers, in and out, she moistened her lips with her tongue. – When, oh, when would it begin?

These few foregoing minutes were the most trying of any. For when, in an ominous hush, Mr Strachey entered and strode to his desk. Laura suddenly grew calm, and could take note of everything that passed.

The Principal raised his hand, to enjoin a silence that was already absolute.

'Will Miss Johns stand up!'

At these words, spoken in a low, impressive tone, Bertha burst into tears and hid her face in her handkerchief. Hundreds of eyes sought the unhappy culprit as she rose, then to be cast down and remain glued to the floor.

The girl stood, pale and silly-looking, and stared at Mr Strachey much as a rabbit stares at the snake that is about to eat it. She was a very ugly girl of fourteen, with a pasty face, and lank hair that dangled to her shoulders. Her mouth had fallen half open through fear, and she did not shut it all the time she was on view.

Laura could not take her eyes off the scene: they travelled, burning with curiosity, from Annie Johns to Mr Strachey, and back again to the miserable thief. When, after a few introductory remarks on crime in general, the Principal passed on to the present case, and described it in detail, Laura was fascinated by his oratory, and gazed full at him. He made it all live vividly before her; she hung on his lips, appreciating his points, the skilful way in which he worked up his climaxes. But then, she herself knew what it was to be poor – as Annie Johns had been. She understood what it would mean to lack your tram-fare on a rainy morning – according to Mr Strachey this was the motor impulse of the thefts – because a lolly shop had stretched out its octopus arms after you. She could imagine, too, with a shiver, how easy it would be, the loss of the first pennies having remained undiscovered, to go on to threepenny-bits, and from these to sixpences. More particularly since the money had been taken, without exception, from pockets in which there was plenty. Not, Laura felt sure, in order to avoid detection, as Mr Strachey supposed, but because to those who had so much a few odd coins could not matter. She wondered if everyone else agreed with him on this point. How did the teachers feel about it? – and she ran her eyes over the row, to learn their opinions from their faces. But these were as stolid as ever. Only good old Chapman, she thought, looked a little

sorry, and Miss Zielinski – yes, Miss Zielinski was crying!
This discovery thrilled Laura – just as, at the play, the fact
of one spectator being moved to tears intensifies his neighbour's
enjoyment. – But when Mr Strachey left the field of personal
narration and went on to the moral aspects of the affair, Laura
ceased to be gripped by him, and turned anew to study the
pale, dogged face of the accused, though she had to crane her
neck to do it. Before such a stony mask as this, she was driven
to imagine what must be going on behind it; and, while thus
engrossed, she felt her arm angrily tweaked. It was Tilly.

'You *are* a beast to stare like that!'

'I'm not staring.'

She turned her eyes away at once, more than half believing
her own words; and then, for some seconds, she tried to do what
was expected of her: to feel a decent unconcern. At her back,
Bertha's purry crying went steadily on. What on earth did she
cry for? She had certainly not heard a word Mr Strachey
said. Laura fidgeted in her seat, and stole a sideglance at Tilly's
profile. She could not, really could not miss the last scene of all,
when, in masterly fashion, the Principal was gathering the
threads together. And so, feeling rather like 'Peeping Tom',
she cautiously raised her eyes again, and this time managed to
use them without turning her head.

All other eyes were still charitably lowered. Several girls
were crying now, but without a sound. And, as the last, awful
moments drew near, even Bertha was hushed, and of all the
odd hundreds of throats not one dared to cough. Laura's heart
began to palpitate, for she felt the approach of the final climax,
Mr Strachey's periods growing ever slower and more massive.

When, after a burst of eloquence which, the child felt, would
not have shamed a Bishop, the Principal drew himself up to
his full height, and, with uplifted arm, thundered forth:
'Herewith, Miss Annie Johns, I publicly expel you from the
school! Leave it, now, this moment, and never darken its doors

again!' – when this happened, Laura was shot through by an ecstatic quiver, such as she had felt once only in her life before; and that was when a beautiful, golden-haired Hamlet, who had held a Ballarat theatre entranced for a whole evening, fell dead by Laertes' sword, to the rousing plaudits of the house. Breathing unevenly, she watched, lynx-eyed, every inch of Annie Johns' progress: watched her pick up her books, edge out of her seat and sidle through the rows of desks; watched her walk to the door with short, jerky movements, mount the two steps that led to it, fumble with the handle, turn it, and vanish from sight; and when it was all over, and there was nothing more to see, she fell back in her seat with an audible sigh.

It was too late after this for the winding of the snaky line about the streets and parks of East Melbourne, which constituted the boarders' daily exercise. They were despatched to stretch their legs in the garden. Here, as they walked round lawns and tennis-courts, they discussed the main event of the afternoon, and were a little more vociferous than usual, in an attempt to shake off the remembrance of a very unpleasant half-hour.

'I bet you Sandy rather enjoyed kicking up that shindy.'

'*Did* you see Puggy's boots again? Girls, he *must* take twelves!'

'And that old blubber of a Ziely's handkerchief! It was filthy. I told you yesterday I was sure she never washed her neck.'

Bertha, whose tears had dried as rapidly as sea-spray, gave Laura a dig in the ribs. 'What's up with you, old Tweedledum? You're as glum as a lubra.'

'No, I'm not.'

'It's my belief that Laura was sorry for that pig,' threw in Tilly.

'Indeed I wasn't!' said Laura indignantly.

'Sorry for a thief?'

'I tell you I *wasn't*!' – and this was true. Among the divers feelings Laura had experienced that afternoon, pity had not been included.

'If you want to be chums with such a mangy beast, you'd better go to school in a lock-up.'

'I don't know what my father'd say, if he knew I'd been in the same class as a pickpocket,' said the daughter of a minister from Brisbane. 'I guess he wouldn't have let me stop here a week.'

Laura went one better. 'My mother wouldn't have let me stop a day.'

Those standing by laughed, and a girl from the Riverina said: 'Oh, no, of course not!' in a tone that made Laura wince, and regret her readiness.

Before tea, she had to practise. The piano stood in an outside classroom, where no one could hear whether she was diligent or idle, and she soon gave up playing and went to the window. Here, having dusted the gritty sill with her petticoat, she leaned her chin on her two palms and stared out into the sun-baked garden. It was empty now, and very still. The streets that lay behind the high palings were deserted in the drowsy heat; the only sound to be heard was a gentle tinkling to vespers in the neighbouring Catholic Seminary. Leaning thus on her elbows, and balancing herself first on her heels, then on her toes, Laura went on, in desultory fashion, with the thoughts that had been set in motion during the afternoon. She wondered where Annie Johns was now, and what she was doing; wondered how she had faced her mother, and what her father had said to her. All the rest of them had gone back at once to their everyday life; Annie Johns alone was cut adrift. What would happen to her? Would she perhaps be turned out of the house? . . . into the streets? – and Laura had a lively vision of the guilty creature, in rags and tatters, slinking along walls and sleeping under bridges, eternally moved on by a ruthless London policeman (her only knowledge of extreme destitution being derived from the woeful tale of 'Little Jo'). – And to think that the beginning of it all had been the want of a trumpery tram-fare. How safe the other girls were! No wonder they could allow themselves to feel shocked and outraged; none of *them* knew what it was not to have threepence in your pocket. While she, Laura ... Yes, and it must be this same incriminating acquaintance with poverty that made her feel differently about Annie Johns and what she had done. For her feelings *had* been different – there was no denying that. Did she now think back over the half-hour spent in Number One, and act honest Injun with herself, she had to admit that her companions' indignant and horrified aversion to the crime had not been hers, let alone their decent indifference towards the criminal. No, to be candid, she had been deeply interested in the whole affair, had even managed to extract an unseemly amount of enter-tainment from it. And that, of course, should not have been. It was partly Mr Strachey's fault, for making it so dramatic; but none the less she genuinely despised herself, for having such a queer inside.

'Pig – pig – pig!' she muttered under her breath, and wrinkled her nose in a grimace.

The real reason of her pleasurable absorption was, she supposed, that she had understood Annie Johns' motive better than anyone else. Well, she had had no business to understand – that was the long and the short of it: nice-minded girls found such a thing impossible, and turned incuriously away. And her companions had been quick to recognise her difference of attitude, or they would never have dared to accuse her of sympathy with the thief, or to doubt her chorusing assertion with a sneer. For them, the gap was not very wide between understanding and doing likewise. And they were certainly right. – Oh! the last wish in the world she had was to range herself on the side of the sinner; she longed to see eye to eye with her comrades – if she had only known how to do it. For there was no saying where it might lead you, if you persisted in having odd and peculiar notions; you might even end by being wicked yourself. Let her take a lesson in time from Annie's fate. For, beginning perhaps with ideas that were no more unlike those of her schoolfellows than were Laura's own, Annie was now a branded thief and an outcast. – And the child's feelings, as she stood at the window, were not very far removed from prayer. Had they found words, they would have taken the form of an entreaty that she might be preserved from having thoughts that were different from other people's; that she might be made to feel as she ought to feel, in a proper, ladylike way – and especially did she see a companion convicted of crime.

Below all this, in subconscious depths, a chord of fear seemed to have been struck in her as well – the fear of stony faces, drooped lids, and stretched, pointing fingers. For that night she started up, with a cry, from dreaming that not Annie Johns but she was being expelled; that an army of spear-like first fingers was marching towards her, and that, try as she would, she could not get her limp, heavy legs to bear her to the schoolroom door.

And this dream often returned.

Chapter Thirteen

On her honourable promotion the following Christmas – she mounted two forms this time – Laura was a thin, middle-sized girl of thirteen, who still did not look her age. The curls had vanished. In their place hung a long, dark plait, which she bound by choice with a red ribbon.

Tilly was the only one of her intimates who skipped a class with her; hence she was thrown more exclusively than before on Tilly's companionship; for it was a melancholy fact: if you were not in the same class as the girl who was your friend, your interests and hers were soon fatally sundered. On their former companions, Tilly and Laura, from their new perch, could not but look down: the two had masters now for all subjects; Euclid loomed large; Latin was no longer bounded by the First Principia; and they fussed considerably, in the others' hearing, over the difficulties of the little blue books that began: *Gallia est omnis divisa in partes tres.*

In the beginning, they held very close together; for their new fellows were inclined to stand on their dignity with the pair of interlopers from Class Two. They were all older than Tilly and Laura, and thought themselves wiser: here were girls of sixteen and seventeen years of age, some of whom would progress no farther along the high-road of education. As for the boarders who sat in this form, they made up a jealous little clique, and it was some time before the younger couple could discover the secret bond.

Then, one morning, the two were sitting with a few others on the verandah bench, looking over their lessons for the day. Mrs Gurley had snatched a moment's rest there, on her way to the secretary's office, and as long as she allowed her withering eye to play upon things and people, the girls conned their pages with a great show of industry. But no sooner had she sailed away than Kate Horner leant forward and called to Maria Morell, who was at the other end of the seat: 'I say, Maria, Genesis LI, 32.' – She held an open Bible in her hand.

Maria Morell frowned caution. 'Dash it, Kate, mind those kids!'

'Oh, they won't savvy.'

But Laura's eyes were saucers of curiosity, for Tilly, who kept her long lashes lowered, had given her a furious nudge. With a wink and a beck to each other, the bigger girls got up and went away.

'I say, what did you poke me so hard for?' inquired Laura as she and Tilly followed in their wake, at the clanging of the public prayer-bell.

'You soft, didn't you hear what she said?'

'Of course I did' – and Laura repeated the reference.

'Let's look it up then.' Under cover of the prayer Tilly sought it out, and together they bent their heads over it.

On this occasion, Tilly was more knowing than Laura; but on this alone; for when Laura once grasped what they were driving at, she was as nimble-witted as any.

Only a day or two later it was she who, in face of Kate and Maria, invited Tilly to turn up chapter and verse.

Both the elder girls burst out laughing.

'By dad!' cried Kate Horner, and smacked her thigh. 'This kid knows a thing or two.'

'You bet! I told you she wasn't born yesterday.' – And Maria laid her arm round Laura's shoulders.

Thus was Laura encouraged, put on her mettle; and soon

there was no more audacious Bible-reader in the class than she.

The girls were thrown thus upon the Book of Books for their contraband knowledge, since it was the only frankly outspoken piece of literature allowed within the College walls: the classics studied were rigidly expurgated; the school library was kept so dull that no one over the age of ten much cared to borrow a volume from it. And, by fair means or unfair, it was necessary to obtain information on matters of sex; for girls most of whom were well across the threshold of womanhood, the subject had an invincible fascination.

Such knowledge as they possessed was a strange jumble, picked up at random: in one direction they were well primed; in another, supremely ignorant. Thus, though they received lectures on what was called 'Physiology', and for these were required to commit to memory the name of every bone and artery in the body, yet all that related to a woman's special organs and chief natural function was studiously ignored. The subject being thus chastely shrouded in mystery, they were thrown back on guesswork and speculation – with the quaintest results. The fancies woven by quite big girls, for instance, round the physical feat of bringing a child into the world, would have supplied material for a volume of fairy-tales. On many a summer evening at this time, in a nook of the garden, heads of all shades might have been seen pressed as close together as a cluster of settled bees; and like the humming of bees, too, were the busy whisperings and subdued buzzes of laughter that accompanied this hot discussion of the 'how' – as a living answer to which, each of them would probably some day walk the world. Innumerable theories were afloat, one more fantastic than another; and the wilder the conjecture, the greater was the respect and applause it gained.

On the other hand, of less profitable information they had amassed a goodly store. Girls who came from up-country could tell a lively tale of the artless habits of the blacks; others, who were at home in mining towns, described the doings in Chinese camps – those unavoidable concomitants of gold-grubbing settlements; rhymes circulated that would have staggered a back-blocker; while the governesses were without exception, young and old, kindly and unkindly, laid under such flamboyant suspicions as the poor ladies had, for certain, never heard breathed – since their own impudent schooldays.

This dabbling in the illicit – it had little in common with the opener grime of the ordinary schoolboy – did not even widen the outlook of these girls. For it was something to hush up and keep hidden away, to have qualms, even among themselves, about knowing; and, like all knowledge that fungus-like shrinks from the sun, it was stunted and unlovely. Their minds were warped by it, their vision was distorted: viewed through its lens, the most natural human relations appeared unnatural. Thus, not the primmest patterns of family life could hope for mercy in their eyes; over the family, too, man, as read by these young rigorists, was held to leave his serpent's trail of desire.

For out of it all rose the vague, crude picture of woman as the prey of man. Man was animal, a composite of lust and cruelty, with no aim but that of brutally taking his pleasure: something monstrous, yet to be adored; annihilating, yet to be sought after; something to flee and, at the same time, to entice, with every art at one's disposal.

As long as it was solely a question of clandestine knowledge and ingenious surmisings, Laura went merrily with the rest: here no barrier shut her off from her companions. Always a very inquisitive little girl, she was now agog to learn new lore. Her mind, in this direction, was like a clean but highly sensitised plate. And partly because of her previous entire ignorance, partly because of her extreme receptiveness, she soon out-stripped her comrades, and before long, was one of the most skilful improvisers of the group: a dexterous theorist; a wicked little adept at innuendo.

But that was all; a step farther, and she ran her head against a stone wall. For the invisible yeast that brought this ferment of natural curiosity to pass, was the girls' intense interest in the opposite sex: a penned-up interest that clamoured for an outlet; an interest which, in the life of these prospective mothers, had already usurped the main place. Laura, on the other hand, had so far had scant experience of boys of a desirable age, nor any liking for such as she had known; indeed she still held to her childish opinion that they were 'silly' – feckless creatures, in spite of their greater strength and size – or downright disagreeable and antagonistic, like God-mother's Erwin and Marmaduke. No breath of their possible dangerous fascination had hitherto reached her. Hence, an experience that came her way, at the beginning of the autumn, was of the nature of an awakening.

Chapter Fourteen

'My cousin Bob's awfully gone on you.'

Laura gaped at Tilly, in crimson disbelief. 'But I've never spoken to him!'

'Doesn't count. He's seen you in church.'

'Go on! – you're stuffing.'

'Word of honour! – And I've promised him to ask aunt if I can bring you with me to lunch next Saturday.'

Laura looked forward to this day with mixed feelings. She was flattered at being invited to the big house in town where Tilly's relatives lived; but she felt embarrassed at the prospect, and she had not the least idea what a boy who was 'gone' on you would expect you to be or to do. Bob was a beautiful youth of seventeen, tall, and dark, and slender, with milk-white teeth and Spanish eyes; and Laura's mouth dried up when she thought of perhaps having to be sprightly or coquettish with him.

On the eventful morning Tilly came to her room while she was dressing, and eyed her critically.

'Oh, I say, don't put on that brown hat . . . for mercy's sake! Bob can't stand brown.'

But the brown was Laura's best, and she demurred.

'Oh well, if you don't care to look nice, you know . . .'

Of course she did; she was burning to. She even accepted the loan of a sash from her friend, because 'Bob loves blue'; and went out feeling odd and unlike herself, in her everyday hat and borrowed plumes.

The Aunt, a pleasant, youthful-looking lady, called for them in a white-hooded wagonette, and set them down at the house with a playful warning.

'Now don't get up to any mischief, you two!'

'No fear!' was Tilly's genial response, as Aunt and cab drove off.

They were going to 'do the block', Tilly explained, and would meet Bob there; but they must first make sure that the drive had not disarranged their hair or the position of their hats; and she led the way to her aunt's bedroom.

Laura, though she had her share of natural vanity, was too impatient to do more than cast a perfunctory glance at her reflected self. At this period of her life when a drive in a hired cab was enough of a novelty to give her pleasure, a day such as the one that lay before her filled her with unbounded anticipation.

She fidgeted from one leg to another while she waited. For Tilly was in no hurry to be gone: she prinked and finicked, making lavish use, after the little swing-glass at school, of the big mirror with its movable wings; she examined her teeth, pulled down her under-lids, combed her eyebrows, twisted her neck this way and that, in an endeavour to view her person from every angle; she took liberties with perfumes and brushes: was, in short, blind and deaf to all but the perfecting of herself – this rather mannish little self, which, despite a most womanly plumpness, affected a boyish bonhomie, and emphasised the rôle by wearing a stiff white collar and cuffs.

Laura was glad when she at last decided that she would 'do', and when they stepped out into the radiant autumn morning.

'What a perfectly scrumptious day!'

'Yes, bully. – I say, *is* my waist all right?'

'Quite right. And ever so small.'

'I know. I gave it an extra pull-in. – Now if only we're lucky enough to get hold of a man or two we know!'

The air, Australian air, met them like a prickling champagne: it was incredibly crisp, pure, buoyant. From the top of the eastern hill the spacious white street sloped speedily down, to run awhile in a hollow, then mount again at the other end. Where the two girls turned into it, it was quiet; but the farther they descended, the fuller it grew – fuller of idlers like themselves, out to see and to be seen.

Laura cocked her chin; she had not had a like sense of freedom since being at school. And besides, was not a boy, a handsome boy, waiting for her, and expecting her? This was the *clou* of the day, the end for which everything was making; yet of such stuff was Laura that she would have felt relieved, could the present moment have been spun out indefinitely. The state of suspense was very pleasant to her.

As for Tilly, that young lady was swinging the shoulders atop of the little waist in a somewhat provocative fashion, only too conscious of the grey-blueness of her fine eyes, and the modish cut of her clothes. She had a knack which seemed to Laura both desirable and unattainable: that of appearing to be engrossed in glib chat with her companion, while in reality she did not hear a word Laura said, and ogled everyone who passed, out of the tail of her eye.

They reached the 'block', that strip of Collins Street which forms the fashionable promenade. Here the road was full of cabs and carriages, and there was a great crowd on the pavement. The girls progressed but slowly. People were meeting their friends, shopping, changing books at the library, eating ices at the confectioner's, fruit at the big fruit-shop round the corner. There were a large number of high-collared young dudes, some Trinity and Ormond men with coloured hat-bands, ladies with little parcels dangling from their wrists, and countless schoolgirls like themselves. Tilly grew momentarily livelier; her big eyes pounced, hawk-like, on every face she met, and her words to Laura became more disjointed than before. Finally, her efforts were crowned with success: she managed, by dint of glance and smile combined, to unhook a youth of her acquaintance from a group at a doorway, and to attach him to herself.

In high good humour now that her aim was accomplished, she set about the real business of the morning – that of promenading up and down. She had no longer even a feigned interest left for Laura, and the latter walked beside the couple a lame and unnecessary third. Though she kept a keen watch for Bob, she could not discover him, and her time was spent for the most part in dodging people, and in catching up with her companions for it was difficult to walk three abreast in the crowd.

Then she saw him – and with what an unpleasant shock. If only Tilly did not see him, too!

But no such luck was hers. 'Look out, there's Bob,' nudged Tilly almost at once.

Alas! there was no question of his waiting longingly for her to appear. He was walking with two ladies, and laughing and talking. He raised his hat to his cousin and her friend, but did not disengage himself, and passing them by disappeared in the throng.

Behind her hand Tilly buzzed: 'One of those Woodwards is awfully sweet on him. I bet he can't get loose.'

This was a drop of comfort. But as, at the next encounter, he still did not offer to join them – could it, indeed, be expected that he would prefer her company to that of the pretty, grown-up girls he was with? – as he again sidled past, Tilly, who had given him one of her most vivacious sparkles, turned and shot a glance at Laura's face.

'For pity's sake, look a little more amiable, or he won't come at all.'

Laura felt more like crying; her sunshine was intercepted,

her good spirits were quenched; had she had her will, she would have turned tail and gone straight back to school. She had not wanted Bob, had never asked him to be 'gone' on her, and if she had now to fish for him, into the bargain . . . However there was no help for it; the thing had to be gone through with; and, since Tilly seemed disposed to lay the blame of his lukewarmness at her door, Laura glued her mouth, the next time Bob hove in sight, into a feeble smile.

Soon afterwards he came up to them. His cousin had an arch greeting in readiness.

'Well, you've been doing a pretty mash, you have!' she cried, and jogged him with her elbow. 'No wonder you'd no eyes for poor us. What price Miss Woodward's gloves this morning!' – at which Bob laughed, looked sly, and tapped his breast pocket.

It was time to be moving homewards. Tilly and her beau led the way. 'For we know you two would rather be alone. – Now, Bob, not too many sheep's-eyes, please!'

Bob smiled, and let fly a wicked glance at Laura from under his dark lashes. Dropping behind, they began to mount the hill. Now was the moment, felt Laura, to say something very witty, or pert, or clever; and a little pulse in her throat beat hard, as she furiously racked her brains. Oh, for just a morsel of Tilly's loose-tonguedness! One after the other she considered and dismissed: the pleasant coolness of the morning, the crowded condition of the street, even the fact of the next day being Sunday – ears and cheeks on fire, meanwhile, at her own slow-wittedness. And Bob smiled. She almost hated him for that smile. It was so assured, and withal so disturbing. Seen close at hand his teeth were whiter, his eyes browner than she had believed. His upper lip, too, was quite dark; and he fingered it incessantly, as he waited for her to make the onslaught.

But he waited in vain; and when they had walked a whole

street-block in this mute fashion, it was he who broke the silence.

'Ripping girls, those Woodwards,' he said, and seemed to be remembering their charms.

'Yes, they looked very nice,' said Laura in a small voice, and was extremely conscious of her own thirteen years.

'Simply stunning! Though May's so slender – May's the pretty one – and has such a jolly figure . . . I believe I could span her waist with my two hands . . . her service is just A1 – at tennis I mean.'

'Is it really?' said Laura wanly, and felt unutterably depressed at the turn the conversation was taking. – Her own waist was coarse, her knowledge of tennis of the slightest.

'Ra-*ther*! Overhand, with a cut on it – she plays with a 14-oz. racquet. And she has a back drive, too, by Jove, that – you play, of course?'

'Oh, yes.' Laura spoke up manfully; but prayed that he would not press his inquiries further. At this juncture his attention was diverted by the passing of a fine tandem; and as soon as he brought it back to her again, she said: 'You're at Trinity, aren't you?' – which was finesse; for she knew he wasn't.

'Well, yes . . . all but,' answered Bob well pleased. 'I start in this winter.'

'How nice!'

There was another pause; then she blurted out: 'We church girls always wear Trinity colours at the boat-race.'

She hoped from her heart, this might lead him to say that he would look out for her there; but he did nothing of the kind. His answer was to the effect that this year they jolly well expected to knock Ormond into a cocked hat.

Lunch threatened to be formidable. To begin with, Laura, whose natural, easy frankness had by this time all but been successfully educated out of her, Laura was never shyer with strangers than at a meal, where every word you said could be

listened to by a tableful of people. Then, too, her vis-à-vis was a
small sharp child of five or six, called Thumbby, or Thumbkin,
who only removed her bead-like eyes from Laura's face to be
saucy to her father. And, what was worse, the Uncle turned out
to be a type that struck instant terror into Laura: a full-fledged
male tease. – He was, besides, very hairy of face, and preter-
naturally solemn.

No sooner had he drawn in his chair to the table than he began.
Lifting his head and thrusting out his chin, he sniffed the air in
all directions with a moving nose – just as a cat does. Everyone
looked at him in surprise. Tilly, who sat next him, went
pink.

'What is it, dear?' his wife at last inquired in a gentle voice;
for it was evident that he was not going to stop till asked why
he did it.

'Mos' extraor'nary smell!' he replied. 'Mother, d'you know,
I could take my appledavy someone has been using my scent.'

'Nonsense, Tom.'

'Silly pa!' said the little girl.

Ramming his knuckles into his eyes, he pretended to cry
at his daughter's rebuke; then bore down on Laura.

'D'you know, Miss Ra . . . Ra . . . Rambotham' – he made
as if he could not get her name out – 'd'you know that I'm a
great man for scent? Fact. I take a bath in it every morning.'

Laura smiled uncertainly, fixed always by the child.

'Fact, I assure you. Over the tummy, up to the chin. – Now,
who's been at it? For it's my opinion I shan't have enough
left to shampoo my eyebrows. – Bob, is it you?'

'Don't be an ass, pater.'

'Cut me some bread, Bob, please,' said Tilly hastily.

'Mos' extraor'nary thing!' persisted the Uncle. 'Or – good
Lord, mother, can it be my monthly attack of D.T.'s beginning
already? They're not due, you know, till next week, Monday,
five o'clock.'

'Dear, *don't* be so silly. Besides it's my scent, not yours. And anyone is welcome to it.'

'Well, well, let's call in the cats! – By the way, Miss Ra . . . Ra . . . Rambotham, are you aware that this son of mine is a professed lady-killer?'

Laura and Bob went different shades of crimson.

'Why has she got so red?' the child asked her mother, in an audible whisper.

'Oh, *chuck* it, pater!' murmured Bob in disgust.

'Fact, I assure you. Put not your trust in Robert! He's always on with the new love before he's off with the old. You ask him whose glove he's still cherishing in the pocket next his heart.'

Bob pushed his plate from him and, for a moment, seemed about to leave the table. Laura could not lift her eyes. Tilly chewed in angry silence.

Here, however, the child made a diversion.

'You're a lady-kilda yourself, pa.'

'Me, Thumbkin? – Mother, d'you hear that? – Then it's the whiskers, Thumbby. Ladies love whiskers – or a fine drooping moustache, like my son Bob's.' He sang: ' "Oh, oh, the ladies loved him so!" '

'Tom, dear, *do* be quiet.'

'Tom, Tom, the piper's son!' chirped Thumbby.

'Well, well, let's call in the cats!' – which appeared to be his way of changing the subject.

It seemed, after this, as though the remainder of lunch might pass off without further hitch. Then however and all of a sudden, while he was peeling an apple, this dreadful man said, as though to himself: 'Ra . . . Ra . . . Rambotham. Now where have I heard that name?'

'Wa . . . Wa . . . Wamboffam!' mocked Thumbkin.

'Monkey, if you're so sharp you'll cut yourself! – Young lady, do you happen to come from Warrenega?' he asked

Laura, when Thumbkin's excited chirrup of: 'I'll cut *you*, pa, into little bits!' had died away.

Ready to sink through the floor, Laura replied that she did.

'Then I've the pleasure of knowing your mother. – Tall, dark woman, isn't she?'

Under the table, Laura locked the palms of her hands and stemmed her feet against the floor. Was here, now, before them all, and Bob in particular, the shameful secret of the embroidery to come to light? She could hardly force her lips to frame an answer.

Her confusion was too patent to be overlooked. Above her lowered head, signs passed between husband and wife, and soon afterwards the family rose from the table.

But Tilly was so obviously sulky that the tease could not let her escape him thus.

He cried: 'For God's sake, Tilly, stand still! What on earth have you got on your back?'

Tilly came from up-country and her thoughts leapt fearfully to scorpions and tarantulas. Affrighted, she tried to peer over her shoulder, and gave a preliminary shriek. 'Gracious! – whatever is it?'

'Hold on!' He approached her with the tongs; the next moment to ejaculate: 'Begad, it's not a growth, it's a bustle!' and as he spoke he tweaked the place where a bustle used to be worn.

Even Bob had to join in the ensuing boohoo, which went on and on till Laura thought the Uncle would fall down in a fit. Then for the third time he invited those present to join him in summoning the cats, murmured something about 'humping his bluey', and went out into the hall, where they heard him swinging Thumbby 'round the world'.

It was all the Aunt could do to mollify Tilly, who was enraged to the point of tears. 'I've never worn a bustle in my life! Uncle's a perfect *fool*! I've never met such a fool as he is!'

Still boiling, she disappeared to nurse her ruffled temper in private; and she remained absent from the room for over half an hour. During this time Laura and Bob were alone together. But even less than before came of their intercourse. Bob, still smarting from his father's banter, was inclined to be stand-offish, as though afraid Laura might take liberties with him after having been made to look so small; Laura, rendered thoroughly unsure to begin with, by the jocular tone of the luncheon-table, had not recovered from the shock of hearing her parentage so bluffly disclosed. And since, at this time, her idea of the art of conversation was to make jerky little remarks which led nowhere, or to put still more jerky questions, Bob was soon stifling yawns, and not with the best success. He infected Laura; and there the two of them sat, doing their best to appear unconscious of the terrible spasms which, every few seconds, distorted their faces. At last Bob could stand it no longer and bolted from the room.

Laura was alone, and seemed to be forgotten. The minutes ticked by, and no one came – or no one but a little grey kitten, which arrived as if from nowhere, with a hop and a skip. She coaxed the creature to her lap, where it joined head to tail and went to sleep. And there she sat, in the gloomy, overfilled drawing-room, and stroked the kitten, which neither cracked stupid jokes nor required her to strain her wits to make conversation.

When at length Tilly came back, she expressed a rather acid surprise at Bob's absence, and went to look for him; Laura heard them whispering and laughing in the passage. On their return to the drawing-room it had been decided that the three of them should go for a walk. As the sky was overcast and the girls had no umbrellas, Bob carried a big one belonging to the Uncle. Tilly called this a 'family umbrella'; and the jokes that were extracted from the pair of words lasted the walkers on the whole of their outward way; lasted so long that Laura, who

was speedily finished with her contribution, grew quite
stupefied with listening to the other two.

Collins Street was now as empty as a bush road. The young
people went into Bourke Street, where, for want of something
better to do, they entered the Eastern Market and strolled
about inside. The noise that rose from the livestock, on ground
floor and upper storey, was ear-splitting: pigs grunted; cocks
crowed, turkeys gobbled, parrots shrieked; while rough human
voices echoed and re-echoed under the lofty roof. There was a
smell, too, an extraordinary smell, composed of all the in-
dividual smells of all these living things: of fruit and vegetables,
fresh and decayed; of flowers, and butter, and grain; of meat,
and fish, and strong cheeses; of sawdust sprinkled with water,
and freshly wet pavements – one great complicated smell, the
piquancy of which made Laura sniff like a spaniel. But after a
very few minutes Tilly, whose temper was still short, called it a
'vile stink' and clapped her handkerchief to her nose; and so
they hurried out, past many enticing little side booths hidden
in dark corners on the ground floor, such as a woman without
legs, a double-headed calf, and the like.

Outside it had begun to rain; they turned into a Waxworks
Exhibition. This was a poor show, and they were merely
killing time when the announcement caught their eye that a
certain room was open to 'Married People Only'. The quips
and jokes this gave rise to again were as unending as those
about the umbrella; and Laura grew so tired of them, and of
pretending to find them funny, that her temper also began to
give way; and she eased her feelings by making the nippy
mental note on her companions, that jokes were evidently
'in the blood'.

When they emerged, it was time for the girls to return to
school. They took a hansom, Bob accompanying them. As
they drove, Laura sitting sandwiched between the other two,
it came over her with a rush what a miserable failure the day

had been. A minute before, her spirits had given a faint flicker, for Bob had laid his arm along the back of the seat. Then she saw that he had done this just to pull at the little curls that grew on Tilly's neck. She was glad when the cab drew up, when Tilly ostentatiously took the fat half-crown from her purse, and Bob left them at the gate with a: 'Well, so long, ladies!'

The boarders spent the evening in sewing garments for charity. Laura had been at work for weeks on a coarse, red flannel petticoat, and as a rule was under constant reprimand for her idleness. On this night, having separated herself from Tilly, she sat down beside a girl with a very long plait of hair and small, narrow eyes, who went by the name of 'Chinky'. Chinky was always making up to her, and could be relied on to cover her silence. Laura sewed away, with bent head and pursed lips, and was so engrossed that the sole rebuke she incurred had to do with her diligence.

Miss Chapman exclaimed in horror at her stiffly outstretched arm.

'How *can* you be so vulgar, Laura? To sew with a thread as long as that!'

Chapter Fifteen

For days Laura avoided even thinking of this unlucky visit. Privately, she informed herself that Tilly's wealthy relations were a 'rude, stupid lot'; and, stuffing her fingers in her ears, memorised pages with a dispatch that deadened thought.

When, however, the first smart had passed and she was able to go back on what had happened, a soreness at her own failure was the abiding result: and this, though Tilly mercifully spared her the 'dull as ditchwater', that was Bob's final verdict. – But the fact that the invitation was not repeated told Laura enough.

Her hurt was not relieved by the knowledge that she had done nothing to deserve it. For she had never asked for Bob's notice or admiration, had never thought of him but as a handsome cousin of Tilly's who sat in a distant pew at St Stephen's-on-the-Hill; and the circumstance that, because he had singled her out approvingly, she was expected to worm herself into his favour, seemed to her of a monstrous injustice. But, all the same, had she possessed the power to captivate him, she would cheerfully have put her pride in her pocket. For, having once seen him close at hand, she knew how desirable he was. Having been the object of glances from those liquid eyes, of smiles from those blanched-almond teeth, she found it hard to dismiss them from her mind. How the other girls would have boasted of it, had they been chosen by such a one as Bob! – they who, for the most part, were satisfied with blotchy-faced, red-handed youths, whose lean wrists dangled from their retreating sleeves. But then, too, they would have known how to keep him. Oh, those lucky other girls!

'I say, Chinky, what do *you* do when a boy's gone on you?'

She would have shrunk from putting an open question of this kind to her intimates; but Chinky could be trusted. For she garnered the few words Laura vouchsafed her, as gratefully as Lazarus his crumbs; and a mark of confidence, such as this, would sustain her for days.

But she had no information to give.

'Me? . . . why, nothing. Boys are dirty, horrid, conceited creatures.'

In her heart Laura was at one with this judgment; but it was not to the point.

'Yes, but s'pose one was awfully sweet on you and you rather liked him?'

'Catch me! If one came bothering round me, I'd do this' – and she set her ten outstretched fingers to her nose and waggled them.

And yet Chinky was rather pretty, in her way.

Maria Morell, cautiously tapped, threw back her head and roared with laughter.

'Bless its little heart! Does it want to know? – 'say, Laura, who's your mash?'

'No one,' answered Laura stoutly. 'I only asked. For I guess you *know*, Maria.'

'By gosh, you bet I do!' cried Maria, italicising the words in her vehemence. 'Well, look here, Kiddy, if a chap's sweet on me I let him be sweet, my dear, and that's all – till he's run to barley-sugar. What I don't let him savvy is, whether I care a twopenny damn for him. Soon as you do that, it's all up. Just let him hang round, and throw sheep's-eyes, till he's as soft as a jellyfish, and when he's right down ripe, roaring mad, go off and pretend to do a mash with someone else. That's the way to glue him, chicken.'

'But you don't have anything of him that way,' objected
Laura.

Maria laughed herself red in the face. 'What'n earth more
d'you want? Why, he'll pester you with letters, world without
end, and look as black as your shoe if you so much as wink at
another boy. As for a kiss, if he gets a chance of one he'll take it –
you can bet your bottom dollar on that.'

'But you never get to know him!'

'Oh, hang it, Laura, but you *are* rich! What d'you think one
has a boy for, I'd like to know. To parlezvous about old
Shepherd's sermons? You loony, it's only for getting lollies, and
letters, and the whole dashed fun of the thing. If you go about
too much with one, you soon have to fake an interest in his
rotten old affairs. Or else just hold your tongue and let him blow.
And that's dull work. D'you think it ever comes up a fellow's
back to talk to you about your new Sunday hat! If it does, you
can teach your grandmother to suck eggs.'

But, despite this wisdom, Laura could not determine how
Maria would have acted had she stood in her shoes.

And then, too, the elder girl had said nothing about another
side of the question, had not touched on the sighs and simpers,
the winged glances, and drooped, provocative lids – all the
thousand and one fooleries, in short, which Laura saw her and
others employ. There was a regular machinery of invitation
and encouragement to be set in motion: for, before it was
safe to ignore a wooer and let him dangle, as Maria advised,
you had first to make quite sure he wished to nibble your bait. –
And it was just in this elementary science that Laura broke
down.

Looking round her, she saw mainly experts. To take the
example nearest at hand: there was Monsieur Legros, the
French master; well, Maria could twist him round her little
finger. She only needed to pout her thick, red lips, or to give a
coquettish twist to her plump figure, or to ogle him with her

fine, bold, blue eyes, and the difficult questions in the lesson were
sure to pass her by. – Once she had even got ten extra marks
added to an examination paper, in this easy fashion. Whereas,
did she, Laura, try to imitate Maria, venture to pout or to smirk,
it was ten to one she would be rebuked for impertinence. No,
she got on best with the women-teachers, to whom red lips
and a full bust meant nothing; while the most elderly masters
could not be relied on to be wholly impartial, where a pair of
magnificent eyes was concerned. Even Mr Strachey, the
unapproachable, had been known, on running full tilt into a
pretty girl's arms in an unlit passage, to be laughingly confused.

Laura was not, of course, the sole outsider in these things;
sprinkled through the College were various others, older, too,
than she, who by reason of demureness of temperament, or
immersion in their work, stood aloof. But they were lost in
the majority, and, as it chanced, none of them belonged to
Laura's circle. Except Chinky – and Chinky did not count. So,
half-fascinated, half-repelled, Laura set to studying her friends
with renewed zeal. She could not help admiring their proficiency in the art of pleasing, even though she felt a little
abashed by the open pride they took in their growing charms.
There was Bertha, for instance, Bertha who had one of the
nicest minds of them all; and yet how frankly gratified she was,
by the visible rounding of her arms and the curving of her bust.
She spoke of it to Laura with a kind of awe; and her voice
seemed to give hints of a coming mystery. Tilly, on the other
hand, lived to reduce her waist-measure: she was always
sucking at lemons, and she put up with the pains of indigestion
as well as a red tip to her nose; for no success in school meant
as much to Tilly as the fact that she had managed to compress
herself a further quarter of an inch, no praise on the part of her
teachers equalled the compliments this earned her from dressmaker and tailor. As for Inez, who had not only a pretty face
but was graceful and slender-limbed as a greyhound, Inez

no longer needed to worry over artificial charms, or to dwell self-consciously on her development; serious admirers were not lacking, and with one of these, a young man some eight years older than herself, she had had for the past three months a sort of understanding. For her, as for so many others, the time she had still to spend at school was as purgatory before paradise. To top all, one of the day-scholars in Laura's class was actually engaged to be married; and in no boy-and-girl fashion, but to a doctor who lived and practised in Emerald Hill: he might some-times be seen, from a peephole under the stairs, waiting to escort her home from school. This fiancée was looked up to by the class with tremendous reverence, as one set apart, oiled and anointed. You really could not treat her as a comrade – her, who had reached the goal. For this *was* the goal; and the thoughts of all were fixed, with an intentness that varied only in degree, on the great consummation which, as planned in these young minds, should come to pass without fail directly the college-doors closed behind them. – And here again Laura was a heretic. For she could not contemplate the future that was to be hers when she had finished her education, but with a feeling of awe: it was still so distant as to be one dense blue haze; it was so vast, that thinking of it took your breath away: there was room in it for the most wonderful miracles that had ever happened; it might contain anything – from golden slip-pers to a Jacob's ladder, by means of which you would scale the skies; and with these marvellous perhapses awaiting you, it was impossible to limit your hopes to one single event, which, though it saved you from derision, would put an end, for ever, to all possible, exciting contingencies.

These thoughts came and went. In the meantime, despite her ape-like study of her companions, she remained where the other sex was concerned a disheartening failure. A further incident drove this home anew.

One Saturday afternoon, those boarders who had not been

invited out were taken to see a cricket-match. They were a mere handful, eight or nine at most, and Miss Snodgrass alone was in charge. All her friends being away that day, Laura had to bring up the rear with the governess and one of the little girls. Though their walk led them through pleasant parks, she was glad when it was over; for she did not enjoy Miss Snodgrass's company. She was no match for this crisply sarcastic governess, and had to be the whole time on her guard. For Miss Snodgrass was not only a great talker, but had also a very inquiring mind, and seemed always trying to ferret out just those things you did not care to tell – such as the size of your home, or the social position you occupied in the township where you lived.

Arrived at the cricket ground, they climbed the Grand Stand and sat down in one of the back rows, to the rear of the other spectators. Before them sloped a steep bank of hats – gaily-flowered and ribbon-banded hats – of light and dark shoulders, of alert, boyish profiles and pale, pretty faces – a representative gathering of young Australia, bathed in the brilliant March light.

Laura's seat was between her two companions, and it was here the malheur occurred. During an interval in the game, one of the girls asked the governess's leave to speak to her cousin; and thereupon a shy lad was the target for twenty eyes. He was accompanied by a friend, who, in waiting, sat down just behind Laura. This boy was addressed by Miss Snodgrass; but he answered awkwardly, and after a pause, Laura felt herself nudged.

'You can speak to him, Laura,' whispered Miss Snodgrass. – She evidently thought Laura waited only for permission, to burst in.

Laura had already fancied that the boy looked at her with interest. This was not improbable; for she had her best hat on, which made her eyes seem very dark – 'like sloes,' Chinky said, though neither of them had any clear idea what a sloe was.

Still, a prompting to speech invariably tied her tongue. She half turned, and stole an uneasy peep at the lad. He might be a year older than herself; he had a frank, sunburnt face, blue eyes, and almost white flaxen hair. She took heart of grace.

'I s'pose you often come here?' she ventured at last.

'You bet!' said the boy; but kept his eyes where they were – on the pitch.

'Cricket's a lovely game . . . don't you think so?'

Now he looked at her; but doubtfully, from the height of his fourteen male years; and did not reply.

'Do you play?'

This was a false move, she felt it at once. Her question seemed to offend him. 'Should rather think I did!' he answered with a haughty air.

Weakly she hastened to retract her words. 'Oh, I meant much – if you played much?'

'Comes to the same thing I guess,' said the boy – he had not yet reached the age of obligatory politeness.

'It must be splendid' – here she faltered – 'fun.'

But the boy's thoughts had wandered: he was making signs to a friend down in the front of the Stand. – Miss Snodgrass seemed to repress a smile.

Here, however, the little girl at Laura's side chimed in. 'I think cricket's awful rot,' she announced, in a cheepy voice.

Now what was it, Laura asked herself, in these words, or in the tone in which they were said, that at once riveted the boy's attention. For he laughed quite briskly as he asked: 'What's a kid like you know about it?'

'Jus' as much as I want to. An' my sister says so 's well.'

'Get along with you! Who's your sister?'

'Ooh! – wouldn't you like to know? You've never seen her in Scots' Church on Sundays I s'pose – oh, no!'

'By jingo! – I should say I have. An' you, too. You're the little sister of that daisy with the simply ripping hair.'

The little girl actually made a grimace at him, screwing up her nose. 'Yes, you can be civil now, can't you?'

'My aunt, but she's a tip-topper – your sister!'

'You go to Scots' Church then, do you?' hazarded Laura, in an attempt to re-enter the conversation.

'Think I could have seen her if I didn't?' retorted the boy, in the tone of: 'What a fool question!' He also seemed to have been on the point of adding. 'Goose,' or 'Sillybones.'

The little girl giggled. 'She's church' – by which she meant episcopalian.

'Yes, but I don't care a bit which I go to,' Laura hastened to explain, fearful lest she should be accounted a snob by this dissenter. The boy, however, was so faintly interested in her theological wobblings that, even as she spoke, he had risen from his seat; and the next moment without another word he went away. – This time Miss Snodgrass laughed outright.

Laura stared, with blurred eyes, at the white-clad forms that began to dot the green again. Her lids smarted. She did not dare to put up her fingers to squeeze the gathering tears away, and just as she was wondering what she should do if one was inconsiderate enough to roll down her cheek, she heard a voice behind her.

'I say, Laura . . . Laura!' – and there was Chinky, in her best white hat.

'I'm sitting with my aunt just a few rows down; but I couldn't make you look. Can I come in next to you for a minute?'

'If you like,' said Laura and, because she had to sniff a little, very coldly: Chinky had no doubt also been a witness of her failure.

The girl squeezed past and shared her seat. 'I don't take up much room.'

Laura feigned to be engrossed in the game. But presently she felt her bare wrist touched, and Chinky said in her ear: 'What pretty hands you've got, Laura!'

She buried them in her dress, at this. She found it in the worst possible taste of Chinky to try to console her.

'Wouldn't you like to wear a ring on one of them?'

'No, thanks,' said Laura, in the same repellent way.

'Truly? I'd love to give you one.'

'You? Where would *you* get it?'

'Would you wear it, if I did?'

'Let me see it first,' was Laura's graceless reply, as she returned to her stony contemplation of the great sunlit expanse.

She was sure Miss Snodgrass, on getting home, would laugh with the other governesses over what had occurred – if not with some of the girls. The story would leak out and come to Tilly's ears; and Tilly would despise her more than she did already. So would all the rest. She was branded, as it was, for not having a single string to her bow. Now, it had become plain to her that she could never hope for one; for, when it came to holding a boy's attention for five brief minutes, she could be put in the shade by a child of eight years old.

Chapter Sixteen

SINCE, however, it seemed that someone had to be loved, if you were to be able to hold up your head with the rest, then it was easier, infinitely easier, to love the curate. With the curate, no personal contact was necessary – and that was more than could be said even of the music-masters. In regard to them, pressures of the hand, as well as countless nothings, were expected and enacted, in the bi-weekly reports you rendered to those of your friends who followed the case. Whereas for the curate it was possible to simulate immense ardour, without needing either to humble your pride or call invention to your aid: the worship took place from afar. The curate was, moreover, no unworthy object; indeed he was quite attractive, in a lean, ascetic fashion, with his spiritual blue eyes, and the plain gold cross that dangled from his black watch-ribbon – though, it must be admitted, when he preached, and grew greatly in earnest, his mouth had a way of opening as if it meant to swallow the church – and Laura was by no means his sole admirer. Several of her friends had a fancy for him, especially as his wife, who was much older than he, was a thin, elderly lady with a tired face.

And now, by her own experience, Laura was led to the following discovery: that, if you imagine a thing with sufficient force, you can induce your imagining to become reality. By dint of pretending that it was so, she gradually worked herself up into an attack of love, which was genuine enough to make her redden when Mr Shepherd was spoken of, and to enjoy being teased about him. And since, at any rate when in church, she was a sincerely religious little girl, and one to whom – notwithstanding her protested indifference to forms of worship – such emotional accessories as flowers, and music, and highly coloured vestments made a strong appeal, her feelings for Mr Shepherd were soon mystically jumbled up with her piety: the eastward slant for the Creed, and the Salutation at the Sacred Name, seemed not alone homage due to the Deity, but also a kind of minor homage offered to and accepted by Mr Shepherd; the school-pew being so near the chancel that it was not difficult to believe yourself the recipient of personal notice.

At home during the winter holidays, his name chanced to cross her lips. Straightway it occurred to Mother that he was the nephew of an old friend whom she had long lost sight of. Letters passed between Warrenega and Melbourne, and shortly after her return to the College Laura learnt that she was to spend the coming monthly holiday at Mr Shepherd's house.

In the agitated frame of mind this threw her into, she did not know whether to be glad or sorry. Her feelings had, of late, got into such a rapt and pious muddle that it seemed a little like being asked out to meet God. On the other hand, she could not but see that the circumstance would raise her standing at school, immeasurably. And this it did. As soon as the first shock had passed she communicated the fact freely, and was shrewd enough not to relate how the invitation had come about, allowing it to be put down, as her friends were but too ready to do, to the effect produced on the minister by her silent adoration.

The Church girls were wild with envy. Laura was dragged up the garden with an arm thrust through each of hers. Mr Shepherd's holy calling and spiritual appearance stood him in small stead here; and the blackest interpretation was put on the matter of the visit.

'Nice things you'll be up to, the pair of you – oh, my aunt!' ejaculated Maria.

'I think it's beastly risky her going at all,' filled in Kate Horner, gobbling a little; for her upper lip overhung the lower. 'These saints are oftenest bad 'uns.'

'Yes, and with an Aunt Sally like that for a wife. – Now look here, Kiddy, just you watch you're not left alone with him in the dark.'

'And mind, you've got to tell us everything – every blessed thing!'

Laura was called for, on Saturday morning, by the maiden sister of her divinity. Miss Isabella Shepherd was a fair, short, pleasant young woman, with a nervous, kindly smile, and a congenital inability to look you in the face when speaking to you; so that the impression she made was that of a perpetual friendliness, directed, however, not at you, but at the inanimate objects around you. Laura was so tickled by this peculiarity, which she spied the moment she entered the waiting-room, that at first she could take in nothing else. Afterwards, when the novelty had worn off, she subjected her companion to a closer scrutiny, and from the height of thirteen years had soon taxed her with being a frumpish old maid; the valiant but feeble efforts Miss Isabella made to entertain her, as they walked along, only strengthening her in this opinion.

Not very far from the College they entered a small, two-storied stone house, which but for an iron railing and a shrub or two gave right on the street.

'Will you come up to the study?' said Miss Isabella, smiling warmly, and ogling the door-mat. 'I'm sure Robby would like to see you at once.'

Robby? Her saint called Robby? – Laura blushed.

But at the head of the stairs they were brought up short by

Mrs Shepherd, who, policeman-like, raised a warning hand.

'Hssh . . . ssh . . . sh!' she breathed, and simultaneously half-closed her eyes, as if imitating slumber. 'Robby has just lain down for a few minutes. How are you, dear?' – in a whisper. 'I'm so pleased to see you.'

She looked even more faded than in church. But she was very kind, and in the bedroom insisted on getting out a clean towel for Laura.

'Now we'll go down. – It's only lunch to-day, for Robby has a confirmation-class immediately afterwards, and doesn't care to eat much.'

They descended to the dining-room, but though the meal was served, did not take their seats: they stood about, in a kind of anxious silence. This lasted for several minutes; then, heavy footsteps were heard trampling overhead; these persisted, but did not seem to advance, and at length there was a loud, impatient shout of: 'Maisie!'

Both ladies were perceptibly flurried. 'He can't find something,' said Miss Isabella in a stage-whisper; while Mrs Shepherd, taking the front of her dress in both hands, set out for the stairs with the short, clumsy jerks which, in a woman, pass for running.

A minute or two later the origin of the fluster came in, looking, it must be confessed, not much more amiable than his voice had been: he was extremely pale, too, his blue eyes had hollow rings round them, and there were tired wrinkles on his forehead. However he offered Laura a friendly hand, which she took with her soul in her eyes.

'Well, and so this is the young lady fresh from the halls of learning, is it?' he asked, after a mumbled grace, as he carved a rather naked mutton-bone: the knife caught in the bone; he wrenched it free with an ill-natured tweak. 'And what do they teach you at college, miss, eh?' he went on. 'French? . . . Greek? . . . Latin? How goes it? *Infandum, Regina, jubes renovare dolorem* – isn't that the way of it? And then . . . let me see! It's so long since I went to school, you know.'

'*Trojanas ut opes et lamentabile regnum eruerint Danai*,' said Laura, almost blind with pride and pleasure.

'Well, well, well!' he exclaimed, in what seemed tremendous surprise; but, even as she spoke, his thoughts were swept away; for he had taken up a mustard-pot and found it empty. 'Yes, yes, here we are again! Not a scrap of mustard on the table.' – His voice was angrily resigned.

'With *mutton*, Robby dear?' ventured Mrs Shepherd, with the utmost humbleness.

'With mutton if I choose!' he retorted violently. '*Will* you, Maisie, be kind enough to allow me to know my own tastes best, and not dictate to me what I shall eat?'

But Mrs Shepherd, murmuring: 'Oh dear! it's that dreadful girl,' had already made a timid spring at the bell.

'Poor Robby . . . so rushed again!' said Isabella in a reproachful tone.

'And while she's here she may bring the water and the glasses as well,' snarled the master of the house, who had run a flaming eye over the table.

'Tch, tch, tch!' said Mrs Shepherd, with so little spirit that Laura felt quite sorry for her.

'*Really*, Maisie!' said Miss Isabella. 'And when the poor boy's so rushed, too.'

This guerilla warfare continued throughout luncheon, and left Laura wondering why, considering the dearth of time, and the distress of the ladies at each fresh contretemps, they did not jump up and fetch the missing articles themselves – as Mother would have done – instead of each time ringing the bell and waiting for the appearance of the saucy, unwilling servant. As it turned out, however, their behaviour had a pedagogic basis. It seemed that they hoped, by constantly summoning the maid, to sharpen her memory. But Mrs Shepherd was also

implicated in the method; and this was the reason why Isabella
– as she afterwards explained to Laura – never offered her a
thimbleful of help.

'My sister-in-law is nothing of a manager,' she said. 'But we
still trust she will improve in time, if she always has her
attention drawn to her forgetfulness – at least Robby does;
I'm afraid I have rather given her up. But Robby's patience is
angelic.' And Laura was of the same opinion, since the couple
had been married for more than seven years.

The moment the meal, which lasted a quarter of an hour,
was over, Mr Shepherd clapped on his shovel-hat and started,
with long strides, for his class, Mrs Shepherd, who had not
been quite ready, scuttling along a hundred yards behind him,
with quick, fussy steps, and bonnet all awry.

Laura and Isabella stood at the gate.

'I ought really to have gone, too,' said Isabella, and smiled
at the gutter. 'But as you are here, Robby said I had better stay
at home to-day. – Now what would you like to do?'

This opened up a dazzling prospect, with the whole of
Melbourne before one. But Laura was too polite to pretend
anything but indifference.

'Well, perhaps you wouldn't mind staying in then? I want
so much to copy out Robby's sermon. I always do it, you know,
for he can't read his own writing. But he won't expect it to-day,
and he'll be so pleased.'

It was a cool, quiet little house, with the slightly unused
smell in the rooms that betokens a lack of children. Laura did
not dislike the quiet, and sat contentedly in the front parlour
till evening fell. Not, however, that she was really within
hundreds of miles of Melbourne; for the wonderful book that
she held on her knee was called *King Solomon's Mines*, and
her eyes never rose from the pages.

Supper, when it came, was as scrappy and as hurried as
lunch had been: a class of working-men was momently

expected, and Robby had just time to gulp down a cup of tea.
Nor could he converse; for he was obliged to spare his throat.

Afterwards the three of them sat listening to the loud talking
overhead. This came down distinctly through the thin ceiling,
and Mr Shepherd's voice – it went on and on – sounded, at such
close quarters, both harsh and rasping. Mrs Shepherd was
mending a stole; Isabella stooped over the sermon, which she
was writing like copperplate. Laura sat in a corner with her
hands before her: she had finished her book, but her eyes were
still visionary. When any of the three spoke, it was in a low
tone.

Towards nine o'clock Mrs Shepherd fetched a little saucepan,
filled it with milk, and set it on the hob; and after this she
hovered undecidedly between door and fireplace, like a distracted moth.

'Now do try to get it right to-night, Maisie,' admonished
Isabella; and, turning her face, if not her glance, to Laura, she
explained: 'It must boil, but not have a scrap of skin on it, or
Robby won't look at it.'

Presently the working-men were heard pounding down the
stairs, and thereupon Maisie vanished from the room.

The next day Laura attended morning and evening service
at St Stephen's-on-the-Hill, and in the afternoon made one of
Isabella's class at Sunday school.

That morning she had wakened, in what seemed to be the
middle of the night, to find Isabella dressing by the light of a
single candle.

'Don't you get up,' said the latter. 'We're all going to early
service, and I just want to make Robby some bread and milk
beforehand. He would rather communicate fasting, but he
has to have something, for he doesn't get home till dinner-
time.'

When midday came, Robby was very fractious. The
mutton-bone – no cooking was done – was harder than ever to

carve with decency; and poor Mrs Shepherd, for sheer fidgetiness, could hardly swallow a bite.

But at nine o'clock that evening, when the labours of the day were behind him, he was persuaded to lie down on the sofa and drink a glass of port. At his head sat Mrs Shepherd, holding the wine and some biscuits; at his feet Isabella, stroking his soles. The stimulant revived him; he grew quite mellow, and presently, taking his wife's hand, he held it in his – and Laura felt sure that all his querulousness was forgiven him for the sake of this moment. Then, finding a willing listener in the black-eyed little girl who sat before him, he began to talk, to relate his travels, giving, in particular, a vivid account of some months he had once spent in Japan. Laura, who liked nothing better than travelling at second hand – since any other way was out of the question – Laura spent a delightful hour, and said so.

'Yes, Robby quite surpassed himself to-night, I thought,' said Isabella as she let down her hair. 'I never heard anyone who could talk as well as he does when he likes. – Can you keep a secret, Laura? We are sure, Maisie and I, that Robby will be a Bishop some day. And he means to be, himself. – But don't say a word about it; he won't have it mentioned out of the house. – And meanwhile he's working as hard as he can, and we're saving every penny, to let him take his next degree.'

'I do hope you'll come again,' she said the following morning, as they walked back to the College. 'I don't mind telling you now, I felt quite nervous when Robby said we were to ask you. I've had no experience of little girls. But you haven't been the least trouble – not a bit. And I'm sure it was good for Robby having something young about the house. So mind you write and tell us when you have another holiday' – and Isabella's smile beamed out once more, none the less kindly because it was caught, on its way to Laura, by the gate they were passing through.

Laura, whose mind was set on a good, satisfying slab of

cake, promised to do this, although her feelings had suffered so great a change that she was not sure whether she would keep her word. She was pulled two ways: on the one side was the remembrance of Mr Shepherd hacking cantankerously at the bare mutton-bone; on the other, the cherry-blossom and the mousmés of Japan.

Chapter Seventeen

A PANTOMIME of knowing smiles and interrogatory grimaces greeted her, when, having brushed the cake-crumbs from her mouth, she joined her class. For the twinkling of an eye Laura hesitated, being unprepared. Then, however, as little able as a comic actor to resist pandering to the taste of the public, she yielded to this hunger for spicy happenings, and did what was expected of her: clapped her hands, one over the other, to her breast, and cast her eyes heavenwards. Curiosity and anticipation reached a high pitch; while Laura, by tragically shaking her head, gave it to be understood that no signs could transmit what she had been through, since seeing her friends last.

In the thick of this message she was, unluckily, caught by Dr Pughson, who, after dealing her one of his butcherly gibes, bade her to the blackboard, to grapple with the Seventh Proposition.

The remainder of the forenoon was a tussle with lessons not glanced at since Friday night. – Besides, Laura seldom forestalled events by thinking over them, choosing rather to trust for inspiration to the spur of the moment.

Morning school at an end, she was laid hands on and hurried off to a retired corner of the garden. Here, four friends squatted round, determined to extract her adventures from her – to the last pip.

Laura was in a pretty pickle. Did she tell the plain truth, state the pedestrian facts – and this she would have been capable of doing with some address; for she had looked through her hosts with a perspicacity uncommon in a girl of her age; had once again put to good use those 'sharp, unkind eyes' which Mother deplored. She had seen an overworked, underfed man, who nagged like any woman, and made slaves of two weak, adoring ladies; and she very well knew that, as often as her thoughts in future alighted on Mr Robby, she would think of him pinching and screwing, with a hawk-like eye on a shadowy bishopric. Of her warm feelings for him, genuine or imaginary, not a speck remained. The first touch of reality had sunk them below her ken, just as a drop of cold water sinks the floating grounds in a coffee-pot . . . But did she confess this, confess also that, save for a handful of monosyllables, her only exchange of words with him had been a line of Virgil; and, still more humbling, that she had liked his wife and sister better than himself: did this come to light, she would forfeit every sou of the prestige the visit had lent and yet promised to lend her. -- And, now that the possible moment for parting with this borrowed support had come, she recognised how greatly she had built on it.

These thoughts whizzed through her mind, as she darted a look at the four predatory faces that hemmed her in. Tilly's was one of them: the lightly mocking smile sat on it that Laura had come to know so well, since her maladroit handling of Bob. She would kill that smile – and if she had to die for it herself.

Still, she must be cautious, wary in picking her steps. Especially as she had not the ghost of an idea how to begin.

Meanwhile cries of impatience buzzed round her.

'She doesn't want to tell.'

'Mean brute!'

'Shouldn't wonder if it's too dashed shady.'

'Didn't I *say* he was a bad 'un?'

'I bet you there's nothing to tell,' said Tilly cockily, and turned up her nose.

'Yes, there is,' flung out Laura, at once put on the defensive, and as she spoke she coloured.

'Look at her! Look how red she's got!'

'And after she promised – the sneak!'

'I'm not a sneak. I *am* going to tell. But you're all in such a blooming hurry.'

'Oh, fire away, slow-coach!'

'Well, girls,' began Laura gamely, breathing a little hard. – 'But, mind, you must never utter a word of what I'm going to tell you. It's a dead secret, and *if* you let on—'

'S' help me God!'

'Ananias and Sapphira!'

'Oh, *do* hurry up.'

'Well . . . well, he's just the most – oh, I don't know how to say it, girls – the *most*—'

'Just scrumptious, I suppose, eh?'

'Just positively scrumptious, and . . .'

'And what'd he do?'

'And what about his old sketch of a wife?'

'Her? Oh' – and Laura squeezed herself desperately for the details that *would* not come – 'oh, why she's just a perfect old . . . old cat. And twenty years older than him.'

'What on earth did he marry her for?'

'Guess he's pretty sick of being tied to an old gin like that?'

'I should say! Perfectly *miserable*. He can't think now why he let himself be induced to marry her. He just despises her.'

'Well, why in the name of all that's holy did he take her?'

Laura cast a mysterious glance round, and lowered her voice. 'Well, you see, she had *lots* of money and he had none. He was ever so poor. And she paid for him to be a clergyman.'

'Go on! As poor as all that?'

'As poor as a church-mouse. – But, oh,' she hastened to add, at the visible cooling-off of the four faces, 'he comes of a *most* distinguished family. His father was a lord or a baronet or

something like that, but he married a beautiful girl who hadn't
a penny against his father's will and so he cut him out of his will.'

'I say!'

'Oh, never mind the father.'

'Yes. Well, now he feels under an awful obligation to her,
and all that sort of thing, you know.'

'And she drives it home, I bet. She looks a nipper.'

'Is always throwing it in his face.'

'What a ghoul!'

'He'd do just *anything* to get rid of her, but— Girls, it's
a dead secret; you must swear you won't tell.'

Gestures of assurance were showered on her.

'Well, he's to be a Bishop some day. It's promised him.'

'Holy Moses!'

'And I suppose he can't divorce her, because of that?'

'No, of course not. He'll have to drag her with him like a
millstone round his neck.'

'And he'd twigged right enough you were gone on him?'

Laura's coy smile hinted many things. 'I should say so.
Since the very first day in church. He said – but I don't like to
tell you what he said.'

'You must!'

'No. You'll only call me conceited.'

'No fear, Kiddy. Out with it!'

'Well, then, he said he saw me as soon as he got in the pulpit,
and he wondered ever so much who the girl was with the
eyes like sloes, and the skin like . . . like cream.'

'Snakes-alive-oh! He went it strong.'

'And how often were you alone with him?'

'Yes, and if he had met me before he was married – but
no, I can't tell any more.'

'Oh, don't be such an ass!'

'No, I can't. – Well, I'll whisper it then . . . but only to
Maria,' and leaning over Laura put her lips to Maria's ear.

The reason for this by-stroke she could not have told: the detail she imparted did not differ substantially from those that had gone before. – But by now she was at the end of her tether.

Here, fortunately for Laura, the dinner-bell rang, and the girls had to take to their heels in order to get their books put away before grace. Throughout the meal, from their scattered seats, they exchanged looks of understanding, and their cheeks were pink.

In the afternoon, Laura was again called on to prove her mettle. Her companion on the daily walk was Kate Horner. Kate had been one of the four, and did not lose this chance of beating up fresh particulars.

After those first few awkward moments, however, which had come wellnigh being a fiasco, Laura had no more trouble with her story. Indeed, the plunge once taken, it was astounding how easy it became to make up things about the Shepherds; the difficulty was, to know where to stop. Fictitious details crowded thick and fast upon her – a regular hotchpotch; she had only to stretch out her hand and seize what she needed. It was simpler than the five-times multiplication-table, and did not need to be learnt. But all the same she was not idle: she polished away at her flimflams, bringing them nearer and nearer probability, never, thanks to her sound memory, contradicting herself or making a slip, and always able to begin again from the beginning.

Such initial scepticism as may have lurked in her hearers was soon got the better of. For, crass realists though these young colonials were, and bluntly as they faced facts, they were none the less just as hungry for romance as the most insatiable novel-reader. Romance in any guise was hailed by them, and swallowed uncritically, though it was no more permitted to interfere with the practical conduct of their lives than it is in the case of just that novel-reader, who puts untruth and unreality from him, when he lays his book aside. – Another and weightier reason was, their slower brains could not conceive the possibility of such extraordinarily detailed lying as that to which Laura now subjected them. Its very elaboration stood for its truth.

And the days passed, and Laura had the happiest ideas. A strange thing about them was that they came to her quite unsought, dropping on her like Aladdin's oranges on his turban. All she had to do was to fit them into their niche in her fabrication.

At first, her tale had been chiefly concerned with the internal rift in Mr Shepherd's home-life, and only in a minor degree with herself. But her public savoured the love-story most, and hence, consulting its taste, as it is the tale-maker's bounden duty to do, Laura was obliged to develop this side of her narrative at the expense of the other. And the more the girls heard, the more they wished to hear. She had early turned Miss Isabella into a staunch ally of her own, in the dissension she had introduced into the curate's household; and one day she arrived at a hasty kiss, stolen in the vestry after evening service, while Mr Shepherd was taking off his surplice. The puzzle had been, to get herself into the vestry; but, once there, she saw what followed as if it had actually happened. She saw Mr Shepherd's arm slipped with diffident alacrity round her waist, and her own virtuous recoil; saw Maisie and Isabella waiting, sheep-like, in their pew, till it should please the couple to emerge; saw the form of the verger moving about the darkening church, as he put the lights out, one by one.

But the success this incident brought her turned Laura's head, making her so foolhardy in her inventions that Maria, who for all her boldness of speech was at heart a prude like the rest, grew uneasy.

'You're not to go to that house again, Kiddy. If you do, I'll peach to old Gurley.'

Laura ran upstairs to dress for tea, taking two steps at a time.

On the top landing, beside the great clothes-baskets, she collided with Chinky, who was coming primly down.

'O ki, John!' she greeted her, being in a vast good-humour. 'What do you look so black for?'

'Dunno. Why do you never walk with me nowadays, Laura? I say, you know about that ring? You haven't forgotten?'

'Course not. When am I to get it? It never turns up.' Her eyes glittered as she asked, for she foresaw a further link in her chain. 'Soon, now?'

Chinky nodded mysteriously. 'Pretty soon. And you promise faithfully never to take it off?'

'But it must be a *nice* one . . . with a red stone in it. And listen, Chink, no one must ever know it was you who gave it me.'

'All right, I swear. You're a darling to say you'll wear it,' and putting her arm round Laura's shoulders, Chinky gave her a hearty kiss.

This was more than Laura had bargained for; she freed herself, ungraciously. 'Oh, don't! – now mind, a red stone, and for the third finger of the left hand.'

'Yes. And Laura, I've thought of something to put inside. *Semper eadem* . . . do you like that, Laura?'

'It'll do. – Look out, there's old Day!' and leaving Chinky standing, she ran down the corridor to her room.

Chapter Eighteen

FOR a month or more, Laura fed like a honeybee on the sweets of success. And throve – even to the blindest eye. What had hitherto been lacking was now hers: the admiration and applause of her circle. And never was a child so spurred and uplifted by praise as Laura. Without it, her nature tended to be wary and unproductive; and those in touch with her, had they wished to make the most of her, would no more have stinted with the necessary incentive, that one stints a delicate rose tree in aids to growth. Laura could swallow praise in large doses, without becoming over-sure. Under the present stimulus she sat top in a couple of classes, grew slightly ruddier in face, and much less shrinking in manner.

'Call her back at once and make her shut that door,' cried Miss Day thickly, from behind one of the long, dining-hall tables, on which were ranged stacks and piles of clean linen. She had been on early duty since six o'clock.

The pupil-teacher in attendance stepped obediently into the passage; and Laura returned.

'Doors are made to be shut, Laura Rambotham, I'd have you remember that!' fumed Miss Day in the same indistinct voice: she was in the grip of a heavy cold, which had not been improved by the draughts of the hall.

'I'm sorry, Miss Day. I thought I had. I was a little late.'

'That's your own lookout,' barked the governess. – 'Oh,

there you are at last, Miss Snodgrass. I'd begun to think you weren't going to appear at all this morning. It's close on a quarter past seven.'

'Sorry,' said Miss Snodgrass laconically. 'My watch must be losing. – Well, I suppose I can begin by marking Laura Rambotham down late. – What on earth are you standing there holding the door for?'

'Miss Day knows – I don't,' sauced Laura, and made her escape.

She did not let Miss Snodgrass's bad mark disturb her. No sooner had she begun her practising than she fell to work again on the theme that occupied all her leisure moments, and was threatening to assume the bulk of an early Victorian novel. But she now built at her top-heavy edifice for her own enjoyment; and the usual fate of the robust liar had overtaken her: she was beginning to believe in her own lies. Still she never ventured to relax her critical alertness, her careful surveillance of detail. For, just a day or two before, she had seen a quick flare-up of incredulity light Tilly's face, and oddly enough this had happened when she tried her audience with a fact, a simple little fact, an incident that had really occurred. She had killed the doubt, instantly, by smothering it with a fiction; but she could not forget that it had existed. It has very perplexing; for otherwise her hearers did not shy at a mortal thing; she could drive them where and how she chose.

At the present moment she was planning a great coup: nothing more or less than a frustrated attempt on her virtue. It was almost ready to be submitted to them – for she had read *Pamela* with heartfelt interest during the holidays – and only a few connecting links were missing, with which to complete her own case.

Then, without the slightest warning, the blow fell.

It was a Sunday afternoon; the half-hour that preceded Sunday school. Laura, in company with several others, was in the garden, getting her Bible chapter by heart, when Maria called her.

'Laura! Come here. I want to tell you something.'

Laura approached, her lips in busy motion. 'What's up?'

'I say, chicken, your nose is going to be put out of joint.'

'Mine? What do you mean?' queried Laura, and had a faint sense of impending disaster.

'What I say. M. Pidwall's asked to the you-know-who's next Saturday.'

'No, she's not!' cried Laura vehemently, and clapped her Bible to.

'S'help me God, she is,' asserted Maria. – 'Look out, don't set the place on fire.'

'How do you know? . . . who told you?'

'M. P. herself. – Gosh, but you are a jealous little cub. Oh, go on, Kiddy, don't take it like that. I guess he won't give you away.' – For Laura was as pale as a moment before she had been scarlet.

Alleging a violent headache, she mounted to her room, and sat down on her bed. She felt stunned, and it took her some time to recover her wits. Sitting on the extreme edge of the bedstead, she stared at the objects in the room without seeing them. 'M. P.'s going there on Saturday . . . M. P.'s going there on Saturday,' she repeated stupidly, and, with her hands pressed on her hips, rocked herself to and fro, after the fashion of an older woman in pain.

The fact was too appalling to be faced; her mind postponed it. Instead, she saw the fifty-five at Sunday school – where they were at this minute – drawn up in a line round the walls of the dining-hall. She saw them rise to wail out the hymn; saw Mr Strachey on his chair in the middle of the floor, perpetually nimming with his left leg. And, as she pictured the familiar scene to herself, she shivered with a sudden sense of isolation: behind each well-known face lurked a possible enemy.

If it had only not been M. P.! – that was the first thought that
crystallised. Anyone else! . . . from any of the rest she might
have hoped for some mercy. But Mary Pidwall was one of
those people – there were plenty such – before whom a nature
like Laura's was inclined, at the best of times, to shrink away,
keenly aware of its own paltriness and ineffectualness. Mary
was rectitude in person: and it cannot be denied that, to Laura,
this was synonymous with hard, narrow, ungracious. Not
quite a prig, though: there was fun in Mary, and life in her;
but it was neither fun nor vivacity of a kind that Laura could
feel at ease with. Such capers as the elder girl cut were only
skin-deep; they were on the surface of her character, had no
real roots in her: just as the pieces of music she played on the
piano were accidents of the moment, without deeper signifi-
cance. To Mary, life was already serious, full of duties. She
knew just what she wanted, too, where she wanted to go and
how to get there; her plans were cut and dried. She was clever,
very industrious, the head of several of her classes. Nor was
she ever in conflict with the authorities: she moved among the
rules of the school as safely as an egg-dancer among his eggs.
For the simple reasons that temptations seemed to pass her by. –
There was, besides, a kind of manly exactness in her habit of
thinking and speaking; and it was this trait her companions
tried to symbolise, in calling her by the initial letters of her
name.

She and Laura, though classmates, had never drawn together.
It is true, Mary was sixteen, and, at that time of life, a couple of
years dig a wide breach. But there was also another reason.
Once, in the innocence of her heart, Laura had let the cat out of
the bag that an uncle of hers lived in the up-country township
to which Mary belonged.

The girl had eyed her coldly, incredulously. 'What? That
dreadful man your uncle?' she had exclaimed: she herself was
the daughter of a church dignitary. 'I should say I did know

him – by reputation at least. And it's quite enough, thank you.'

Now Laura had understood that Uncle Tom – he needed but a pair of gold earrings to pose as the model for a Spanish Grandee – that Uncle Tom *was* odd, in this way: he sometimes took more to drink than was good for him; but she had never suspected him of being 'dreadful', or a byword in Wanta-badgery. Colouring to the roots of her hair, she murmured something about him of course not being recognised by the rest of the family; but M. P., she was sure, had never looked on her with the same eyes again.

Such was the rigid young moralist into whose hands her fate was given.

She sat and meditated these things, in spiritless fashion. She would have to confess to her fabrications – that was plain. M. P.'s precise mind would bring back a precise account of how matters stood in the Shepherd household: not by an iota would the truth be swerved from. Why, oh why, had she not foreseen this possibility? What evil spirit had prompted her and led her on? – But, before her brain could contemplate the awful necessity of rising and branding herself as a liar, it sought desperately for a means of escape. For a wink, she even nursed the idea of dragging in a sham man, under the pretence that Mr Shepherd had been but a blind, used by her to screen some-one else. But this yarn, twist it as she might, would not pass muster. Against it was the mass of her accumulated detail.

She sat there, devising scheme after scheme. Not one of them would do.

When, at tea-time, she rose to wash her face before going downstairs, the sole point on which she had come to clearness was, that just seven days lay between her and detection. – Yet after all, she reminded herself, seven days made a week, and a week was a good long time. Perhaps something would happen between now and Saturday. M. P. might have an accident and break her leg, and not be able to go. Or thin, poorly-fed Mr

Shepherd fall ill from overwork. – Oh, how she would rejoice to hear of it!

And, if the worst came to the worst and she *had* to tell, at least it should not be to-day. To-day was Sunday; and people's thoughts were frightfully at liberty. To-morrow they would be engaged again; and, by to-morrow, she herself would have grown more accustomed to the idea. – Besides, how foolish to have been in too great a hurry, should something come to pass that rendered confession needless.

On waking next morning, however, and accounting, with a throb, for the leaden weight on her mind, she felt braver, and quite determined to make a clean breast of her misdoings. Things could not go on like this. But no sooner was she plunged into the routine of the day than her decision slackened: it was impossible to find just the right moment to begin. Early in the morning everyone was busy looking over lessons, and would not thank you for the upset, the dinner-hour was all too short; after school, on the walk, she had a partner who knew nothing about the affair, and after tea she practised. – Hence, on Monday her purpose failed her.

On Tuesday it was the same; the right moment never presented itself.

In bed that night she multiplied the remaining days into hours. They made one hundred and twenty. That heartened her a little; considered thus, the time seemed very much longer; and so she let Wednesday slip by, without over-much worry.

On Thursday she not only failed to own up, but indulged anew.

All the week, as if Mary Pidwall's coming visit worked upon them, the girls had been very greedy for more love-story, and had shown themselves decidedly nettled by Laura's refusal to continue; for this was the week when the great revelation she had hinted at should have been made. And one afternoon when the four were twitting her, and things were looking very

black, Laura was incited by some devil to throw them, not,
it is true, the savoury incident their mouths watered for, but a
fresh fiction – just as the beset traveller throws whatever he has
at hand, to the ravenous wolves that press round the sledge.
At the moment, the excitement that accompanies inspiration
kept her up; but afterwards she had a stinging fit of remorse;
and her self-reproaches were every whit as bitter as those of
the man who has again broken the moral law he has vowed
to respect, and who now sees that he is powerless against
recurring temptation.

When she remembered those four rapacious faces, Laura
realised that, come what might, she would never have the
courage to confess. To them, at least. That night in deep
humility she laid her sin bare to God, imploring Him, even
though He could not pardon it, to avert the consequences
from her.

The last days were also darkened by her belief that M. P.
had got wind of her romancings: as, indeed, was quite likely;
for the girls' tongues were none too safe. Mary looked at her
from time to time with such a sternly suspicious eye that
Laura's very stomach quailed within her.

And meanwhile the generous hours had declined to less
than half.

'Twice more to get up, and twice to go to bed,' she reckoned
aloud to herself on Saturday morning.

She was spending that week-end at Godmother's. It was
as dull as usual; she had ample leisure to brood over what lay
before her. It was now a certainty, fixed, immovable; for,
by leaving school that day without having spoken, she had
burned her ships behind her. When she went back on Monday
M. P. would be there, and every loophole closed. On Sunday
evening she made an excuse and went down into the garden.
There was no moon; but, overhead, the indigo-blue was a
prodigal glitter of stars – myriads of silver eyes that perforated

the sky. They sparkled with a cold disregard of the small girl standing under the mulberry tree; but Laura, too, was only half-alive to their magnificence. Her thoughts ran on suicide, on making an end of her blighted career. God was evidently not going to be generous or long-suffering enough to come to her aid; and in imagination she saw the fifty-five gaining on her like a pack of howling hyaenas; saw Mrs Gurley, Mr Strachey – Mother. Detection and exposure, she knew it now, were the most awful things the world held. But she had nothing handy: neither a rope, nor poison, nor was there a dam in the neighbourhood.

That night she had the familiar dream that she was being 'stood up' and expelled, as Annie Johns had been: thousands of tongues shouted her guilt; she was hunted like a wallaby. She wakened with a scream, and Marina, her bedfellow, rose on one elbow and lighted the candle. Crumpled and dishevelled, Laura lay outside the sheet that should have covered her; and her pillow had slipped to the floor.

'What on earth's the matter? Dreaming? Then depend on it you've eaten something that's disagreed with you.'

How she dragged her legs back to school that morning, Laura never knew. At the sight of the great stone building her inner disturbance was such that she was nearly sick. Even the unobservant Marina was forced to a remark.

'You do look a bit peaky. I'm sure your stomach's out of order. Your should take a dose of castor-oil to-night, before you go to bed.'

Though it was a blazing November day, her fingers were cold as she took off her hat and changed her white frock. 'For the last time,' she murmured; by which she meant the last time in untarnished honour. And she folded and hung up her clothes, with a neatness that was foreign to her.

Classes were in full swing when she went downstairs; nothing could happen now till the close of morning school.

But Laura signalised the beginning of her downfall, the end of her comet-like flight, by losing her place in one form after another, the lessons she had prepared on Friday evening having gone clean out of her head.

Directly half-past twelve struck, she ran to the top of the garden and hid herself under a tree. There she crouched, her fingers in her ears, her heart thumping as if it would break, Till the dinner-bell rang. Then she was forced to emerge – and no tottering criminal, about to face the scaffold, has ever had more need of Dutch courage than Laura in this moment. Peeping round the corner of the path she saw the fateful group: M. P. the centre of four gesticulating figures. She loitered till they had scattered and disappeared; then with shaking legs crept to the house. At the long tables the girls still stood, waiting for Mr Strachey; and the instant Laura set foot in the hall, five pairs of eyes caught her, held her, pinned her down, as one pins a butterfly to a board. She was much too far gone to think of tossing her head and braving things out, now that the crisis had come. Pale, guilty, wretched, she sidled to her seat. This was near Maria's, and, as she passed, Maria leant back.

'You *vile* little liar !'

'How's that shy little mouse of a girl we had here a month or two ago?' Mr Shepherd had inquired. 'Let me see – what was her name again?'

To which Miss Isabella had replied: 'Well, you know, Robby dear, you really hardly saw her. You had so much to do, poor boy, just when she was here. Her name was Laura – Laura Rambotham.'

And Mrs Shepherd gently: 'Yes, a nice little girl. But very young for her age. And *so* shy.'

'You wretched little lying sneak !'
In vain Laura wept and protested.

'You made me do it. I should never have told a word, if it hadn't been for you.'

This point of view enraged them. 'What? You want to put it on us now, do you? . . . you dirty little skunk! To say *we* made you tell that pack of lies? – Look here: as long as you stay in this blooming shop, I'll never open my mouth to you again!'

'Someone ought to tell old Gurley and have her expelled. That's all she's fit for. Spreading disgusting stories about people who've been kind to her. They probably only asked her there out of charity. She's as poor as dirt.'

'Wants her bottom smacked – that's what I say!'

Thus Maria, and, with her, Kate Horner.

Tilly was cooler and bitterer. 'I was a dashed fool ever to believe a word. *I* might have known her little game. She? Why, when I took her out to see my cousin Bob, she couldn't say boo to a goose. He laughed about her afterwards like anything; said she ought to have come in a perambulator, with a nurse. – *You* make anyone in love with you – you!' And Tilly spat, to show her disdain.

'What have they been saying to you, Laura?' whispered Chinky, pale and frightened. 'Whatever is the matter?'

'Mind your own business and go away,' sobbed Laura.

'I am, I'm going,' said Chinky humbly. – 'Oh, Laura, I *wish* you had that ring.'

'Oh, blow you and your ring! I hate the very name of it,' cried Laura, maddened. – And retreating to a lavatory, which was the only private place in the school, she wept her full.

They all, every girl of them, understood white lies, and practised them. They might also have forgiven her a lie of the good, plain, straightforward, thumping order. What they could not forgive, or get over, was the extraordinary circumstantiality of the fictions which with she had gulled them: to be able to invent lies with such proficiency meant that you had been born with a criminal bent. – And as a criminal she was accordingly treated.

Even the grown-up girls heard a garbled version of the story.

'Why ever did you do it?' one of them asked Laura curiously; it was a very pretty girl, called Evelyn, with twinkling brown eyes.

'I don't know,' said Laura abjectly; and this was almost true.

'But I say! . . . nasty tarradiddles about people who's been so nice to you? What made you tell them?'

'I don't *know*. They just came.'

The girl's eyes smiled. 'Well, I never! Poor little Kiddy,' she said as she turned away.

But this was the only kind word Laura heard. For many and many a night after, she cried herself to sleep.

Chapter Nineteen

THUS Laura went to Coventry. – Not that the social banishment she now suffered was known by that name. To the majority of the girls Coventry was just a word in the geography-book, a place where ribbons were said to be made, and where, for a better-read few, someone had hung with grooms and porters on a bridge; this detail, odd to say, making a deeper impression on their young minds than the story of Lady Godiva, which was looked upon merely as a naughty anecdote.

But, by whatever name it was known, Laura's ostracism was complete. She had been sampled, tested, put on one side. And not the softest-hearted could find an excuse for her behaviour.

It was but another instance of how misfortune dogs him who is down, that Chinky should choose this very moment to bring further shame upon her.

On one of the miserable days that were now the rule, when Laura would have liked best to be a rabbit, hid deep in its burrow; as she was going upstairs one afternoon, she met Jacob, the man-of-all-work, coming down. He had a trunk on his shoulder. Throughout the day she had been aware of a subdued excitement among the boarders; they had stood about in groups, talking in low voices – talking about her, she believed, from the glances that were thrown over shoulders at her as she passed. She made herself as small as she could; but when tea-time came, and then supper, and Chinky had not appeared at either meal, curiosity got the better of her, and she tried to pump one of the younger girls.

Maria came up while she was speaking, and the child ran away; for the little ones aped their elders in making Laura taboo.

'What, liar? You want to stuff us you don't know why she's gone?' said Maria. 'No, thank you, it's not good enough. You can't bamboozle us this time.'

'Sapphira up to her tricks again, is she?' threw in the inseparable Kate, who had caught the last words. 'No, by dad, we don't tell liars what they know already. – So put that in your pipe and smoke it!'

Only bit by bit did Laura dig out their meaning: then, the horrible truth lay bare. Chinky had been dismissed – privately because she was a boarder – from the school. Her crime was: she had taken half-a-sovereign from the purse of one of her room-mates. When taxed with the theft, she wept that she had not taken it for herself, but to buy a ring for Laura Rambotham; and, with this admission on her lips, she passed out of their lives, leaving Laura, her confederate, behind. – Yes, confederate; for, in the minds of most, liar and thief were synonymous.

Laura had not cared two straws for Chinky; she found what the latter had done, 'mean and disgusting', and said so, stormily; but of course was not believed. Usually too proud to defend herself, she here returned to the charge again and again; for the hint of connivance had touched her on the raw. But she strove in vain to prove her innocence: she could not get her enemies to grasp the abysmal difference between merely making up a story about people, and laying hands on others' property; if she could do the one, she was capable of the other; and her companions remained convinced that, if she had not actually had her fingers in someone's purse, she had, by a love of jewellery, incited Chinky to the theft. And so, after a time, Laura gave up the attempt and suffered in silence; and it *was* suffering; for her schoolfellows were cruel with that intolerance, that unimaginative dullness, which makes a woman's cruelty so hard to bear. Laura had to accustom herself to hear every word she said doubted; to hear someone called to, before her face, to attest her statements; to see her room-mates lock up their purses under her very nose.

However, only three weeks had still to run till the Christmas holidays. She drew twenty-one strokes on a sheet of paper, which she pinned to the wall above her bed; and each morning she ran her pencil through a fresh line. She was quite resolved to beg Mother not to send her back to school: if she said she was not getting proper food, that would be enough to put Mother up in arms.

The boxes were being fetched from the lumber-rooms and distributed among their owners, when a letter arrived from Mother saying that the two little boys had sandy blight, and that Laura would not be able to come home under two or three weeks, for fear of infection. These weeks she was to spend, in company with Pin, at a watering-place down the Bay, where one of her aunts had a cottage.

The news was welcome to Laura: she had shrunk from the thought of Mother's searching eye. And at the cottage there would be none of her grown-up relatives to face; only an old housekeeper, who was looking after a party of boys.

Hence, when speech day was over, instead of setting out on an up-country railway journey, Laura, under the escort of Miss Snodgrass, went on board one of the steamers that ploughed the Bay.

'I should say sea-air'll do you good – brighten you up a bit,' said the governess affably as they drove: she was in great good-humour at the prospect of losing sight for a time of the fifty-five. 'You seem to be always in the dumps nowadays.'

Laura dutifully waved her handkerchief from the deck of the *Silver Star*; and the paddles began to churn. As Miss

Snodgrass's back retreated down the pier, and the breach between ship and land widened, she settled herself on her seat with a feeling of immense relief. At last – at last she was off. The morning had been a sore trial to her: in all the noisy and effusive leave-taking, she was odd man out; no one had been sorry to part from her; no one had extracted a promise that she would write. Her sole valediction had been a minatory shaft from Maria: if she valued her skin, to learn to stop telling crams before she showed up there again. Now, she was free of them; she would not be humiliated afresh, would not need to stand eye to eye with anyone who knew of her disgrace, for weeks to come; perhaps never again, if Mother agreed. Her heart grew momentarily lighter. And the farther they left Melbourne behind them, the higher her spirits rose.

But then, too, was it possible, on this radiant December day, long to remain in what Miss Snodgrass had called 'the dumps'? – The sea was a blue-green mirror, on the surface of which they swam. The sky was a stretched sheet of blue, in which the sun hung a very ball of fire. But the steamer cooled the air as it moved; and none of the white-clad people who, under the stretched white awnings, thronged the deck, felt oppressed by the great heat. In the middle of the deck, a brass band played popular tunes.

At a pretty watering-place where they stopped, Laura rose and crossed to the opposite railing. A number of passengers went ashore, pushing and laughing, but almost as many more came on board, all dressed in white, and with eager, animated faces. Then the boat stood to sea again and sailed past high, grass-grown cliffs, from which a few old cannons, pointing their noses at you, watched over the safety of the Bay – in the event, say, of the Japanese or the Russians entering the Heads – past the pretty township, and the beflagged bathing-enclosures on the beach below. They neared the tall, granite lighthouse at the point, with the flagstaff at its side where incoming steamers were signalled; and as soon as they had rounded this corner they were in view of the Heads themselves. From the distant cliffs there ran out, on either side, brown reefs, which made the inrushing water dance and foam, and the entrance to the Bay narrow and dangerous: on one side, there projected the portion of a wreck which had lain there as long as Laura had been in the world. Then, having made a sharp turn to the left, the boat crossed to the opposite coast, and steamed past barrack-like buildings lying asleep in the fierce sunshine of the afternoon; and, in due course, it stopped at Laura's destination.

Old Anne was waiting on the jetty, having hitched the horse to a post: she had driven in, in the 'shandrydan', to meet Laura. For the cottage was not on the front beach, with the hotels and boarding-houses, the fenced-in baths and great gentle slope of yellow sand: it stood in the bush, on the back beach, which gave to the open sea.

Laura took her seat beside the old woman in her linen sunbonnet, the body of the vehicle being packed full of groceries and other stores; and the drive began. Directly they were clear of the township the road as good as ceased, became a mere sandy track, running through a scrub of ti-trees. – And what sand! White, dry, sliding sand, through which the horse shuffled and floundered, in which the wheels sank and stuck. Had one of the many hillocks to be taken, the two on the box-seat instinctively threw their weight forward; old Anne, who had a stripped wattle-bough for a whip, urged and cajoled; and more than once she handed Laura the reins and got down, to give the horse a pull. They had always to be ducking their heads, too, to let the low ti-tree branches sweep over their backs.

About a couple of miles out, the old woman alighted and slipped a rail; and having passed the only other house within cooee, they drove through a paddock, but at a walking-pace, because of the thousands of rabbit-burrows that perforated the ground. Another slip-rail lowered, they drew up at the foot of a steepish hill, beside a sandy little vegetable garden, a shed and a pump. The house was perched on the top of the hill, and directly they sighted it they also saw Pin flying down, her sunbonnet on her neck.

'Laura, Laura! Oh, I *am* glad you've come. What a time you've been!'

'Hullo, Pin. – Oh, I say, let me get out first.'

'And pull up your bonnet, honey. D'you want to be after gettin' sunstruck?'

Glad though Laura was to see her sister again, she did not manage to infuse a very hearty tone into her greeting; for her first glimpse of Pin had given her a disagreeable shock. It was astonishing, the change the past half-year had worked in the child; and as the two climbed the hill together, to the accompaniment of Pin's bubbly talk, Laura stole look after look at her little sister, in the hope of growing used to what she saw. Pin had never been pretty, but now she was 'downright hideous' – as Laura phrased it to herself. Eleven years of age, she had at last begun to grow in earnest: her legs were as of old mere spindleshanks, but nearly twice as long; and her fat little body, perched above them, made one think of a shrivelled-up old man who has run all to paunch. Her face, too, had increased in shapelessness, the features being blurred in the fat mass; her blue eyes were more slit-like than before; and, to cap everything, her fine skin had absolutely no chance, so bespattered was it with freckles. And none of your pretty little sun-kisses; but large, black, irregular freckles that disfigured like moles. Laura felt quite distressed; it outraged her feelings that anyone belonging to her should be so ugly; and as Pin, in happy ignorance of her sister's reflections, chattered on, Laura turned over in her mind what she ought to do. She would have to tell Pin about herself – that was plain: she must break the news to her, in case others should do it, and more cruelly. It

was one consolation to know that Pin was not sensitive about
her looks; so long as you did not tease her about her legs,
there was no limit to what you might say to her: the grieving
was all for the onlooker. But not today: this was the first day;
and there were pleasanter things to think of. And so, when they
had had tea – with condensed milk in it, for the cow had gone
dry, and no milkman came out so far – when tea was over – and
that was all that could be undertaken in the way of refreshment
after the journey; washing your face and hands, for instance,
was out of the question; every drop of water had to be carried
up the hill from the pump, and old Anne purposely kept the
ewers empty by day; if you *would* wash, you must wash in the
sea – as soon, then, as tea was over, the two sisters made for
the beach.

The four-roomed, weatherboard cottage, to which at a
later date a lean-to had been added, faced the bush: from the
verandah there was a wide view of the surrounding country.
Between the back of the house and the beach rose a huge
sand-hill, sparsely grown with rushes and coarse grass. It took
you some twenty minutes to toil over this, and boots and
stockings were useless impedimenta; for the sand was once
more of that loose and shifting kind in which you sank at times
up to the knees, falling back one step for every two you climbed.
But then, sand was the prevailing note of this free and easy life:
it bestrewed verandah and floors; you carried it in your clothes;
the beds were full of it; it even got into the food; and you were
soon so accustomed to its presence that you missed the grit of
it underfoot, or the prickling on your skin, did old Anne happen
to take a broom in her hand, or thoroughly re-make the beds. –
When, however, on your way to the beach you had laboriously
attained the summit of the great dune, the sight that met you
almost took your breath away: as far as the eye could reach,
the bluest of skies melting into the bluest of seas, which broke
its foam-flecked edge against the flat, brown reefs that fringed

the shore. Then, downhill – with a trip and a flounder that
sent the sand man-high – and at last you were on what Laura
and Pin thought the most wonderful beach in the world. What
a variety of things was there! Whitest, purest sand, hot to the
touch as a zinc roof in summer; rocky caves, and sandy caves
hung with crumbly stalactites; at low tide, on the reef, lakes
and ponds and rivers deep enough to make it unnecessary for
you to go near the ever-angry surf at all; seaweeds that ran
through the gamut of colours: brown and green, pearl-pink
and coral-pink, to vivid scarlet and orange; shells, beginning
with tiny grannies and cowries, and ending with the monsters
in which the breakers had left their echo; the bones of cuttle-
fish, light as paper, and shaped like javelins. And, what was
best of all, this beach belonged to them alone; they had not to
share its treasures with strangers; except the inhabitants of the
cottage, never a soul set foot upon it.

The chief business of the morning was to bathe. If the girls
were alone and the tide full, they threw off their clothes and
ran into a sandy, shallow pool, where the water never came
above their waists, and where it was safe to let the breakers
dash over them. But if the tide were low, the boys bathed, too,
and then Pin and Laura tied themselves up in old bathing-
gowns that were too big for them, and all went in a body to the
'Half-Moon Hole'. This pool, which was about twenty feet
long and ten to fifteen deep, lay far out on the reef, and, at
high tide, was hidden beneath surf and foam; at low water,
on the other hand, it was like a glass mirror reflecting the sky,
and so clear that you could see every weed that waved at the
bottom. Having cast off your shoes, you applied your soles
gingerly to the prickles of the rock; then plop! – and in you
went. Pin often needed a shove from behind, for nowhere,
of course, could you get a footing; but Laura swam with the
best. Some of the boys would dive to the bottom and bring
up weeds and shells, but Laura and Pin kept on the surface of

the water; for they had the imaginative dread common to children who know the sea well – the dread of what may lurk beneath the thick, black horrors of seaweed.

Then, after an hour or so in the water, home to dinner, hungry as swagmen, though the bill of fare never varied: it was always rabbit for dinner, crayfish for tea; for the butcher called only once a week, and meat could not be kept an hour without getting flyblown. The rabbits were skinned and in the stew-pot before they were cold; the crayfish died an instant death: one that drove the blood to Laura's head, and made Pin run away and cry, with her fingers to her ears; for she believed the sizzling of the water, as the fish were dropped in, to be the shriek of the creatures in their death-agony.

Except in bathing, the girls saw little of the boys. Both were afraid of guns, so did not go out on the expeditions which supplied the dinner-table; and old Anne would not allow them to join the crayfishing excursions. For these took place by night, off the end of the reef, with nets and torches; and it sometimes happened, if the surf were heavy, that one of the fishers was washed off the rocks, and only hauled up again with considerable difficulty.

Laura took her last peep at the outside world, every evening, in the brief span of time between sunset and dark. Running up to the top of one of the hills, and letting her eyes range over sky and sea, she would drink in the scents that were waking to life after the burning heat of the day: salt water, warmed sand and seaweeds, ti-scrub, sour-grass, and the sturdy berry-bushes, high as her knee, through which she had ploughed her way. That was one of the moments she liked best, that, and lying in bed at night listening to the roar of the surf, which went on and on like a cannonade, even though the hill lay between. It made her flesh crawl, too, in delightful fashion, did she picture to herself how alone she and Pin were, in their room: the boys slept in the lean-to on the other side of the kitchen;

old Anne at the back. For miles round, no house broke the solitude of the bush; only a thin wooden partition separated her from possible bushrangers, from the vastness and desolation of the night, the eternal booming of the sea.

Such was the life into which Laura now threw herself heart and soul, forgetting, in the sheer joy of living, her recent tribulation.

But even the purest pleasures *will* pall; and after a time, when the bloom had worn off and the newness and her mind was more at leisure again, she made some disagreeable discoveries which ruffled her tranquillity.

It was Pin, poor, fat, little well-meaning Pin, who did the mischief.

Pin was not only changed in looks; her character had changed, too; and in so marked a way that before a week was out the sisters were at loggerheads. Each day made it plainer to Laura that Pin was developing a sturdy independence; she had ceased to look up to Laura as a prodigy of wisdom, and had begun to hold opinions of her own. She was, indeed, even disposed to be critical of her sister; and criticism from this quarter was more than Laura could brook: it was just as if a slave usurped his master's rights. At first speechless with surprise, she ended by losing her temper; the more, because Pin was prone to be mulish, and could not be got to budge, either by derision or by scorn, from her espoused views. They were those of the school at which for the past half-year she had been a day-pupil, and seemed to her unassailable. Laura found them ridiculous, as she did much else about Pin at this time: her ugliness, her setting herself up as an authority: and she jeered unkindly whenever Pin came out with them. – A still more ludicrous thing was that, despite her plainness, Pin actually had an admirer. True, she did not say so outright; perhaps she was not even aware of it; but Laura gathered from her talk that a boy at her school, a boy some three years older than herself, had given her a silk handkerchief and liked to help her with her sums. – And to Laura this was the most knock-down blow of all.

One day it came to an open quarrel between them.

They were lying on the beach after bathing, trying to protect their bare and blistered legs from the sandflies. Laura, flat on her back, had spread a towel over hers; Pin sat Turk-fashion with her legs beneath her and fought the flies with her hands. Having vainly endeavoured to draw from the reticent Laura some of those school-tales of which, in former holidays, she had been so prodigal, Pin was now chattering, to her heart's content, about the small doings of home. Laura listened to her with the impatient toleration of one who has seen the world: she really could not be expected to interest herself in such trifles; and she laughed in her sleeve at Pin's simpleness. When, however, her little sister began to enlarge anew on some wonderful orders Mother had lately had, she could not refrain from saying crossly: 'You've told me that a dozen times already. And you needn't bawl it out for everyone to hear.'

'Oh, Laura! there isn't anyone anywhere near us ... and even if there were – why, I thought you'd be so pleased. Mother's going to give you an extra shilling pocket-money, 'cause of it.'

'Of course I'm pleased. Don't be so silly, Pin.'

'I'm not *always* silly, Laura,' protested Pin. 'And I don't believe you *are* glad, a bit. Old Anne was, though. She said: "Bless her dear heart!"'

'Old Anne? Well, I just wonder what next! It's none of her dashed business.'

'Oh, Laura!' began Pin, growing tearful both at words and tone. 'Why, Laura, you're not ashamed of it, are you? – that mother does sewing?' – and Pin opened her lobelia-blue eyes to their widest, showing what very big eyes they would be, were they not so often swollen with crying.

'Of course not,' said Laura tartly. 'But I'm blessed if I can see what it's got to do with old Anne.'

'But she asked me . . . what mother was working at – and if she'd got any new customers. She just loves mother.'

'Like her cheek!' snapped Laura. 'Poking her ugly old nose into what doesn't concern her. You should just have said you didn't know.'

'But that would have been a story, Laura!' cried Pin, horrified 'I did know – quite well.'

'Goodness gracious, Pin, you—'

'I've never told a story in my life,' said Pin hotly. 'And I'm not going to either, for you or anyone. I think you ought to be ashamed of yourself.'

'Hold your silly tongue!'

'I shan't, Laura. And I think you're very wicked. You're not a bit like what you used to be. And it's all going to school that's done it – Mother says it is.'

'Oh, don't be such a blooming ass!' and Laura, stung to the quick, retaliated by taunting Pin with the change that had come to pass in her appearance. To her surprise, she found Pin grown inordinately touchy about her looks: at Laura's brutal statement of the truth she cried bitterly.

'I'm not, no, I'm not! I haven't got a full moon for a face! It's no fatter than yours. Sarah said last time you were home how fat you were getting.'

'I'm sure I'm not,' said Laura, indignant in her turn.

'Yes, you are,' sobbed Pin. 'But you only think other people are ugly, not yourself. I'll tell mother what you've said as soon as ever I get home. And I'll tell her, too, you want to make me tell stories. And that I'm sure you've done something naughty at school, 'cause you won't ever talk about it. And how you're always saying bad words like blooming and gosh and golly – yes, I will!'

'You were always a sneak and a tell-tale.'

'And you were always a greedy, selfish, deceitful thing.'

'You don't know anything about me, you numbskull, you!'

'I don't want to! I know you're a bad, wicked girl.'

After this exchange of home truths, they did not speak to each other for two days: Pin had a temper that smouldered, and could not easily forgive. So she stayed at old Anne's side, helping to bake scones and leather-jackets; or trotted after the boys, who had dropped into the way of saying: 'Come on, little Pin!' as they never said: 'Come on, Laura!' – and Laura retired in lonely dudgeon to the beach.

She took the estrangement so much to heart that she eased her feelings by abusing Pin in thought; Pin was a pig-headed little ignoramus, as timid as ever of setting one foot before the other. And the rest of them would be just the same – old stick-in-the muds, unchanged by a hair, or, if they *had* changed, then changed for the worse. Laura had somehow never foreseen the day on which she would find herself out of tune with her home circle; with unthinking assurance she had expected that Pin, for instance, would always be eager to keep pace with her. Now, she saw that her little sister would probably never catch up to her again. Such progress as Pin might make – if she were not already glued firm to her silly notions – would be in quite another direction. For the quarrel had made one thing plain to Laura: with regard to her troubles, she need not look to Pin for sympathy: if Pin talked such gibberish at the hint of putting off an inquisitive old woman, what would she – and not she alone – what would they all say to the tissue of lies Laura had spun round Mr Shepherd, a holy man, a clergyman, and a personal friend of Mother's into the bargain? She could not blink the fact that, did it come to their ears, they would call her in earnest, what Pin had called her in her temper – bad and wicked. Home was, alas! no longer the snug nest in which she was safe from the slings and shanghais of the world.

And then there was another thing: did she stay at home,

she would have to re-live herself into the thousand and one
gimcrack concerns, which now, as set forth by Pin, so bored
her: the colic Leppie had brought on by eating unripe fruit;
the fact that another of Sarah's teeth had dropped out without
extraneous aid. It was all very well for a week or two, but,
at the idea of shutting herself wholly up with such mopokes,
of cutting herself off from her present vital interests, Laura
hastily reconsidered her decision to leave school. No: badly as
she had suffered at her companions' hands, much as she
dreaded returning, it was at school she belonged. All her heart
was there: in the doings of her equals, the things that really
mattered – who would be promoted, who prefect, whose seat
changed in the dining-hall. – Besides, could one who had
experienced the iron rule of Mr Strachey, or Mrs Gurley, ever
be content to go back and just form one of a family of children?
She not, at any rate!

Thus she lay, all day long, her hands clasped under her neck,
a small white speck on the great wave-lapped beach. She
watched the surf break, watched the waves creep up and hide
the reef, watched the gulls vanish in the sun-saturated blue
overhead. Sometimes she rose to her elbow to follow a ship
just inside the horizon; and it pleased her to think that this
great boat was sailing off, with a load of lucky mortals, to
some unknown, fairer world, while she, a poor Cinderella,
had to stop behind – even though she knew it was only the
English mail going on to Sydney. Of Pin she preferred not to
think; nor could she dwell with equanimity on her late mis-
fortunes at school and the trials that awaited her on her re-
appearance; and since she *had* to think of something, she fell
into the habit of making up might-have-beens, of narrating to
herself how things would have fallen out had her fictions been
fact, her ascetic hero the impetuous lover she had made of
him. – In other words, lying prostrate on the sand, Laura
went on with her story.

When, towards the end of the third week, she and Pin were summoned to spend some days with Godmother, she had acquired such a gusto for this occupation, that she preferred to shirk reality, and let Pin pay the visit alone.

Chapter Twenty

SEA, sun and air did their healing work, as did also the long, idle days in the home garden; and Laura drank in health and vigour with every breath.

She had need of it all when, the golden holidays over, she returned to school; for the half-year that broke was, in many ways, the most trying she had yet had to face. True, her dupes' first virulence had waned -- they no longer lashed her openly with their tongues -- but the quiet, covert insults, that were now the rule, were every bit as hard to bear; and before a week had passed Laura was telling herself that, had she been a Christian Martyr, she would have preferred to be torn asunder with one jerk, rather than submit to the thumbkin. Not an eye but looked askance at her; on every face was painted a reminder of her moral inferiority; and even newcomers among the boarders soon learnt, without always knowing what her crime had been, that Laura Rambotham was 'not the thing'.

This system of slight and disparagement was similar to what she had had to endure in her first school term; but its effect upon her was different. Then, in her raw timidity, she had bowed her head beneath it; now, she could not be so lamb-like. In thought, she never ceased to lay half the blame of what had happened on her companions' shoulders; and she was embittered by their injustice in making her alone responsible, when all she had done was to yield to their craving for romance. She became a rebel, wrapping herself round in the cloak of bitterness which the outcasts of fortune wear, feeding on her hate of those within the pale. Very well then, she said to herself: if her fellows chose to shut her out like this, she would stop outside, and never see eye to eye with them again. And it gave her an unholy pleasure to mock, in secret, at all they set store by.

Her outward behaviour for many a day was, none the less, that of a footlicker; and by no sign did she indicate what she really was – a very unhappy girl. Like most rebels of her sex, she ardently desired to re-enter the fold of law and order; and it was to this end she worked, although, wherever she approached it, the place seemed to bristle with spears. But she did not let herself be daunted; she pocketed injuries, pretended not to hear them, played the spaniel to people she despised; and it soon became open talk, that no matter what you said to her, Laura Rambotham would not take offence. You could also rely on her to do a dirty job for you. – A horrid little toady was the verdict; especially of those who had no objection to be toadied to.

Torn thus, between mutinous sentiments on the one hand, a longing for restitution on the other, Laura grew very sly – a regular little tactician. In these days, she was for ever considering what she ought to do, what to leave undone. She learnt to weigh her words before uttering them, instead of blurting out her thoughts in the childish fashion that had exposed her to ridicule; she learnt, too, at last, to keep her real opinions to herself, and to make those she expressed tally with her hearers'. And she was quick to discover that this was a short-cut towards regaining her lost place: to conceal what she truly felt – particularly if her feelings ran counter to those of the majority. For, the longer she was at school, the more insistently the truth was driven home to her, that the majority is always in the right.

In the shifting of classes that took place at the year's end, she left the three chief witnesses of her disgrace – Tilly, Maria, Kate – behind her. She was again among a new set of girls.

But this little piece of luck was outweighed by the fact that, shortly after Christmas, her room was changed for the one occupied by M. P., and M. P.'s best friend.

So far, Laura had hardly dared to lift her eyes in Mary Pidwall's presence. For Mary knew not only the sum of her lies, but also held – or so Laura believed – that she came of a thoroughly degenerate family; thanks to Uncle Tom. And the early weeks spent at close quarters with her bore out these fears. The looks both M. P. and her friend bent on Laura said as plainly as words: if we are forced to tolerate this obnoxious little insect about us, we can at least show it just what a horrid little beast it is. – M. P. in particular was adamant, unrelenting; Laura quailed at the sound of her step.

And yet she soon felt, rightly enough, it was just in the winning over of this stern, rigid nature that her hope of salvation lay. If she could once get M. P. on her side, all might yet be well again.

So she began to lay siege to Mary's good-will – to Mary, who took none but the barest notice of her, even in the bedroom ignoring her as if she did not exist, and giving the necessary orders, for she was the eldest of the three, in tones of ice. But it needed a great wariness on Laura's part. And, in the beginning, she made a mistake. She was a toadeater here, too, seeking to curry favour with M. P. as with the rest, by fawning on her, in a way for which she could afterwards have hit herself. For it did not answer; M. P. had only a double disdain for the cringer, knowing nothing herself of the pitfalls that lie in wait for a temperament like Laura's. Mary's friendship was extended to none but those who had a lofty moral standard; and truthfulness and honesty were naturally the head virtues on her list. Laura was sharp enough to see that, if she wished to gain ground with M. P. she must make a radical change in her tactics. It was not enough, where Mary was in question, to play the echo. Did she, Laura, state an opinion, she must say what she meant, above all, mean what she said, and stick manfully to it, instead of, at the least hint, being ready to fly over to Mary's point of view: always though, of course, with the disquieting proviso in the background that her own opinions were such as she ought to have, and not heretical leanings that shocked and dismayed. In which case, there was nothing for it but to go on being mum.

She ventured, moreover, little unobtrusive services, to which she thought neither of the girls could take exception; making their beds for them in the morning, and staying up last at night to put out the light. And once she overheard the friend, who was called Cupid, say: 'You know, M. P., she's not such a bad little stick after all.' – But then Cupid was easy-going, and inclined to be original. –

May answered: 'She's no doubt beginning to see she can't lie to *us*. But she's a very double-faced child.'

It was also with an eye to M. P.'s approval that Laura threw herself, with renewed zeal, upon her work. And in those classes that called only for the exercise of her memory, she soon sat high. The reason why she could not mount still higher was that M. P. occupied the top place, and was not to be moved, even had Laura dreamed of attempting it.

And at length, after three months of unremitting exertion – in the course of which, because she had little peeps of what looked like success, the rebel in her went to sleep again – at length Laura had her reward. One Sunday morning M. P. asked her to be her partner on the walk to church. This was as if a great poet should bend from his throne to take a younger brother-singer by the hand; and, in her headlong fashion, Laura all but fell at the elder girl's feet. From this day forward she out-heroded Herod, in her efforts to make of herself exactly what Mary thought she ought to be.

Deep within her, none the less, there lurked a feeling which sometimes made as if to raise its head: a feeling that she did not really like M. P., or admire her, or respect her; one which, had it come quite to life, would have kicked against Mary's authority, been contemptuous of her unimaginative way of seeing and saying things, on the alert to remind its owner that *her* way, too, had a right to existence. But is was not strong enough to make itself heard, or rather Laura refused to hear it, and turned a deaf ear whenever it tried to hint at its presence. – For Mr Worldly-Wiseman was her model just now.

Whereas Cupid – there was something in Cupid that was congenial to her. A plain girl, with irregular features – how she had come by her nickname no one knew – Cupid was three years older than Laura, and one of the few in the school who loved reading for its own sake. In a manner, she was cleverer even than M. P.; but it was not a school-booky way, and hence was not thought much of. However, Laura felt drawn to her at once – even though Cupid treated her as quite a little girl – and they sometimes got as far as talking of books they had read. From this whiff of her, Laura was sure that Cupid would have had more understanding than M. P. for her want of veracity; for Cupid had a kind of a dare-devil mind in a hidebound character, and was often very bold of speech.

Yet it was not Cupid's good opinion she worked for, with might and main.

The rate of her upward progress in Mary's estimation could be gauged by the fact that the day came when the elder girl spoke openly to her of her crime. At the first merciless words Laura winced hotly, both at and for the tactlessness of which Mary was guilty. But, the first shameful stab over, she felt the better of it; yes, it was a relief to speak to someone of what she had borne alone for so long. To speak of it, and even to argue round it a little; for, like most wrongdoers, Laura soon acquired a taste for dwelling on her misdeed. And Mary, being entirely without humour, and also unversed in dealing with criminals, did not divine that this was just a form of self-indulgence.

It was Cupid who said: 'Look here, Infant, you'll be getting cocky about what you did, if you don't look out.'

Mary would not allow that a single one of Laura's excuses held water.

'That's the sheerest nonsense. You don't seem to realise that you tried to defame another person's moral character,' she said, in the assured, superior way that so impressed Laura. – And this aspect of the case, which had never once occurred to her, left Laura open-mouthed; and yet a little doubtful: Mr Shepherd was surely too far above her, and too safely ensconced in holiness, to be injured by anything she might say. But the idea gave her food for thought; and she even tentatively developed her story along these unfamiliar lines, just to see how it might have turned out.

One night as they were undressing for bed, Mary spoke, with the same fireless depreciation, of the behaviour of a classmate which had been brought to her notice that day. This girl was said to have nefariously 'copied' from another, in the course of a written examination; and, as prefect of her class, Mary was bound to track the evil down. 'I shall make them both show me their papers as soon as they get them back; and then, if I find proof of what's being said, I must tackle her. – Just as I tackled you, Laura.'

Laura flushed. 'Oh, M. P., I've never "copied" in my life!' she cried.

'Probably not. But those things all belong in the same box: lying, and "copying", and stealing.'

'You never *will* believe me when I say I didn't know anything about that horrid Chinky. I only told a few crams – that was quite different.'

'I think it's most unfortunate, Laura, that you persist in clinging to that idea.'

Here M. P. was obliged to pause; for she had put a lock of hair between her teeth while she did something to a plait at the back. As soon as she could speak again, she went on: 'You and your few crams! Have you ever thought, pray, what a state of things it would be, if we all went about telling false-hoods, and saying it didn't matter, they were merely a few little fibs? – What are you laughing at?'

'I'm not laughing. I mean . . . I just smiled. I was only thinking how funny it would be – Sandy, and old Gurley, and Jim Chapman, all going round making up things that had never happened.'

'You've a queer notion of what's funny. Have you utterly no respect for the truth?'

'Yes, of course I have. But I say' – Laura, who always slipped quickly out of her clothes, was sitting in her nightgown on the edge of the bed, hugging her knees. 'I say, M. P., if everybody told stories, and everybody knew everybody else was telling them, then truth wouldn't be any good any more at all, would it? If nobody used it?'

'What rubbish you do talk!' said Mary serenely, as she shook her toothbrush on to a towel and rubbed it dry.

'As if truth were a soap!' remarked Cupid who was already in bed, reading *Nana*, and trying to smoke a cigarette under the blankets.

'You can't do away with truth, child.'

'But why not? Who says so? It isn't a law.'

'Don't try to be so sharp, Laura.'

'I don't mean to, M. P. – But what *is* truth, anyhow?' asked Laura.

'The Bible is truth. Can you do away with the Bible, pray?'

'Of course not. But M. P. . . . The Bible isn't quite all truth, you know. My father—' here she broke off in some confusion, remembering Uncle Tom.

'Well, what about him? You don't want to say, I hope, that he didn't believe in the Bible?'

Laura drove back the: 'Of course not!' that was all but over her lips. 'Well, not exactly,' she said, and grew very red. 'But you *know*, M. P., whales don't have big enough throats *ever* to have swallowed Jonah.'

'Little girls shouldn't talk about what they don't understand. The Bible is God's Word; and God is Truth.'

'You're a silly infant,' threw in Cupid, coughing as she spoke. 'Truth has got to be – and honesty, too. If it didn't exist, there couldn't be any state, or laws, or any social life. It's one of the things that makes men different from animals, and the people who boss us know pretty well what they're about, you bet, when they punish the ruffians who don't practise it.'

'Yes, now *that* I see,' agreed Laura eagerly. 'Then truth's a useful thing. – Oh, and that's probably what it means, too, when you say: Honesty is the best Policy.'

'I never heard such a child,' said M. P., shocked. 'Cupid, you really shouldn't put such things into her head. – You're downright immoral, Laura.'

'Oh, how *can* you say such a horrid thing?'

'Well, your ideas are simply dreadful. You ought to try your hardest to improve them.'

'I do, M. P., really I do.'

'You don't succeed. I think there must be a screw loose in you somewhere.'

'Anyhow, I vote we adjourn this meeting,' said Cupid, recovering from a fresh cough and splutter. 'Or old Gurley'll be coming in to put me on a mustard plaster. – As for you, Infant, if you take the advice of a chap who has seen life, you'll keep your ideas to yourself: they're too rude for this elegant world.'

'Right you are!' said Laura cheerfully.

She was waiting by the gas-jet till M.P. had folded her last garment, and she shuffled her bare feet one over the other as she stood; for it was a cold night. The light out, she hopped into bed in the dark.

Chapter Twenty-One

BUT the true seal was set on her regeneration when she was invited to join the boarders' Literary Society; of which Cupid and Mary were the leading spirits. This carried her back, at one stroke, into the swing of school life. For everybody who was anybody belonged to the society. And, despite her friendship with the head of her class, Laura still knew what it was to get the cold shoulder.

But this was to some extent her own fault. At the present stage of her career she was an extraordinarily prickly child, and even to her two sponsors did not at times present a very amiable outside: like a hedgehog, she was ever ready to shoot out her spines. With regard, that is, to her veracity. She had been so badly grazed, in her recent encounter, that she was now constantly seeing doubt where no doubt was; and this wakeful attitude of suspicion towards others did not make for brotherly love. The amenity of her manners suffered, too: though she kept to her original programme of not saying all she thought, yet what she was forced to say she blurted out in such a precise and blunt fashion that it made a disagreeable impression. At the same time, a growing pedantry in trifles warped both her imagination and her sympathies: under the aegis of M. P., she rapidly learned to be the latter's rival in an adherence to bald fact, and in her contumely for those who departed from it. Indeed, before the year spent in Mary's company was out, Laura was well on the way towards becoming one of those

uncomfortable people who, concerned only for their own
salvation, fire the truth at you on every occasion, without
regard for your tender places. – So she remained but scantly
popular.

Hence, her admission to the Literary Society augured well.

Her chief qualifications for membership were that she could
make verses, and was also very fond of reading. At school,
however, this taste had been quiescent; for books were few.
Still, she had read whatever she could lay hands on, and for the
past half-year or more she had fared like a little pig in a clover
field. Since Christmas, she was one of the few permitted to do
morning practice on the grand piano in Mrs Strachey's
drawing-room – an honour, it is true, not overmuch valued
by its recipients, for Mrs Gurley's bedroom lay just above, and
that lady could swoop down on whoever was weak enough
to take a little rest. But Laura snapped her fingers at such a
flimsy objection; for this was the wonderful room 'round the
walls of which low, open bookshelves ran; and she was soon
bold enough, on entering, hastily to select a book to read while
she played, always on the alert to pop it behind her music,
should anyone come into the room.

For months, she browsed unchecked. As her choice had to
be made with extreme celerity, and from those shelves nearest
the piano, it was in the nature of things that it was not invariably
a happy one. For some time she had but moderate luck, and
sampled queer foods. To these must be reckoned a translation
of *Faust*, which she read through, to the end of the First Part
at least, with a kind of dreary wonder why such a dull thing
should be called great. For her next repast, she sought hard,
and it was in the course of this rummage that she had the
strangest find of all. Running a skilled eye over the length of
a shelf close at hand, she hit on a slim, blue volume, the title
of which at once arrested her attention. For, notwithstanding
her fourteen years, and her dabblings in Richardson and Scott,

Laura's liking for a real child's book was as strong as it had ever been; and *A Doll's House* seemed to promise good things. Deftly extracting the volume, she struck up her scales and began to read.

This was the day on which, after breakfast, Mrs Gurley pulverised her with the remark: 'A new, and, I must say, extremely interesting, fashion of playing scales, Laura Rambotham! To hold, the forte pedal down, from beginning to end!'

Laura was unconscious of having sinned in this way. But it might quite well be so. For she had spent a topsy-turvy, though highly engrossing hour. In place of the children's story she anticipated, she had found herself, on opening the book, confronted by the queerest stuff she had ever seen in print. From the opening sentence on. To begin with, it was a play – and Laura had never had a modern prose play in her hand before – and then it was all about the oddest, yet the most commonplace people. It seemed to her amazingly unreal – how these people spoke and behaved – she had never known anyone like them; and yet again so true, in the way it dragged in everyday happenings, so petty in its rendering of petty things, that it bewildered and repelled her: why, someone might just as well write a book about Mother or Sarah! Her young, romantic soul rose in arms against this, its first bluff contact with realism, against such a dispiriting sobriety of outlook. Something within her wanted to cry out in protest as she read – for read she did, on three successive days, with an interest she could not explain. And that was not all. It was worse that the people in this book – the extraordinary person who was married, and had children, and yet ate biscuits out of a bag and said she didn't; the man who called her his lark and his squirrel – as if any man ever did call his wife such names! – all these people seemed eternally to be meaning something different from what they said; something that was for ever eluding her. It was most irritating. – There was, moreover, no mention of a doll's house in the whole three acts.

The state of confusion this booklet left her in, she allayed with a little old brown leather volume of Longfellow. And *Hyperion* was so much more to her liking that she even ventured to borrow it from its place on the shelf, in order to read it at her leisure, braving the chance that her loan, were it discovered, might be counted against her as a theft.

It hung together, no doubt, with the after-effects of her dip into Ibsen that, on her sitting down to write the work that was to form her passport to the Society, her mind should incline to the most romantic of romantic themes. Not altogether, though: Laura's taste, such as it was, for literature had, like all young people's, a mighty bias towards those books which turned their backs on reality: she sought not truth, but the miracle. However, though she had thus taken sides, there was still a yawning gap to be bridged between her ready acceptance of the honourable invitation, and the composition of a masterpiece. Thanks to her wonted inability to project her thoughts beyond the moment, she had been so unthinking of possible failure that Cupid had found it necessary to interject: 'Here, I say, don't blow!' Whereas, when she came to write, she sat with her pen poised over the paper for nearly half an hour, without bringing forth a word. First, there was the question of form: she considered, then abruptly dismissed, the idea of writing verses: the rhymes with love and dove, and heart and part, which could have been managed, were, she felt, too silly and sentimental to be laid before her quizzical audience. Next, what to write about – a simple theme, such as a fairy-tale, was not for a moment to be contemplated. No, Laura had always flown her hawk high, and she was now bent on making a splutter. It ended by being a toss-up between a play in the Shakesperian manner and a novel after Scott. She decided on the novel. It should be a romance of Venice, with abundant murder and mystery in it, and a black, black villain, such as her soul loved – no macaroon-nibblers or rompers with children for her! And having thus attuned her mind to scarlet deeds, she set to work. But she found it tremendously difficult to pin her story to paper: she saw things clearly enough, and could have related them by word of mouth; but did she try to write them down they ran to mist; and though she toiled quite literally in the sweat of her brow, yet when the eventful day came she had but three niggardly pages to show for her pains.

About twenty girls formed the Society, which assembled one Saturday evening in an empty music-room. All were not, of course, equally productive: some had brought it no further than a riddle: and it was just these drones who, knowing nothing of the pother composition implied, criticised most stringently the efforts of the rest. Several members had pretty enough talents, Laura's two room-mates among the number: on the night Laura made her debut, the weightiest achievement was, without doubt, M. P.'s essay on 'Magnanimity'; and Laura's eyes grew moist as she listened to its stirring phrases. Next best – to her thinking, at least – was a humorous episode by Cupid, who had a gift that threw Laura into a fit of amaze; and this was the ability to expand infinitely little into infinitely much; to rig out a trifle in many words, so that in the end it seemed ever so much bigger than it really was – just as a thrifty merchant boils his oranges, to swell them to twice their size.

Laura being the youngest member, her affair came last on the programme: she had to sit and listen to the others, her cheeks hot, her hands very cold. Presently all were done, and then Cupid, who was chairman, called on 'a new author, Rambotham, who it is hoped will prove a valuable acquisition to the Society, to read us his maiden effort'.

Laura rose to her feet and, trembling with nervousness, stuttered forth her prose. The three little pages shot past like a flash; she had barely stood up before she was obliged to sit down again, leaving her hearers, who had only just re-adopted their listening attitudes, agape with astonishment. She could have endured, with phlegm, the ridicule this malheur earned her: what was harder to stomach was that her paper heroics made utterly no impression. She suffered all the humiliation of a flabby fiasco, and, till bedtime, shrank out of her friends' way.

'You were warned not to be too cocky, you know,' Mary said judicially, on seeing her downcast air.

'I didn't mean to be, really. – Then you don't think what I wrote was up to much, M. P.?'

'Mm,' said the elder girl, in a non-committal way.

Here Cupid chimed in. 'Look here, Infant, I want to ask you something. Have you ever been in Venice?'

'No.'

'Ever seen a gondola?'

'No.'

'Or the Doge's palace? – or a black-cloaked assassin? – or a masked lady?'

'You know I haven't,' murmured Laura, humbled to the dust.

'And probably never will. Well then, why on earth try to write wooden, second-hand rubbish like that?'

'Second-hand? . . . But Cupid . . . think of Scott! He couldn't have seen half he told about?'

'My gracious!' ejaculated Cupid, and sat down and fanned herself with a hairbrush. 'You don't imagine you're a Scott, do you? Here, hold me, M. P., I'm going to faint!' – and at Laura's quick and scarlet denial, she added: 'Well, why the unmentionable not use the eyes the Lord has given you, and write about what's before them every day of your life?'

'Do you think that would be better?'

'I don't think – I know it would.'

But Laura was not so easily convinced as all that.

Ever a talented imitator, she next tried her hand at an essay on an abstract subject. This was a failure: you could *see* things, when you wrote about, say, 'Beneficence'; and Laura's thinking was done mainly in pictures. Matters were still worse when she tinkered at Cupid's especial genre: her worthless little incident stared at her, naked and scraggy, from the sheet; she had no wealth of words at her disposal in which to deck it out. So, with a sigh, she turned back to the advice Cupid had given her, and prepared to make a faithful transcript of actuality. She called what she now wrote: 'A Day at School', and conscientiously set down detail on detail; so fearful, this time, of over-brevity, that she spun the account out to twenty pages; though the writing of it was as distasteful to her as her reading of *A Doll's House* had been.

At the subsequent meeting of the Society, expression of opinion was not lacking.

'Oh, Jehoshaphat! How much more?'

'Here, let me get out. I've had enough.'

'I say, you forgot to count how many steps it took you to come downstairs.'

Till the chairman had pity on the embarrassed author and said: 'Look here, Laura, I think you'd better keep the rest for another time.'

'It was just what you told me to do,' Laura reproached Cupid that night: she was on the brink of tears.

But Cupid was disinclined to shoulder the responsibility. 'Told you to be as dull and long-winded as that? Infant, it's a whacker!'

'But it was *true* what I wrote – every word of it.'

Neither of the two elder girls was prepared to discuss this vital point. Cupid shifted ground. 'Good Lord, Laura, but it's hard to drive a thing into *your* brain-pan. – You don't need to be *all* true on paper, silly child!'

'Last time you said I had to.'

'Well, if you want it, my candid opinion is that you haven't any talent for this kind of thing. – Now turn off the gas.'

As the light in the room went out, a kind of inner light seemed to go up in Laura; and both then and on the following days she thought hard. She was very ambitious, anxious to shine, not ready to accept defeat; and to the next literary contest she brought the description of an excursion to the hills and gullies that surrounded Warrenega; into which she had worked an adventure with some vagrant blacks. She and Pin and the boys had often picnicked on these hills, with their lunches packed in billies; and she had seen the caves and rocky holes where blackfellows were said to have hidden themselves in early times; but neither this particular excursion, nor the exciting incident which she described with all the aplomb of an eyewitness, had ever taken place. That is to say: not a word of her narration was true, but every word of it might have been true.

And with this she had an unqualified success.

'I believe there's something in you after all,' said Cupid to her that night. 'Anyhow, you know now what it is to be true, yet not dull and prosy.'

And Laura manfully choked back her desire to cry out that not a word of her story was fact.

She was long in falling asleep. Naturally, she was elated and excited by her success; but also a new and odd piece of knowlege had niched itself in her brain. It was this. In your speech, your talk with others, you must be exact to the point of pedantry, and never romance or draw the long-bow; or you would be branded as an abominable liar. Whereas, as soon as you put pen to paper, provided you kept one foot planted on probability, you might lie as hard as you liked: indeed, the more vigorously you lied, the louder would be your hearers' applause.

And Laura fell asleep over a chuckle.

Chapter Twenty-Two

AND then, alas! just as she rode high on this wave of appro-
bation, Laura suffered another of those drops in the esteem of
her fellows, another of those mental upsets, which from time
to time had thrown her young life out of gear.

True, what now came was not exactly her own fault; though
it is doubtful whether a single one of her companions would
have made her free of an excuse. They looked on, round-eyed,
mouths a-stretch. Once more, the lambkin called Laura saw
fit to sunder itself from the flock, and to cut mad capers in sight
of them all. And their delectation was as frank as their former
wrath had been. – As for Laura, as usual she did not stop to think
till it was too late; but danced lightly away to her own undoing.

The affair began pleasantly enough. A member of the
Literary Society was the girl with the twinkly brown eyes – she
who had gone out of her way to give Laura a kindly word
after the Shepherd debacle. This girl, Evelyn Souttar by name,
was also the only one of the audience who had not joined in
the laugh provoked by Laura's first appearance as an author.
Laura had never forgotten this; and she would smile shyly at
Evelyn when their looks met. But a dozen reasons existed why
there should have been no further rapport between them.
Although now in the fifth form, Laura had remained childish
for her age: whereas Evelyn was over eighteen, and only
needed to turn up her hair to be quite grown-up. She had
matriculated the previous Christmas, and was at present

putting away a rather desultory half-year, before leaving school for good. In addition, she was rich, pampered and very pretty – the last comrade in the world for drab little Laura.

One evening, as the latter was passing through the dining-hall, she found Evelyn, who studied where she chose, disconsolately running her fingers through her gold-brown hair.

'I say, Kiddy,' she called to Laura. 'You know Latin, don't you? Just give us a hand with this.' – Latin had not been one of Evelyn's subjects, and she was now employing some of her spare time in studying the language with Mr Strachey, who taught it after a fashion of his own. 'How on earth would you say: "We had not however rid here so long, but should have tided it up the river"? What's the old fool mean by that?' and she pushed an open volume of *Robinson Crusoe* towards Laura.

Laura helped to the best of her ability.

'Thanks awfully,' said Evelyn. 'You're a clever chickabiddy. But you must let me help you with something in return. What's hardest?'

'Filling baths and papering rooms,' replied Laura candidly.

'Arithmetic, eh? Well, if ever you want a sum done, come to me.'

But Laura was temperamentally unable to accept so vague an invitation; and here the matter closed.

When, consequently, Miss Chapman summoned her one evening to tell her that she was to change her present bedroom for Evelyn's, the news came as a great shock to her.

'Change my room?' she echoed, in slow disgust. 'Oh, I can't, Miss Chapman!'

'You've got to, Laura, if Mrs Gurley says so,' expostulated the kindly governess.

'But I won't! There *must* be some mistake. Just when I'm so comfortably settled, too. – Very well, then, Miss Chapman, I'll speak to Mrs Gurley myself.'

She carried out this threat, and, for daring to question orders, received the soundest snubbing she had had for many a long day.

That night she was very bitter about it all, and the more so because Mary and Cupid did not, to her thinking, show sufficient sympathy.

'I believe you're both glad I'm going. It's a beastly shame. Why must I always be odd man out?'

'Look here, Infant, don't adopt that tone, please,' said Cupid magisterially. 'Or you'll make us glad in earnest. People who are always up in arms about things are the greatest bores in the world.'

So the following afternoon Laura wryly took up armfuls of her belongings, mounted a storey higher, and deposited them on the second bed in Evelyn's room.

The elder girl had had this room to herself for over a year now, and Laura felt sure would be chafing inwardly at her intrusion. For days she stole mousily in and out, avoiding the hours when Evelyn was there, getting up earlier in the morning, hurrying into bed at night and feeling very sore indeed at the sufferance on which she supposed herself to be.

But once Evelyn caught her and said: 'Don't, for gracious' sake, knock each time you want to come in, child. This is your room now as well as mine.'

Laura reddened, and blurted out something about knowing how she must hate to have *her* stuck in there.

Evelyn wrinkled up her forehead and laughed. 'What rot! Do you think I'd have asked to have you, if I hated it so much?'

'You asked to have me?' gasped Laura.

'Of course – didn't you know? Old Gurley said I'd need to have someone; so I chose you.'

Laura was too dumbfounded, and too diffident, to ask the grounds of such a choice. But the knowledge that it was so, worked an instant change in her.

In all the three years she had been at school, she had not got

beyond a surface friendliness with any of her fellows. Even
those who had been her 'chums' had wandered like shades
through the groves of her affection: rough, teasing Bertha;
pretty, lazy Inez; perky Tilly, slangily frank Maria and Kate,
Mary and her moral influence, clever, instructive Cupid: to
none of them had she been drawn by any deeper sense of
affinity. And though she had come to believe, in the course of
the last, more peaceful year, that she had grown used to being
what you would call an unpopular girl – one, that is, with whom
no one ever shared a confidence – yet seldom was there a child
who longed more ardently to be liked, or suffered more
acutely under dislike. Apart however from the brusque manner
she had contracted, in her search after truth, it must be admitted
that Laura had but a small talent for friendship; she did not
grasp the constant give-and-take intimacy implies; the liking
of others had to be brought to her, unsought, she, on the other
hand, being free to stand back and consider whether or no
the feeling was worth returning. And friends are not made in
this fashion.

But Evelyn had stoutly, and without waiting for permission,
crossed the barrier; and each new incident in her approach was
pleasanter than the last. Laura was pleased, and flattered, and
round the place where her heart was, she felt a warm and
comfortable glow.

She began to return the liking, with interest, after the manner
of a lonely, bottled-up child. And everything about Evelyn
made it easy to grow fond of her. To begin with, Laura loved
pretty things and pretty people; and her new friend was out
and away the prettiest girl in the school. Then, too, she was
clever, and that counted; you did not make a friend of a fool.
But her chief characteristics were a certain sound common
sense, and an inexhaustible fund of good-nature – a careless,
happy, laughing sunniness, that was as grateful to those who
came into touch with it as a rare ointment is grateful to the skin.

This kindliness arose, it might be, in the first place from indolence: it was less trouble to be merry and amiable than to put oneself out to be selfish, which also meant standing a fire of disagreeable words and looks; and then, too, it was really hard for one who had never had a whim crossed to be out of humour. But, whatever its origin, the good-nature was there, ever-lastingly; and Laura soon learnt that she could cuddle in under it, and be screened by it, as a lamb is screened by its mother's woolly coat.

Evelyn was the only person who did not either hector her, or feel it a duty to clip and prune at her: she accepted Laura for what she was – for herself. Indeed, she even seemed to lay weight on Laura's bits of opinions, which the girl had grown so chary of offering; and, under the sunshine of this treatment, Laura shot up and flowered like a spring bulb. She began to speak out her thoughts again; she unbosomed herself of dark little secrets; and finally did what she would never have believed possible: sitting one night in her nightgown, on the edge of Evelyn's bed, she made a full confession of the pickle she had got herself into, over her visit to the Shepherds.

To her astonishment, Evelyn, who was already in bed, laughed till the tears ran down her cheeks. At Laura's solemn-faced incredulity she said:

'I say, Kiddy, but that *was* rich. To think a chicken of your size sold them like that. It's the best joke I've heard for an age. Tell us again – from the beginning.'

Nothing loath Laura started in afresh, and in this, the second telling, embroidered the edge of her tale with a few fancy stitches, in a way she had not ventured on for months past; so that Evelyn was more tickled than before.

'No wonder they were mad about being had like that. You little rascal!'

She was equally amused by Laura's description of the miser-able week she had spent, trying to make up her mind to confess.

'You ridiculous sprat! Why didn't you come to me? We'd have let them down with a good old bump.'

But Laura could not so easily forget the humiliations she had been forced to suffer, and delicately hinted to her friend at M. P.'s moral strictures. With her refreshing laugh, Evelyn brushed these aside as well.

'Tommyrot! Never mind that old jumble-sale of all the virtues. It was jolly clever of a mite like you to bamboozle them as you did – take my word for that.'

This jocose way of treating the matter seemed to put it in an entirely new light; Laura could even smile at it herself. In the days that followed, she learned, indeed, to laugh over it with Evelyn, and to share the latter's view that she had been superior in wit to those she had befooled. This meant a great and healthy gain in self-assurance for Laura. It also led to her laying more and more weight on what her friend said. For it was not as if Evelyn had a low moral standard; far from that: she was honest and straightforward, too proud, or, it might be, too lazy to tell a lie herself – with all the complications lying involved – and Laura never heard her say a harder thing of anyone than what she had just said about Mary Pidwall.

The two talked late into every night after this, Laura perched, monkey-fashion, on the side of her friend's bed. Evelyn had all the accumulated wisdom of eighteen, and was able to clear her young companion up on many points about which Laura had so far been in the dark. But when, in time, she came to relate the mortifications she had suffered – and was still called on to suffer – at the hands of the other sex, Evelyn pooh-poohed the subject.

'Time enough in a couple of years for that. Don't bother your head about it in the meantime.'

'I don't now – not a bit. I only wanted to know why. Sometimes, Evvy, do you know, they liked to talk to quite little kids of seven and eight better than me.'

'Perhaps you talked too much yourself – and about your-self?'

'I don't think I did. And if you don't talk something, they yawn and go away.'

'You've got to let them do the lion's share, child. Just you sit still, and listen, and pretend you like it – even though you're bored to extinction.'

'And they never need to pretend anything, I suppose? No, I think they're horrid. You don't like them either, Evvy, do you?... any more than I do?'

Evelyn laughed.

'Say what you think they are,' persisted Laura and waggled the other's arm, to make her speak.

'Mostly fools,' said Evelyn, and laughed again – laughed in all the conscious power of lovely eighteen.

Overjoyed at this oneness of mind, Laura threw her arms round her friend's neck and kissed her. 'You dear!' she said.

And yet, a short time afterwards, it was on this very head that she had to bear the shock of a rude awakening.

Evelyn's people came to Melbourne that year from the Riverina. Evelyn was allowed considerable freedom; and one night, by special permit, Laura also accepted an invitation to dinner and the theatre. The two girls drove to a hotel, where they found Evelyn's mother, elegant but a little stern, and a young lady-friend. Only the four of them were present at dinner, and the meal passed off smoothly; though the strange-ness of dining in a big hotel had the effect of tying Laura's tongue. Another thing that abashed her was the dress of the young lady, who sat opposite. This person – she must have been about the ripe age of twenty-five – was nipped into a tight little pink satin bodice, which, at the back, exposed the whole of two very bony shoulder-blades. But it was the front of the dress that Laura faced; and, having imbibed strict views of propriety from Mother, she wriggled on her chair whenever she raised her eyes.

They drove to the theatre – though it was only a few doors off. The seats were in the dress circle. The ladies sat in the front row, the girls, who were in high frocks, behind.

Evelyn made a face of laughing discontent. 'It's so ridiculous the mater won't let me dress.'

These words gave Laura a kind of stab. 'Oh Evvy, I think you're *ever* so much nicer as you are,' she whispered, and squeezed her friend's hand.

Evelyn could not answer, for the lady in pink had leant back and tapped her with her fan. 'It doesn't look as if Jim were coming, my dear.'

Evelyn laughed, in a peculiar way. 'Oh, I guess he'll turn up all right.'

There had been some question of a person of this name at dinner; but Laura had paid no great heed to what was said. Now, she sat up sharply, for Evelyn exclaimed: 'There he is!'

It was a man, a real man – not a boy – with a drooping, fair moustache, a single eyeglass in one eye, and a camellia-bud in his buttonhole. For the space of a breathless second Laura connected him with the pink satin; then he dropped into a vacant seat at Evelyn's side.

From this moment on, Laura's pleasure in her expensive seat, in the pretty blue theatre and its movable roof, in the gay trickeries of the *Mikado*, slowly fizzled out. Evelyn had no more thought for her. Now and then, it is true, she would turn in her affectionate way and ask Laura if she were all right – just as one satisfies oneself that a little child is happy – but her real attention was for the man at her side. In the intervals, the two kept up a perpetual buzz of chat, broken only by Evelyn's low laughs. Laura sat neglected, sat stiff and cold with disappointment, a great bitterness welling up within her. Before the performance had dragged to an end, she would have liked to put her head down and cry.

'Tired?' queried Evelyn noticing her pinched look, as they drove home in the wagonette. But the mother was there, too, so Laura said no.

Directly, however, the bedroom door shut behind them, she fell into a tantrum, a fit of sullen rage, which she accentuated till Evelyn could not but notice it.

'What's the matter with you? Didn't you enjoy yourself?'

'No, I hated it,' returned Laura passionately.

Evelyn laughed a little at this, but with an air of humorous dismay. 'I must take care, then, not to ask you out again.'

'I wouldn't go. Not for anything!'

'What on earth's the matter with you?'

'Nothing's the matter.'

'Well, if that's all, make haste and get into bed. You're overtired.'

'Go to bed yourself!'

'I am, as fast as I can. I can hardly keep my eyes open;' and Evelyn yawned heartily.

When Laura saw that she meant it, she burst out: 'You're nothing but a story-teller – that's what you are! You said you didn't like them ... that they were mostly fools ... and then ... then, to go on as you did to-night.' Her voice was shaky with tears.

'Oh, that's it, is it? Come now, get to bed. We'll talk about it in the morning.'

'I never want to speak to you again.'

'You're a silly child. But I'm really too sleepy to quarrel with you to-night.'

'I hate you – hate you!'

'I shall survive it.'

She turned out the light as she spoke, settled herself on her pillow, and composedly went to sleep.

Laura's rage redoubled. Throwing herself on the floor she burst into angry tears, and cried as loudly as she dared, in the hope of keeping her companion awake. But Evelyn was a magnificent sleeper; and remained undisturbed. So after a time Laura rose, drew up the blind, opened the window and sat down on the sill.

It was a bitterly cold night, of milky-white moonlight; each bush and shrub carved its jet-black shadow on paths and grass. Across Evelyn's bed fell a great patch of light: this, or the chill air would, it was to be trusted, wake her. Meanwhile Laura sat in her thin nightgown and shivered, feeling the cold intensely after the great heat of the day. She hoped with all her heart that she would be lucky enough to get an inflammation of the lungs. Then, Evelyn would be sorry she had been so cruel to her.

It was nearly two o'clock, and she had several times found herself nodding, when the sleeper suddenly opened her eyes and sat bolt upright in bed.

'Laura, good heavens, what are you doing at the window? Oh, you wicked child, you'll catch your death of cold! Get into bed at once.'

And, the culprit still maintaining an immovable silence, Evelyn dragged her to bed by main force, and tucked her in as tightly as a mummy.

Chapter Twenty-Three

'LAURA, you're a cipher!'

'I'm nothing of the sort!' threw back Laura indignantly. 'You're one yourself. – What does she mean, Evvy?' she asked getting out of earshot of the speaker.

'Goodness knows. Don't mind her, Poppet.'

It was an oppressive evening: all day long a hot north wind had scoured the streets, veiling things and people in clouds of gritty dust; the sky was still like the prolonged reflection of a great fire. The hoped-for change had not come, and the girls who strolled the paths of the garden were white and listless. They walked in couples, with interlaced arms; and members of the Matriculation Class carried books with them, the present year being one of much struggling and heartburning, and few leisured moments. Mary Pidwall and Cupid were together under an acacia tree at the gate of the tennis-court; and it was M. P. who had cast the above gibe at Laura. At least Laura took it as a gibe, and scowled darkly; for she could never grow hardened to ridicule.

As she and Evelyn re-passed this spot in their perambulation, a merry little lump of a girl called Lolo, who darted her head from side to side when she spoke, with the movements of a watchful bird – this Lolo called: 'Evelyn, come here, I want to tell you something.'

'Yes, what is it?' asked Evelyn, but without obeying the summons; for she felt Laura's grip of her arm tighten.

'It's a secret. You must come over here.'

'Hold on a minute, Poppet,' said Evelyn persuasively, and crossed the lawn with her characteristically lazy saunter.

Minutes went by; she did not return.

'Look at her Laura-ship!' said a saucebox to her partner. The latter made 'Hee-haw, hee-haw!' and both laughed derisively.

The object of their scorn stood at the farther end of the wire-net fence: all five fingers of her right hand were thrust through the holes of the netting, and held oddly and unconsciously outspread; she stood on one leg, and with her other foot rubbed up and down behind her ankle; mouth and brow were sullen, her black eyes bent wrathfully on her faithless friend.

'A regular moon-calf!' said Cupid, looking up from *The Tempest*, which was balanced breast-high on the narrow wooden top of the fence.

'Mark my words, that child'll be plucked in her "tests",' observed M. P.

'Serve her right, say I, for playing the billy-ass,' returned Cupid, and killed a giant mosquito with such a whack that her wrist was stained with its blood. 'Ugh, you brute! . . . gorging yourself on me. But I'm dashed if I know how Evelyn can be bothered to have her always dangling round.'

'She's a cipher,' repeated Mary, in so judicial a tone that it closed the conversation.

Laura, not altogether blind to externals, saw that her companions made fun of her. But at the present pass, the strength of her feelings quite out-ran her capacity for self-control; she was unable to disguise what she felt, and though it made her the laughing-stock of the school. What scheme was the birdlike Lolo hatching against her? Why did Evelyn not come back? – these were the thoughts that buzzed round inside her head, as the mosquitoes buzzed outside. – And meanwhile the familiar, foolish noises of the garden at evening knocked at her ear. On the other side of the hedge a batch of third-form girls were whispering, with choked laughter, a doggerel rhyme which was hard to say, and which meant something quite different did the tongue trip over a certain letter. Of two girls who were playing tennis in half-hearted fashion, the one next Laura said 'Oh, damn!' every time she missed a ball. And over the parched, dusty grass the hot wind blew, carrying with it, from the kitchens, a smell of cabbage, of fried onions, of greasy dish-water.

Then Evelyn returned, and a part, a part only of the cloud lifted from Laura's brow.

'What did she want?'

'Oh, nothing much.'

'Then you're not going to tell me?'

'I can't.'

'What business has she to have secrets with you?' said Laura furiously. And for a full round of the garden she did not open her lips.

Her companions were not alone in eyeing this lopsided friendship with an amused curiosity. The governesses also smiled at it, and were surprised at Evelyn's endurance of the tyranny into which Laura's liking had degenerated. On this particular evening, two who were sitting on the verandah-bench came back to the subject.

'Just look at that Laura Rambotham again, will you?' said Miss Snodgrass in her tart way. 'Sulking for all she's worth. What a little fool she is!'

'I'm sure I wonder Mrs Gurley hasn't noticed how badly she's working just now,' said Miss Chapman; and her face wore it best-meaning, but most uncertain smile.

'Oh, you know very well if Mrs Gurley doesn't want to see a thing she doesn't,' retorted Miss Snodgrass. 'A regular talent for going blind, I call it – especially where Evelyn Souttar's concerned.'

'Oh, I don't think you should talk like that,' urged Miss Chapman nervously.

'I say what I think,' asserted Miss Snodgrass. 'And if I had my way, I'd give Laura Rambotham something she wouldn't forget. That child'll come to a bad end yet. – How do you like that colour, Miss C.?' She had a nest of cloth-patterns in her lap, and held one up as she spoke.

'Oh, you shouldn't say such things,' remonstrated Miss Chapman. 'There's many a true word said in jest.' She settled her glasses on her nose. 'It's very nice, but I think I like a bottle-green better.'

'Of course, I don't mean she'll end on the gallows, if that's what troubles you. But she's frightfully unbalanced, and, to my mind, ought to have some sense knocked into her before it's too late. – That's a better shade, isn't it?'

'Poor little Laura,' said Miss Chapman, and drew a sigh. – 'Yes, I like that. Where did you say you were going to have the dress made?'

Miss Snodgrass named, not without pride, one of the first warehouses in the city. 'I've been saving up my screw for it, and I mean to have something decent this time. Besides, I know one of the men in the shop, and I'm going to make them do it cheap.' And here they fell to discussing price and cut.

Thus the onlookers laughed and quizzed and wondered; no one was bold enough to put an open question to Evelyn, and Evelyn did not offer to take anyone into her confidence. She held even hints and allusions at bay, with her honeyed laugh; which was *her* shield against the world. Laura was the only person who ever got behind this laugh, and what she discovered there, she did not tell. As it was, varying motives were suggested for Evelyn's long-suffering, nobody being ready to believe that it could really be fondness, on her part, for the Byronic atom of humanity she had attracted to her.

However that might be, the two girls, the big fair one and

the little dark one, were, outside class-hours, seldom apart. Evelyn did not often, as in the case of the birdlike Lolo, give her young tyrant cause for offence; if she sometimes sought another's company, it was done in a roguish spirit – from a feminine desire to tease. Perhaps, too, she was at heart not averse to Laura's tantrums, or to testing her own power in quelling them. On the whole, though, she was very careful of her little friend's sensitive spots. She did not repeat the experiment of taking Laura out with her; as her stay at school drew to a close she went out less frequently herself; for the reason that, no matter how late it was on her getting back, she would find Laura obstinately sitting up in bed, wide-awake. And it went against the grain in her to keep the pale-faced girl from sleep.

On such occasions, while she undid her pretty muslin dress, unpinned the flowers she was never without, and loosened her gold-brown hair, which she had put up for the evening: while she undressed, Evelyn had to submit to a rigorous cross-examination. Laura demanded to know where she had been, what she had done, whom she had spoken to; and woe to her if she tried to shirk a question. Laura was not only jealous, she was extraordinarily suspicious; and the elder girl had need of all her laughing kindness to steer her way through the shallows of distrust. For a great doubt of Evelyn's sincerity had implanted itself in Laura's mind: she could not forget the incident of the 'mostly fools'; and, after an evening of this kind, she never felt quite sure that Evelyn was not deceiving her afresh – out of sheer goodness of heart, of course – by assuring her that she had had a 'horrid time', been bored to death, and would have much preferred to stay with her; when the truth was that, in the company of some moustached idiot or other, she had enjoyed herself to the top of her bent.

On the night Laura learned that her friend had again met the loathly 'Jim', there was a great to-do. In vain Evelyn laughed, reasoned, expostulated. Laura was inconsolable.

'Look here, Poppet,' said Evelyn at last, and was so much in earnest that she laid her hairbrush down, and took Laura by both her bony little shoulders. 'Look here, you surely don't expect me to be an old maid, do you? – *me*?' The pronoun signified all she might not say: it meant wealth, youth, beauty, and an unbounded capacity for pleasure.

'Evvy, you're not going to *marry* that horrid man?'

'Of course not, goosey. But that doesn't mean that I'm never going to marry at all, does it?'

Laura supposed not – with a tremendous sniff.

'Well, then, what *is* all the fuss about?'

It was not so easy to say. She was of course reconciled, she sobbed, to Evelyn marrying some day: only plain and stupid girls were left to be old maids: but it must not happen for years and years and years to come, and when it did, it must be to someone much older than herself, someone she did not greatly care for: in short, Evelyn was to marry only to escape the odium of the single life.

Having drawn this sketch of her future word by word from the weeping Laura, Evelyn fell into a fit of laughter which she could not stifle. 'Well, Poppet,' she said when she could speak, 'if that's your idea of happiness for me, we'll postpone it just as long as ever we can. I'm all there. For I mean to have a good time first – a jolly good time – before I tie myself up for ever, world without end, amen.'

'That's just what I hate so – your good time, as you call it,' retorted Laura, smarting under the laughter.

'Everyone does, child. You'll be after it yourself when you're a little older.'

'Me? – never!'

'Oh, yes, indeed you will.'

'I won't. I hate men and I always shall. And oh, I thought' – with an upward, sobbing breath – 'I thought you liked me best.'

'Of course I like you, you silly child! But that's altogether different. And I don't like you any less because I enjoy having some fun with them, too.'

'I don't want your old leavings!' said Laura savagely. It hurt, almost as much as having a tooth pulled out, did this knowledge that your friend's affection was wholly yours only as long as no man was in question. And out of the sting, Laura added: 'Wait till I'm grown up, and I'll show them what I think of them – the pigs!'

This time Evelyn had to hold her hand in front of her mouth. 'No, no, I don't mean to laugh at you. Come, be good now,' she petted. 'And you really must go to bed, Laura. It's past twelve o'clock, and that infernal machine'll be going off before you've had any sleep at all.'

The 'machine' was Laura's alarum, which ran down every night just now at two o'clock. For, if one thing was sure, it was that affairs with Laura were in a sorry muddle. In this, the last and most momentous year of her school life, at the close of which, like a steep wall to be scaled, rose the university examination, she was behindhand with her work, and occupied a mediocre place in her class. So steadfastly was her attention pitched on Evelyn that she could link it to nothing else: in the middle of an important task, her thoughts would stray to contemplate her friend or wonder what she was doing; while, if Evelyn were out for the evening, Laura gave up her meagre pretence of study altogether, and moodily propped her head in her hand. This was why she had hit on the small hours for the necessary cramming; then, there were no distractions: the great house was as still as an empty church; and Evelyn lay safe and sound before her. So, punctually at two o'clock Laura was startled, with a pounding heart, out of her first sleep; and lighting the gas she sat up in bed and pored over her books. Evelyn was not disturbed by the light, or at least she did not complain; and it was certainly a famous time for committing things to memory: the subsequent hours of sleep seemed rather to etch the facts into your brain than to blur them.

You cannot however rob Peter to pay Paul, with impunity, and in the weeks that followed, despite her nightly industry, Laura made no headway.

As the term tapered to an end, things went from bad to worse with her; and since, besides, the parting with Evelyn was at the door, she was often to be seen with red-rimmed eyelids, which she did not even try to conceal.

'As if she'd lost her nearest relation!' laughed her school-fellows. And did they meet her privately, on the stairs or in a house-corridor, they crossed their hands on their breasts and turned up their eyes, in tragedy-fashion.

Laura hardly saw them; for once in her life ridicule could not have her. The nearer the time drew, the more completely did the coming loss of Evelyn push other considerations into the background. It was bitter to reflect that her present dear friendship had no more strength to endure than the thin pretences of friendship she had hitherto played at. Evelyn and she would, no doubt, from time to time meet and take pleasure in each other again; but their homes lay hundreds of miles apart; and the intimacy of the schooldays was passing away, never to return. And no one could be held to blame for this. Evelyn's mother and father thought, rightly enough, that it was time for their daughter to leave school – but that was all. They did not really miss her, or need her. No, it was just a stupid, crushing piece of ill-luck, which happened one did not know why. The ready rebel in Laura sprang into being again; and she fought hard against the lesson that there are events in life – bitter, grim, and grotesque events – beneath which one can only bow one's head. – A further effect of the approaching separation was to bring home to her a sense of the fleetingness of things; she began to grasp that, everywhere and always, even while you revelled in them, things were perpetually rushing to a close; and the fact of them being things you loved, or enjoyed, was powerless to diminish the speed at which they escaped you.

Of course, though, these were sensations rather than thoughts; and they did not hinder Laura from going on her knees to Evelyn, to implore her to remain. Day after day Evelyn kindly and patiently explained why this could not be; and if she sometimes drew a sigh at the child's persistence, it was too faint to be audible. Now Laura knew that it was possible to kill animal-pets by surfeiting them; and, towards the end, a suspicion dawned on her that you might perhaps damage feelings in the same way. It stood to reason: no matter how fond two people were of each other, the one who was about to emerge, like a butterfly from its sheath, could not be asked to regret her release; and, at moments – when Laura lay sobbing face downwards on her bed, or otherwise vented her pertinacious and disruly grief – at these moments she thought she scented a dash of relief in Evelyn, at the prospect of deliverance.

But such delicate hints on the part of the hidden self are rarely able to gain a hearing; and, as the days dropped off one by one, like over-ripe fruit, Laura surrendered herself more and more blindly to her emotions. The consequence was, M. P.'s prediction came true: in the test-examinations which took place at midwinter, Laura, together with the few dunces of her class, was ignominiously plucked. And still staggering under this blow, she had to kiss Evelyn good-bye, and to set her face for home.

Chapter Twenty-Four

MOTHER did not know or understand anything about 'tests'; and Laura had no idea of enlightening her. She held her peace, and throughout the holidays hugged her disgraceful secret to her, untold. She had never before failed to pass an examination, having always lightly skimmed the surface of them on the wings of her parrot-like memory; hence, at home no one suspected that anything was amiss with her. The knowledge weighed the more heavily on her own mind. And, as if her other troubles were not enough, she was now beset by nervous fears about the future. She saw chiefly rocks ahead. If she did not succeed in getting through the final examination in summer, she would not be allowed to present herself for matriculation, and, did this happen, there would be the very devil to pay. All her schooling would, in Mother's eyes, have been for naught. For Mother was one of those people who laid tremendous weight on prizes and examinations, as offering a tangible proof that your time had not been wasted or misspent. Besides this, she could not afford in the event of a failure, to pay the school-fees for another year. The money which, by hook and by crook, had been scraped together and hoarded up for Laura's education was now coming to an end; as it was, the next six months would mean a terrible pinching and screwing. The other children, too, were growing day by day more costly; their little minds and bodies clamoured for a larger share of attention. And Laura's eyes were rudely opened to the struggle

Mother had had to make both ends meet, while her first-born was acquiring wisdom; for Mother spoke of it herself, spoke openly of her means and resources, perhaps with some idea of rousing in Laura a gratitude that had so far been dormant.

If this was her intention she failed. Laura was much too fast entangled in her own troubles, to have leisure for such a costly feeling as gratitude; and Mother's outspokenness only added a fresh weight to her pack. It seemed as if everybody and everything were ranged against her; and guilty, careworn, lonely, she shrank into her shell. About school affairs she again kept her lips shut, enduring, like a stubborn martyr, the epithets 'close' and 'deceitful' this reticence earned her. Her time was spent in writing endless, scrawly letters to Evelyn, which covered days; in sitting moodily at the top of the fir tree – which she climbed in defiance of her length of petticoat – glaring at sunsets, and brooding on dead delights; in taking long, solitary, evening walks, by choice on the heel of a thunderstorm, when the red earth was riddled by creeklets of running water; till Mother, haunted by a lively fear of encounters with 'swags', or other rough types, put her foot down and forbade them.

Sufferers are seldom sweet-tempered; and Laura formed no exception. Pin, her most frequent companion, had to bear the brunt of her acrimony: hence the two were soon at war again. For Pin was tactless, and took small heed of her sister's grumpy moods, save to cavil at them. Laura's buttoned-upness, for instance, and her love of solitude, were perverse leanings to Pin's mind; and she spoke out against them with the assurance of one who has public opinion at his back. Laura retaliated by falling foul of little personal traits in Pin: a nervous habit she had of clearing her throat – her very walk. They quarrelled passionately, having branched as far apart as the end-points of what is ultimately to be a triangle, between which the connecting lines have not yet been drawn.

Sometimes they even came to blows.

'I'll fetch your ma to you – that I will!' threatened Sarah, called by the noise of the scuffle. 'Great girls like you – fightin' like bandicoots! You ought to be downright ashamed o' yourselves.'

'I don't know what's come over you two, I'm sure,' scolded Mother, when the combatants had been parted and brought before her in the kitchen, where she was rolling pastry. 'You never used to go on like this. – Pin, stop that noise. Do you want to deafen me?'

'She hit me first,' sobbed Pin. 'It's always Laura who begins.'

'I'll teach her to cheek me like that!'

'Well, all I can say is,' said Mother exasperated, and pushed a lock of hair off her perspiring forehead with the back of her hand. 'All I say is, big girls as you are, you deserve to have the nonsense whipped out of you. – As for you, Laura, if this is your only return for all the money I've spent on you, then I wish from my heart you'd never seen the inside of that Melbourne school.'

'How pretty your eyes look, mother, when your eyelashes get floury!' said Laura, struck by the vivid contrast of black and white. She merely stated the fact, without intent to flatter, her anger being given to puffing out as suddenly as it kindled.

'Oh, get along with you!' said Mother, at the same time skilfully lifting and turning a large, thin sheet of paste. 'You can't get round *me* like that.'

'You used to have nice, ladylike manners,' she said on another occasion, when Laura, summoned to the drawing-room to see a visitor, had in Mother's eyes disgraced them both. 'Now, you've no more idea how to behave than a country bumpkin. You sit there, like a stock or a stone, as if you didn't know how to open your mouth.' – Mother was very cross.

'I didn't want to see that old frump anyhow,' retorted Laura, who inclined to charge the inhabitants of the township with an extreme provinciality. 'And what else was there to say, but yes or no? She asked me all things I didn't know anything about. You don't want me to tell stories, I suppose?'

'Well, if a child of mine doesn't know the difference between being polite and telling stories,' said Mother, completely outraged, 'then, all I can say is, it's a . . . a great shame!' she wound up lamely, after the fashion of hot-tempered people who begin a sentence without being clear how they are going to end it. – 'You were a nice enough child once. If only I'd never let you leave home.'

This jeremiad was repeated by Mother and chorused by the rest till Laura grew incensed. She was roused to defend her present self, at the cost of her past perfections; and this gave rise to new dissensions.

So that in spite of what she had to face at school, she was not altogether sorry, when the time came, to turn her back on her unknowing and hence unsympathetic relations.

She journeyed to Melbourne on one of those pleasant winter days when the sun shines from morning till night in a cloudless sky, and the chief mark of the season is the extraordinary greenness of the grass; returned a pale, determined, lanky girl, full of the grimmest resolutions.

The first few days were like a bad dream. The absence of Evelyn came home to her in all its crushing force. A gap yawned drearily where Evelyn had been – but then, she had been everywhere. There was now a kind of emptiness about the great school – except for memories, which cropped up at each turn. Laura was in a strange room, with strange, indifferent girls; and for a time she felt as lonely as she had done in those unthinkable days when she was still the poor little green 'new chum'.

Her companions were not wilfully unkind to her – her last

extravagance had been foolish, not criminal – and two or three were even sorry for the woebegone figure she cut. But her idolatrous attachment to Evelyn had been the means of again drawing round her one of those magic circles, which held her schoolfellows at a distance. And the aroma of her eccentricity still clung to her. The members of her class were deep in study, too; little was now thought or spoken of but the approaching examinations. And her first grief over, Laura set her teeth and flung herself on her lessons like a dog on a bone, endeavouring to pack the conscientious work of twelve months into less than six.

The days were feverish with energy. But at night the loneliness returned, and was only the more intense because, for some hours on end, she had been able to forget it.

On one such night when she lay wakeful, haunted by the prospect of failure, she turned over the leaves of her Bible – she had been memorising her weekly portion – and read, not as a school-task, but for herself. By chance she lighted on the Fourteenth Chapter of St John, and the familiar, honey-sweet words fell on her heart like caresses. Her tears flowed; both at the beauty of the language and out of pity for herself; and before she closed the Book, she knew that she had found a well of comfort that would never run dry.

In spite of a certain flabbiness in its outward expression, deep down in Laura the supreme faith of childhood still dwelt intact: she believed, with her whole heart, in the existence of an all-knowing God, and just as implicitly in His perfect power to succour His human children at will. But thus far on her way she had not greatly needed Him: at the most, she had had recourse to Him for forgiveness of sin. Now, however, the sudden withdrawal of a warm, human sympathy seemed to open up a new use for Him. An aching void was in her and about her; it was for Him to fill this void with the riches of His love. – And she comforted herself for her previous lack of warmth, by the reminder that His need also was chiefly of the heavy-laden and oppressed.

In the spurt of intense religious fervour that now set in for her, it was to Christ she turned by preference, rather than to the remoter God the Father. For of the latter she carried a kind of Michelangelesque picture in her brain: that of an old, old man with a flowing grey beard, who sat, Turk-fashion, one hand plucking at this beard, the other lying negligently across His knees. Christ, on the contrary, was a young man, kindly of face, and full of tender invitation.

To this younger, tenderer God, she proffered long and glowing prayers, which vied with one another in devoutness. Soon she felt herself led by Him, felt herself a favourite lying on His breast; and, as the days went by, her ardour so increased that she could not longer consume the smoke of her own fire: it overspread her daily life – to the renewed embarrassment of her schoolfellows. Was it then impossible, they asked themselves, for Laura Rambotham to do anything in a decorous and ladylike way. Must she at every step put them out of countenance? It was not respectable to be so fervent. Religion, felt they, should be practised with modesty; be worn like an indispensable but private garment. Whereas she committed the gross error in taste of, as it were, parading it outside her other clothes.

Laura, her thoughts turned heavenwards, did not look low enough to detect the distaste in her comrades' eyes. The farther she spun herself into her intimacy with the Deity, the more indifferent did she grow to the people and things of this world.

Weeks passed. Her feelings, in the beginning a mere blissful certainty that God was Love and she was God's, ceased to be wholly passive. Thus, her first satisfaction at her supposed election was soon ousted by self-righteousness, did she contemplate her unremitting devotion. And one night, when her own eloquence at prayer had brought the moisture to her eyes – one night the inspiration fell. Throughout these weeks, she had faithfully worshipped God without asking so much as a pin's head from Him in return; she had given freely; all she had, had been His. Now the time had surely come when she might claim to be rewarded. Now it was for Him to show that He had appreciated her homage. – Oh, it was so easy a thing for Him to help her, if He would . . . if He only would!

Pressing her fingers to her eyeballs till the starry blindness was effected that induces ecstasy, she prostrated herself before the mercy-seat, not omitting, at this crisis, to conciliate the Almighty by laying stress on her own exceeding unworthiness.

'Oh, dear Lord Jesus, have mercy upon me, miserable sinner! Oh, Christ, I ask Thy humble pardon! For I have been weak, Lord, and have forgotten to serve Thy Holy Name. My thoughts have erred and strayed like . . . like lost sheep. But I loved Thee, Jesus, all the time, my heart seemed full as it would hold . . . no, I didn't mean to say that. But I was not ever thus, nor prayed that Thou shouldst lead me on. But now, dear Jesus, if Thou wilt only grant me my desire, I will never forget Thee or be false to Thee again. I will love Thee and serve Thee, all the days of my life, till death us do . . . I mean, only let me pass my examinations, Lord, and there is nothing I will not do for Thee in return. Oh, dear Lord Jesus, Son of Mary, hear my prayer, and I will worship Thee and adore Thee, and never forget Thee, and that Thou hast died to save me! Grant me this my prayer, Lord, for Christ's sake, Amen.'

It came to this: Laura made a kind of pact with God, in which His aid at the present juncture guaranteeed her continued, unswerving allegiance.

The idea once lodged in her mind, she wrestled with Him night after night, filling His ears with her petitions, and remaining on her knees for such an immoderate length of time that her room-mates, who were sleepy, openly expressed their impatience.

'Oh, draw it mild, Laura!' said the girl in the neighbouring bed, when it began to seem as if the supplicant would never rise to her feet again. 'Leave something to ask Him to-morrow.'

But Laura, knowing very well that the Lord our God is a jealous God, was mindful not to scrimp in lip-service, or to shirk the minutest ceremony by means of which He might be propitiated and won over. Her prayers of greeting and farewell, on entering and leaving church, were drawn out beyond anyone else's; she did not doze or dream over a single clause of the Litany, with its hypnotising refrain; and she not only made the sign of the Cross at the appropriate place in the Creed, but also privately at every mention of Christ's name.

Meanwhile, of course, she worked at her lessons with unflagging zeal, for it was by no means her intention to throw the whole onus of her success on the Divine shoulders. She overworked; and on one occasion had a distressing lapse of memory.

And at length spring was gone and summer come, and the momentous week arrived on which her future depended. Now, though, she was not alone in her trepidation. The eyes of even the surest members of the form had a steely glint in them, and mouths were hard. Dr Pughson's papers were said to be far more formidable than the public examination: if you got happily through these, you were safe.

Six subjects were compulsory; high-steppers took nine. Laura was one of those with eight, and since her two obligatory mathematics were not to be relied on, she could not afford to fail in a single subject.

In the beginning, things, with the exception of numbers, went pretty well with her. Then came the final day, and with it the examination in history. Up to the present year Laura had cut a dash in history; now her brain was muddled, her memory overtaxed, by her having had to cram the whole of

Green's *History of the English People* in a few months, besides a large dose of *Greece* and *Rome*. Reports ran of the exceptionally 'catchy' nature of Dr Pughson's questions; and Laura's prayer, the night before, was more like a threat than a supplication.

The class had only just entered the Headmaster's room on the eventful morning, and begun to choose desks, when there came a summons to Laura to take a music-lesson. This was outside consideration, and Dr Pughson made short work of the intruder – a red-haired little girl, who blushed meekly and unbecomingly, and withdrew. Here, however, Laura rose and declared that, under these circumstances, some explanation was due to Monsieur Boehmer, the music-master, to-day's lesson being in fact a rehearsal for the annual concert.

Dr Pughson raised his red-rimmed eyes from his desk and looked very fierce.

'Tch, tch, tch!' he snapped, in the genial Irish fashion that made him dreaded and adored. 'How like a woman that is! Playing at concerts when she can't add two and two together! – Your arithmetic paper's fit for *Punch*, Miss Rambotham.'

The smile he looked for went round.

'Have you seen the questions? – no? Well, give them here then. You've got to go, I suppose, or we might deprive the concert of your shining light. – Hurry back, now. Stir your stumps!'

But this Laura had no intention of doing. In handling the printed slip, her lagging eye had caught the last and most vital question: 'Give a full account of Oliver Cromwell's Foreign Policy.' – And she did not know it! She dragged out her interview with the music-master, put questions wide of the point, insisted on lingering till he had arranged another hour for the postponed rehearsal; and, as she walked, as she talked, as she listened to Monsieur Boehmer's ridiculous English, she strove in vain to recall jot or tittle of Oliver's relations to foreign powers. – Oh, for just a peep at the particular page of

Green! For, if once she got her cue, she believed she could go on.

The dining-hall was empty when she went through it on her way back to the classroom: her history looked lovingly at her from its place on the shelf. But she did not dare to go over to it, take it out, and turn up the passage: that was too risky. What she did do, however, when she had almost reached the door, was to dash back, pull out a synopsis – a slender, medium-sized volume – and hastily and clumsily button this inside the bodice of her dress. The square, board-like appearance it gave her figure, where it projected beyond the sides of her apron, she concealed by hunching her shoulders.

Her lightning plan was, to enter a cloakroom, snatch a hurried peep at Oliver's confounded policy, then hide the book somewhere till the examination was over. But on emerging from the dining-hall she all but collided with the secretary, who had come noiselessly across the verandah; and she was so overcome by the thought of the danger she had run, and by Miss Blount's extreme surprise at Dr Pughson's leniency, that she allowed herself to be driven back to the examination-room without a word.

The girls were hard at it; they scarcely glanced up when she opened the door. From her friends' looks, she could judge of the success they were having. Cupid, for instance, was smirking to herself in the peculiar fashion that meant satisfaction; M. P.'s cheeks were the colour of monthly roses. And soon Laura, crouching low to cover her deformity, was at work like the rest.

Had only Oliver Cromwell never been born! – thus she reflected, when she had got the easier part of the paper behind her. Why could it not have been a qustion about Bourke and Wills, or the Eureka Stockade, or the voyages of Captain Cook? . . . something about one's own country, that one had heard hundreds of times and was really interested in. Or a big, arresting thing like the Retreat of the Ten Thousand, or

Hannibal's March over the Alps? Who cared for old Oliver, and his shorn head, and his contempt for baubles! What did it matter now to anyone what his attitude had been, more than two hundred years ago, to all those far-away, dream-like countries? ... Desperately she pressed her hand to her eyes. She knew the very page of Green on which Cromwell's foreign relations were set forth; knew where the paragraph began, near the foot of the page: what she could not get hold of was the opening sentence that would have set her mechanical memory a-rolling.

The two hours drew steadily to a close. About half an hour beforehand the weakest candidates began to rise, to hand in their papers and leave the room; but it was not till ten minutes to twelve that the 'crack' girls stopped writing. Laura was to be allowed an extra twenty minutes, and it was on this she relied. At last, she was alone with the master. But though he was already dipping into the examination-papers, he was not safe. She had unbuttoned two buttons and was at a third, when he looked up so unexpectedly that she was scared out of her senses, and fastened her dress again with all the haste she could. Three or four of the precious minutes were lost.

At this point, the door opened and Mr Strachey strode into the room. Dr Pughson blinked up from the stacks of papers, rose, and the two spoke in low tones. Then, with a glance at Laura, they went together to the door, which Dr Pughson held to behind him, and stood just over the threshold. As they warmed to their talk, the master let the door slip into the latch.

Laura could see them from where she sat, without being seen. A moment later they moved stealthily away, going down the verandah in the direction of the office.

Now for it! With palsied hands she undid her bodice, clutched at the book, forced her blurred eyes to find the page, and ran them over it. A brief survey: five or six heads to remember: a few dates. Flapped to again; tucked under her apron; shoved into her bosom.

And not a second too soon. There he came, hurrying back. And three buttons were still undone. But Laura's head was bent over her desk: though her heart was pummelling her ribs, her pen now ran like lightning; and by the time the order to stop was given, she had covered the requisite number of sheets.

Afterwards she had adroitly to rid herself of the book, then to take part – a rather pale-eyed, distracted part – in the lively technical discussions that ensued; when each candidate was as long-winded on the theme of her success, or non-success, as a card-player on his hand at the end of a round. Directly she could make good her escape, she pleaded a headache, climbed to her bedroom and stretched herself flat on her bed. She was through – but at what a cost! She felt quite sore. Her very bones seemed to hurt her.

Not till she was thoroughly rested, and till she had assured herself that all risk attaching to the incident was over, did she come to reflect on the part God had played in the business. And then, it must be admitted, she found it a sorry one. Just at first, indeed, her limpid faith was shocked into a reluctance to believe that He had helped her at all: His manner of doing it would have been so inexpressibly mean. But, little by little, she dug deeper, and eventually she reached the conclusion that He had given her the option of this way, throwing it open to her and then standing back and watching to see what she would do, without so much as raising an eyelid to influence her decision. In fact, the more she pondered over it, the more inclined she grew to think that it had been a kind of snare on the part of God, to trap her afresh into sin, and thus to prolong her dependence on Him after her crying need was past. But, if this were true, if He had done this, then He must *like* people to remain miserable sinners, so that He might have them always crawling to His feet. And from this view of the case her ingenuous young mind shrank appalled. She could not go on loving and worshipping a God who was capable of double dealing; who could behave in such a mean fashion. Nor would she ever forget His having forced her to endure the moments of torture she had come through that day.

Lying on her bed, she grappled with these thoughts. A feeling of deep resentment was their abiding result. Whatever His aim, it had been past expression pitiless of Him, Him who had at His command thousands of pleasanter ways in which to help her, thus to drive a poor unhappy girl to extremities: one, too, whose petition had not been prompted by selfish ends alone. What she had implored of Him touched Mother even more nearly than herself: her part prayer to Him had been to save Mother – whose happiness depended on things like examinations – from a bitter disappointment. That much at least He had done – she would give Him His due – but at the expense of her entire self-respect. Oh, He must have a cold, calculating heart . . . could one only see right down into it. The tale of His clemency and compassion, which the Bible told, was not to be interpreted literally: when one came to think of it, had He ever – outside the Bible – been known to stoop from His judgment-seat, and lovingly and kindly intervene? It was her own absurd mistake: she had taken the promises made through His Son, for gospel truth; had thought He really meant what He said, about rewarding those who were faithful to Him. Her companions – the companions on whom, from the heights of her piety, she had looked pityingly down – were wiser than she. They did not abase themselves before Him, and vow a lifelong devotion; but neither did they make any but the most approved demands on Him. They satisfied their consciences by paying Him lip-homage, by confessing their sins, and by asking for a vague, far-distant mercy, to which they attached no great importance. Hence, they never came into fierce personal conflict with Him. Nor would she, ever again; from this time forward, she would rival the rest in lukewarmness. – But, before she could put this resolve into force, she had to let her first indignation subside: only then was it possible for her to recover the shattering of her faith, and settle down to practise religion after the glib and shallow mode of her friends. She did not, however, say her prayers that night, or for many a night to come; and when, at church, Christ's name occurred in the Service, she held her head erect, and shut the ears and eyes of her soul.

Chapter Twenty-Five

THE school year had ebbed; the ceremonies that attended its conclusion were over. A few days beforehand, the fifth-form boarders, under the tutelage of a couple of governesses, drove off early in the morning to the distant university. On the outward journey the candidates were thoughtful and subdued; but as they returned home, in the late afternoon, their spirits were not to be kept within seemly bounds. They laughed, sang, and rollicked about inside the wagonette, Miss Zielinski weakly protesting unheard – were so rowdy that the driver pushed his cigar-stump to the corner of his mouth, to be able to smile at ease, and flicked his old horse into a canter. For the public examination had proved as anticipated, child's play, compared with what the class had been through at Dr Pughson's hands; and its accompanying details were of an agreeable nature: the weather was not too hot; the examination-hall was light and airy; through the flung-back windows trees and flowering shrubs looked in; the students were watched over by a handsome Trinity man, who laid his straw hat on the desk before him.

Then came the annual concert, at which none of the performers broke down; Speech Day, when the body of a big hall was crowded with relatives and friends, and when so many white, blue-beribboned frocks were massed together on the platform, that this looked like a great bed of blue and white

flowers; and, finally, trunks were brought out from boxrooms
and strewn through the floors, and upper-form girls emptied
cupboards and drawers into them for the last time.

On the evening before the general dispersion, Laura, Cupid,
and M. P. walked the well-known paths of the garden once
again. While the two elder girls were more loquacious than
their wont, Laura was quieter. She had never wholly recovered
her humour since the day of the history-examination; and she
still could not look back, with composure, on the jeopardy
in which she had placed herself: one little turn of the wheel in
the wrong direction, and the end of her schooldays would have
been shame and disgrace. – And just as her discovery of God's
stratagem had damped her religious ardour, so her antipathy
to the means she had been obliged to employ had left a feeling
of enmity in her, towards the school and everything connected
with it: she had counted the hours till she could turn her back
on it altogether. None the less, now that the time had come,
there was a kind of ache in her at having to say good-bye; for it
was in her nature to let go unwillingly of things, places and
people once known. Besides, glad as she felt to have done with
learning, she was unclear what was to come next. The idea
of life at home attracted her as little as ever – Mother had even
begun to hint as well that she would now be expected to
instruct her young brothers. Hence, her parting was effected
with very mixed feelings; she did not know in the least where
she really belonged, or under what conditions she would be
happy; she was conscious only of a mild sorrow at having to
take leave of the shelter of years.

Her two companions had no such doubts and regrets; for
them the past was already dead and gone; their talk was all of
the future, so soon to become the present. They forecast this,
mapping it out for themselves with the iron belief in their
power to do so, which is the hall-mark of youth.

Laura, walking at their side, listened to their words with the deepest interest, and with the reverence she had learned to extend to all opinions save her own.

M. P. proposed to return to Melbourne at the end of the vacation; for she was going on to Trinity, where she intended to take one degree after another. She hesitated only whether it was to be in medicine or arts.

'Oogh! . . . to cut off people's legs!' ejaculated Laura. 'M. P., how awful.'

'Oh, one soon gets used to that, child. – But I think, on the whole, I should prefer to take up teaching. Then I shall probably be able to have a school of my own some day.'

'I shouldn't wonder if you got Sandy's place here,' said Laura, who was assured that M. P.'s massy intellect would open all doors.

'Who knows?' answered Mary, and set her lips in a determined fashion of her own. 'Stranger things have happened.'

Cupid, less enamoured of continual discipline, intended to be a writer. 'My cousin says I've got the stuff in me. And he's a journalist and ought to know.'

'I should rather think he ought.'

'Well, I mean to have a shot at it.'

'And you, Laura?' M. P. asked suavely.

'Me? – Oh, goodness knows!'

'Close as usual, Infant.'

'No, really not, Cupid.'

'Well, you'll soon have to make up your mind to something now. You're nearly sixteen. – Why not go on working for your B.A.?'

'No thanks! I've had enough of that here.' And Laura's thoughts waved their hands, as it were, to the receding figure of Oliver Cromwell.

'Be a teacher, then.'

'M. P.! I never want to hear a date or add up a column of figures again.'

'Laura!'

'It's the solemn truth. I'm fed up with all those blessed things.'

'Fancy not having a single wish!'

'Wish? . . . oh, I've tons of wishes. First I want to be with Evvy again. And then, I want to *see* things – yes, that most of all. Hundreds and thousands of things. People, and places, and what they eat, and how they dress, and China, and Japan . . . just tons.'

'You'll have to hook a millionaire for that, my dear.'

'And perhaps you'll write a book about your travels for us stay-at-homes.'

'Gracious! I shouldn't know how to begin. But you'll send me all you write – all *your* books – won't you, Cupid? And, M. P., you'll let me come and see you get your degrees – every single one.'

With these and similar promises the three girls parted. They never met again. For a time they exchanged letters regularly, many-sheeted letters, full of familiar, personal detail. Then the detail ceased, the pages grew fewer in number, the time-gap longer. Letters in turn gave place to mere notes and postcards, scribbled in violent haste, at wide intervals. And ultimately even these ceased; and the great silence of separation was unbroken. Nor were the promises redeemed: there came to Laura neither gifts of books nor calls to be present at academic robings. Within six months of leaving school, M. P. married and settled down in her native township; and thereafter she was forced to adjust the rate of her progress to the steps of halting little feet. Cupid went a-governessing, and spent the best years of her life in the obscurity of the bush.

And Laura? . . . In Laura's case, no kindly Atropos snipped the thread of her aspirations: these, large, vague, extemporary, one and all achieved fulfilment; then withered off to make room for more. But this, the future still securely hid from her.

She went out from school with the uncomfortable sense of being a square peg, which fitted into none of the round holes of her world; the wisdom she had got, the experience she was richer by, had, in the process of equipping her for life, merely seemed to disclose her unfitness. She could not then know that, even for the squarest peg, the right hole may ultimately be found; seeming unfitness prove to be only another aspect of a peculiar and special fitness. But, of the after years, and what they brought her, it is not the purport of this little book to tell. It is enough to say: many a day came and went before she grasped that, oftentimes, just those mortals who feel cramped and unsure in the conduct of everyday life, will find themselves to rights, with astounding ease, in that freer, more spacious world where no practical considerations hamper, and where the creatures that inhabit dance to their tune: the world where are stored up men's best thoughts, the hopes, and fancies; where the shadow is the substance, and the multitude of business pales before the dream.

In the meantime, however, the exodus of the fifty-five turned the College upside-down.

Early the following morning Laura made her final preparations for departure. This, alas! was not to be on so imposing a scale as the departures of her schoolfellows. They, under special escort, would have a cab apiece, and would drive off with flying handkerchiefs and all their luggage piled high in front. Whereas Laura's box had gone by van: for she and Pin, who was in Melbourne on a visit, were to spend a couple of days at Godmother's before starting up-country. Even her farewells, which she had often rehearsed to herself with dramatic emphasis, went off without éclat. Except for Miss Chapman, the governesses were absent when the moment came, and Miss Chapman's mind was so full of other things that she went on giving orders while she was shaking hands.

But Laura was not destined to leave the walls, within the shadow of which she had learned so much, as tamely as all this. There was still a surprise in waiting for her. As she whisked about the corridors in search of Mrs Gurley, she met two girls, one of whom said: 'I say, Laura Rambotham, you're fetched. Your pretty sister's come for you.'

'My . . . who?' gaped Laura.

'Your sister. By gum, there's a nose for you – and those whopping eyes! You'll have to play second fiddle to *that*, all your days, my dear.'

On entering the reception-room Laura tried hard to see Pin with the eyes of a stranger. Pin rose from her chair – awkwardly, of course, for there were other people present, and Laura's violent stare was disconcerting in the extreme: it made Pin believe her hat was crooked, or that she had a black speck on her nose. As for Laura, she could see no great change in her sister; the freckles were certainly paler, and the features were perhaps beginning to emerge a little, from the cushiony fat in which they were bedded; but that was all. Still, if outsiders, girls in particular, were struck by it . . .

A keener stab than this – really, she did not grudge Pin being pretty: it was only the newness of the thing that hurt – a keener stab was it that, though she had ordered Pin repeatedly, and with all the stress she was master of, to come in a wagonette to fetch her, so that she might at least drive away like the other girls; in spite of this, the little nincompoop had after all arrived on foot. Godmother had said the idea of driving was stuff and nonsense – a quite unnecessary expense. Pin, of course, had meekly given in; and thus Laura's last brave attempt to be comfortably like her companions came to naught. She went out of the school in the same odd and undignified fashion in which she had lived there.

The wrangle caused by Pin's chicken-heartedness lasted the sisters down the garden-path, across the road, and over into the precints of a large, public park. Only when they were some distance through this, did Laura wake to what was happening to her. Then, it came over her with a rush: she was free, absolutely free; she might do any mortal thing she chose.

As a beginning she stopped short.

'Hold on, Pin . . . take this,' she said, giving her sister the heavy leather bag they were carrying in turns to the tramway.

Pin obediently held out her hand, in its little white cotton glove.

'And my hat.'

'What are you going to do, Laura?'

'You'll see.'

'You'll get sunstroke!'

'Fiddles! – it's quite shady. Here're my gloves. – Now, Pin, you follow your nose and you'll find me – *where* you find me!'

'Oh, what *are* you going to do, Laura?' cried Pin, in anxiety.

'I'm going to have a good run,' said Laura; and tightened her hair-ribbon.

'Oh, but you can't run in the street! You're too big. People'll see you.'

'Think I care? – If you'd been years only doing what you were allowed to, I guess you'd want to do something you weren't allowed to, too. – Good-bye!'

She was off, had darted away into the leaden heat of the December morning, like an arrow from its bow, her head bent, her arms close to her sides, fleet-footed as a spaniel: Pin was faced by the swift and rhythmic upturning of her heels. There were not many people abroad at this early hour, but the few there were, stood still and looked in amazement after the half-grown girl in white, whose thick black plait of hair sawed up and down as she ran; and a man with mop and bucket, who was washing statues, stopped his work and whistled, and winked at Pin as she passed.

Cross and confused Pin trudged after her sister, Laura's hat and gloves in one hand, the leather bag in the other.

Right down the central avenue ran Laura, growing smaller and smaller in the distance, the area of her movements decreasing as she ran, till she appeared to be almost motionless, and not much larger than a figure in the background of a picture. Then came a sudden bend in the long, straight path. She shot round it, and was lost to sight.

VIRAGO MODERN CLASSICS

The first Virago Modern Classic, *Frost in May* by Antonia White, was published in 1978. It launched a list dedicated to the celebration of women writers and to the rediscovery and reprinting of their works. Its aim was, and is, to demonstrate the existence of a female tradition in fiction which is both enriching and enjoyable. The Leavisite notion of the 'Great Tradition', and the narrow, academic definition of a 'classic', has meant the neglect of a large number of interesting secondary works of fiction. In calling the series 'Modern Classics' we do not necessarily mean 'great' — although this is often the case. Published with new critical and biographical introductions, books are chosen for many reasons: sometimes for their importance in literary history; sometimes because they illuminate particular aspects of womens' lives, both personal and public. They may be classics of comedy or storytelling; their interest can be historical, feminist, political or literary.

Initially the Virago Modern Classics concentrated on English novels and short stories published in the early decades of this century. As the series has grown it has broadened to include works of fiction from different centuries, different countries, cultures and literary traditions. In 1984 the Victorian Classics were launched; there are separate lists of Irish, Scottish, European, American, Australian and other English speaking countries; there are books written by Black women, by Catholic and Jewish women, and a few relevant novels by men. There is, too, a companion series of Non-Fiction Classics constituting biography, autobiography, travel, journalism, essays, poetry, letters and diaries.

By the end of 1986 over 250 titles will have been published in these two series, many of which have been suggested by our readers.